*Praise for* Baby Love:

'Danks at her considerable best' *Crime Time*

'A brilliant, believable, sleep-robbing thriller . . . An acute sense of bad social weather . . . One of those rare books which gives the genre a chance to exercise both its mind and its muscle' *Literary Review*

'. . . a story Hitchcock would have loved . . . A small *tour de force*' *Observer*

'Fictional techno-crime is fashionable, but Denise Danks makes most other writers of the genre seem crude and amateurish . . . an absorbing mystery'
Susanna Yager, *Saturday Telegraph*

'A super Brit crime novel, which will do Miss Danks's excellent reputation no harm at all'
*Independent on Sunday*

'Her six books featuring Georgina Powers, sexy techno-journo and sleuth, are uniformly racy, witty, exciting and technologically convincing' *The Times*

Denise Danks has been shortlisted twice for the CWA Gold Dagger, for *Phreak* and *Baby Love*, and has been shortlisted for a Sherlock Award for Best Detective. She was recently described by *The Times* as one of the six best crime writers in the UK. *Baby Love* is her sixth novel featuring Georgina Powers.

*By Denise Danks*

FEATURING GEORGINA POWERS

The Pizza House Crash
Better Off Dead
Frame Grabber
Wink a Hopeful Eye
Phreak
Baby Love

OTHER NOVELS

Torso

# BABY LOVE

*Denise Danks*

An Orion paperback

First published in Great Britain in 2001
by Orion,
This paperback edition published in 2002
by Orion Books Ltd,
Orion House, 5 Upper Saint Martin's Lane
London, WC2H 9EA



A CIP catalogue record for this book is available from the British Library.

ISBN 075284 803 8

Typeset by Deltatype Ltd, Birkenhead, Merseyside

Printed in Great Britain by
Clays Ltd, St Ives plc

For my three stars – Georgie, Alex, and Nick.

ACKNOWLEDGEMENTS

Many thanks for their time and tolerance to Amanda Callaghan of the BPAS, Ross Anderson, Computer Laboratory, University of Cambridge, and Paul Thomas, Dierdre Gillon and Doug Howe of The John Ellicot Centre.

CHAPTER ONE

# HIT-AND-RUN

It was hard to remember exactly what had happened that night. The black car had come at us out of nowhere. All I could recall was the sound of its accelerator and a shove in the back. I didn't see it hit Richard. I heard it. I was face down on the floor trying to grab my bag and get up, but my legs wouldn't support me. My world had narrowed to the spinning concrete space between the bleeding palms of my hands. I knew that I wasn't dead, and that Richard wasn't dead, because he was screaming.

I remember getting to my feet, half crawling towards him. I remember the unnatural angle of his lower leg. I don't remember his face, or even the rest of his body, just the impossible geometry of his limbs. I remember a white bone protruding through the blackish-grey material of his trousers as if it were a broken strut from a discarded umbrella. I remember throwing up, sobering up, eager people coming out of their houses, and the ambulance, the police, the red, the blue, the orange and then the hospital.

We had been coming back from the tube station. We should have got a cab from there home but we'd decided to walk it, arm in arm, lurching and laughing along the slick, wet pavements. It's the sort of decision you make when you are drunk. You underestimate distance. You underestimate danger. You overestimate the kindness of strangers.

It had been a rip-roaring night. *Technology Week*'s online news service had gone live after months of preparation and there had been money behind the bar at the Crown, a smoky old Soho boozer round the corner from the company offices in Old Compton Street. Richard had been promoted to editor-in-chief with a flattering salary hike and a set of golden handcuffs by way of share options to make sure he didn't stray. There was nothing in it for me but a free beer. I was a freelance. I didn't even have a particular speciality. I used to have a talent for nailing front-page exclusives but it was hard to know what they meant any more in an online world where everyone knows everything, or can if they choose to. Real news was buried so deep in the twenty-four-hour spin machine that it was getting hard to detect. Things happened so fast that it didn't seem so important who got there first because everyone would have it a nanosecond later. You didn't even have time to check, only report, for fear of losing the tiniest of leads. The checks came later, if anyone cared to do them, by which time decisions had already been made and it didn't matter because everyone had reacted the same way. In the market economy, the important thing was not to miss the rush. Yesterday's news was truly history, and only a fraction of it ever really mattered. There was no use for it. You couldn't even wrap fish in it.

'No one investigates any more,' Richard had said, throwing his heavy arm around my shoulder and squeezing me close. His new salary had given him an arrogant new confidence in his old opinions.

'We hire monkeys who can search sites. The information is out there just waiting to be harvested. People pay us so they don't have to do it. They want our opinions. That's what news is for them – someone sifting through oven-ready information that they could get for themselves if they had the time.'

'Or the inclination,' I said.

'What you can do,' he said, circling his index finger around until he steadied it an inch from my nose, 'What you *do*, George, is give us that Factor X. The stuff people *don't* want published, that doesn't get posted on websites. The stuff other people know they'll find on ours. News. Real news. That's always worth money.'

'So what are we talking?'

'Sixty grand a year, but you have to come in from the cold. It's a full-time job, you can't work for anyone else.'

There was a roar of laughter from the group of new kids next to us. They swayed, knocking us sideways so that Richard had to grab me to keep upright. We seemed to move backwards together and came to a stop against the bar. It occurred to me as I looked around at all the new faces that Richard and I were now the old guard. Just ten years covering the computer business was the equivalent of several lifetimes in any other, and the worst thing about it was that nothing we had seen and learned counted for anything. What the new kids had learned about the business in the last six weeks would do as well. After all, six weeks was a lifetime in Internet time.

Richard was looking around just like I was.

'What's our edge, Richard?' I said.

'I have no fucking idea,' he replied.

I took the beer bottle that I had been sucking on and pointed it at a tall, good-looking lad in a distressed leather jacket, who had glanced over at us more than a couple of times.

'Who's he?' I said. Richard turned and tried to focus on the boy in the crowd. The place was dark and packed with journalists and sales people, but you could tell who was who because sales wore chain-store suits and the journalists looked like they were still paying off their student loans. The lad I was pointing at was talking to Mary Stow, Richard's sometime girlfriend. It looked to me like she was flirting with him.

'Him? Danny Morgan, one of my monkeys,' Richard said, and he started to laugh.

Like I said, rip-roaring. Only I wasn't laughing with Richard, because at that moment, I was one of his monkeys too. I knew that because, as they say, I got paid peanuts and, unlike Monkey Boy in the leather jacket, I got paid them three months late. The job on offer was worth thinking about.

I was about to move away when I noticed a girl pushing through the crowd towards Danny Morgan. She tugged at his sleeve. He turned, grinned, and leaned towards her. They kissed mouth to mouth while Mary kept smiling like a woman who was trying too hard not to care about losing.

'Who's she?'

'Jo Casey. Fresh up from the provinces.'

'What's she like?'

Richard wiped his mouth with the back of his hand and ordered a couple more beers.

'Bit like you, I'd say.'

She was a brunette, bigger round the bust than me

but as tall and as close to twenty as I was to thirty. She stood by her man but her gaze shifted restlessly around the room until her eyes caught mine. We stared at each other for a few seconds and she seemed to connect with me. It was almost a challenge.

'What's she looking at?' I said.

'You?'

'She better look away soon. I might get the wrong idea.'

'You've got a reputation, George. You're the one they want to be like.'

'God help them.'

Richard stuck his hand in front of my face and waggled his fingers at her. She smiled at him, a kind of tired, willing smile that you save for your superiors when you're off duty.

'Mind how you go, Richard old boy,' I said, but he had already gone, pushing his way through the crowd towards her and never reaching his destination. Two hours later, we just had each other to stagger home with; and one month later and twenty-four shopping days to Christmas, here we were, hurt in body and mind, lying on his double bed together, sharing five pillows between us and watching *The Jerry Springer Show*.

Three grossly overweight people were describing their worthless marriages. The two women appeared to be related. As far as I could work out, one fat lady was the other fat lady's mother, and the lover of the latter had made the former pregnant. He was the fat guy sitting in the middle.

'Look, why don't you go?' Richard said.

'I'm all right.'

'I'm all right too. Go out somewhere. You're as bad as her.'

He meant Mary. I glanced at him sprawled across his double bed and calculated how long it would be before she was back in it. She'd made herself busy when she'd heard about the accident, come over so fast you'd think she'd followed the ambulance. I reckoned a month, when he'd got his leg out of plaster.

'I've got nowhere to go,' I said.

'Go to the office. They'll pay a day rate. They need someone. Better still, take the job. Sixty grand, for fuck's sake, what's there to think about?'

'Can you smoke in editorial still?'

'No, the hard-core wheezers go out on the fire escape. Except Max. The bossman has his own office now.'

I had a pack on the side. I picked it up and worried at it but Richard wouldn't relent and let me smoke. He was right. What was there to think about? I wasn't going to turn sixty grand down. It was the phrase 'go to the office' that was the brake. Since the hit-and-run, it was all I could do to force myself up here from the basement below. In one month, apart from my planned escapes to Richard's upstairs, I had managed to leave my basement three times to take the dog for a walk, and I'd stopped that altogether. I just opened the back door now and let her run about in the garden, hoping she wouldn't dive in the canal like she did in the summer. She'd stink like a dead rat and I hated washing her. She wasn't even my dog. She was Tony Levi's. He was my ex, and he didn't want her because he said that I had spoiled her. It wasn't as if I had given her a good home or anything. I hadn't even given her a proper name. The bloody animal thrived on benign neglect.

Richard and I were prisoners, good as, him with his

broken leg and me with my broken spirit. It was like we'd died that night and gone to some sort of purgatory where sinners watched daytime television and got on each other's nerves while Time, cheesy as a cheap continuity man, dragged on.

The studio audience were going crazy. Two of Springer's guests had thrust their stomachs out and were bouncing off each other. The floor manager seemed to be injured. It had to be fake, I thought, like professional wrestling.

'This is it. It's going to go down,' I said, but Richard wasn't paying attention any more. He was sorting through some letters on his bed. He handed me a white card with black italic writing on it. It was a lunchtime invitation to a Gecko Games press conference at the White House Club, which was probably the hippest dance venue in town. It was a nice idea, but these places look so shabby in the sober light of day, like a tired face that has failed to take off its make-up the night before the morning after.

'Go,' Richard said. 'It's addressed to you. If you go now you'll just about make it.'

I'd moved downstairs to the basement a year ago and Richard still got fifty per cent of my mail. I ignored him. I wasn't interested in the invitation. I wanted to stay home and watch television. The fat people had turned very nasty. Springer had sprung between them, unwisely, in my opinion. It was the climax of the show but Richard spoiled the tension by moving and making the bed dip. I tried to focus on the screen violence, but his anaerobic struggle was distracting. He made little gasping noises as he leaned on one arm, levered himself up slightly and stretched his other arm across his body to fiddle about underneath a book that was on the bedside table. When he finally dragged out what he was searching for with the tips of his fingers, it was just about all over.

He threw a postcard on the bed before slumping back exhausted on the pillows. 'It came yesterday,' he said.

It was a blank, fogged view of nothing, with a caption that said 'London By Night'. I threw the Gecko invitation on to the bed and picked up the postcard, but a letter that Richard had dislodged from underneath the book caught my eye. It was from the National Road Traffic Accident Claims Centre. I pointed at it with the edge of the card.

'What's that about?'

'The hospital wants to know if I'll be claiming personal injury compensation.'

'What's it to them?'

'They want to get back their expenses.'

'So they sent your medical details to a call centre up north?'

I wanted to say something about that, but I could see Richard was not in the mood. He looked at the television and I looked at the card.

'Read it,' he said.

I flipped it over. There was a West End postmark. The handwriting on the back was a black, angular script that I didn't recognise. It had a one-line unsigned message: *Be seeing you.*

'I have no idea who this is from,' I said.

Richard levered his body up again a few inches, this time shifting from one buttock to the other. His face was slick with perspiration and his tone was sour.

'How about one of your weird boyfriends?'

'What do you mean?'

'You tell me. What does *that* mean? "Be seeing you"?'

I knew what he was getting at. Ever since the car had mown us down that night, I had got the feeling that he blamed me.

He'd pushed me out of the way, so he was the *hero* and I was the *victim*, which meant I was to blame. 'The car accelerated towards her,' was what he'd said when the dough-faced policeman who had come to the hospital had asked him what he could remember. There was an undercurrent of bitterness in everything he said. It was in his tone of voice every time he asked me if the police had got back to me, which he did every day. He was hurting and he blamed his pain on me. He'd even told them about my past. 'Poor choice of companion, let's say,' he'd said, and I'd interrupted and asked him if he fancied *two* broken legs instead of just the one.

'You think *this* has something to do with the accident?'

'It's odd, isn't it? It's a strange sort of card to send someone, isn't it?'

'You think someone I know tried to run us over?'

'Well, I doubt if it's anyone *I* know.'

'That's right. Mary can't drive, can she?'

Richard grabbed the television controller and changed channels like he was firing a gun. There were only five channels but he seemed to find forty until he was back with Jerry Springer, and by then the fat people were all seated and someone had brought them some towels. The phone next to the bed began to ring. I ignored it and Richard ignored it, but whoever it was wouldn't let up.

'You don't have to,' he said when he finally answered

it. 'Mary, I'm OK, really. No, she's gone out. No, you don't have to.'

He put the receiver down.

'She coming over anyway?'

'Yes.'

I picked up the postcard and the invitation and swung my legs off the bed.

'That her mobile?'

'Yes.'

'That gives me two minutes,' I said, and my breathing started to quicken.

'You OK?' he said.

'I'm OK,' I said.

I stood by Richard's front door and it took me a minute to prepare myself. When I opened it, I kept my head down and ran down the steps like I was under enemy fire.

CHAPTER TWO

# NO NEWS IS GOOD NEWS

I heard her arrive as I sat in my office at my machine. I was logged on to the Net. What had been a small regular duty before the accident had become a daily compulsion. It was one hour at first, then two, then more. I slept a great deal and I surfed a great deal. If I didn't go looking, there were email alerts telling me to.

At first, I trawled through web sites and newsgroups looking for something that might interest me, or that I might recycle, like those South American kids you see picking over huge, hot, stinking heaps of urban waste for something to eat or deal. At first. Now I didn't have to have a reason. I just let myself go with it. I imagined that a smell of data-mining clung to me, like the odour of garbage-hunting clung to those little scavengers, a whiff of stale information that hinted of warm electronics, cigarettes, chilli chicken and mayo, cold coffee on the side.

As usual, I lost track of time. It was only when I hit a site for flights to Bali that I realised that I was drifting. A banner ad flicked its tail as if it were trailing across an indigo sky, the neon words *Bali by Night* shone with the glow of false starlight.

The postcard was propped up on my keyboard, leaning against the bottom of the screen, next to the invitation from Gecko Games. I tried to focus on the invitation and ignore the postcard. The invitation said briefly that the company was entering into a £2 million charity sponsorship. If I was going to go and get there on time, I had twenty minutes to make up my mind. I knew I wasn't going to even try to make it, but I had to go through the motions of coming to a decision. It was something to do with self-respect.

I told myself it was a worthy story but I couldn't see myself earning from it. The press release would have been posted on the web site in any case. In fact, the best reason that I could find for going to the Gecko press conference was that I'd be fed. The second best reason was that Cherry Shankar would be there, and she was a friend that I hadn't seen in a long while, too long a while.

I'd met her partner in business and in bed, Douglas 'Gecko' Samuels, five years ago. He'd just started the company with £50,000 worth of venture capital and a half-decent games distribution business that was worth practically nothing. It was Cherry, a hotter than hot games designer, who turned it into a world-class games creation company worth millions. Everyone had interviewed Cherry but I had been the first to tell the world that she would be to the games software business what Spielberg was to Hollywood.

I searched out the details. Gecko Games' turnover was clocked at an enviable £27 million, but its share price had fallen slightly on the day. Four anonymous analysts judged it a strong to moderate *buy* despite its recent losses in revenues as a result of Dreamcast, the latest games station launch. I tried to log on to Gecko's site, but it was achingly slow to load.

I lost patience as the minutes passed and the Gecko

site still hadn't made it down the line. I clicked back to the technology stocks and saw that the Gecko share price had fallen ten per cent and some. I clicked through for some technology news but nothing was coming through that would explain the dive in Gecko stock. One thing was certain. Something big had hit the company broadsides. I have to go, I thought. There was something happening. Everyone would be there at the conference and I should be there too, asking questions. My fingers brushed anxiously across the keyboard. It would have meant leaving the house.

I sat in the gloom for a long time, clicking through the online news, watching other people's work feeding me what I could have been doing myself. The dog gave a great sigh outside the door like an abandoned lover. I'd have to let her out eventually, but that would mean opening the door to the garden, to the outside, where the colours of the trees and grass were unfamiliar and intense and the water lay still in the distance like a bottomless lake of nightmares.

It was worse opening that door than opening my front door and going upstairs to Richard's. I knew exactly what I was going to do then and I could plan. I didn't look around when I opened the front door, or the gate. I just walked straight up to street level, turned quickly right, up the steps to his door, key *in*. There was the road to think about, and beyond that the large park behind the steel railings, but my moves were rehearsed and it was over quickly. When I opened the door to the garden, it could seem to me like a jungle or a prairie: too wide, too narrow, too congested, too spare, and the dog's movements were unpredictable. Worse still, I had to wait at the door for her to mooch around in and out of the shadows and do her thing. The waiting killed me because I could never get her to come until she was finished, which meant I had no control over events and all the time I could see the tower block looming above the terraces and the houses that backed on to the canal. Their windows were like eyes, and sometimes, people came to those windows. People that I didn't know and who made me afraid.

I wanted for nothing. I ordered grass, amphetamines, cigarettes and takeaways over the phone. Beer and wine and whatever groceries I needed I ordered online and had delivered. My connection with the outside world was the phone, the modem, the computer, the radio, the TV. Richard was the only person I could visit, and it had got so his was the only voice I heard without a machine interface.

I wasn't exactly delighted to be in my own place, either. I'd bought it a year back, when Mary and Richard had decided that two was company and three, me, was a crowd. I was stuck here now, but even before the accident, I'd found it hard living on my own, being asset-rich but suddenly cash-poor. I wasn't used to spending my money on decor instead of decadence. If I was honest, I missed sharing with Richard too. Despite his nagging, we'd been good together. We'd tolerated each other's hangovers and, before Mary had hustled into the place with her tobacco-neutralising pot pourri and hellish high-fibre recipes, we'd been happy. In fact, I could only think of two things that made up for the cash-strapped isolation and the takeaways. One, I didn't have to bump into Richard's drab women in the bathroom, and two, there was no one to nag me about my personal habits any more, although the way the dog looked at me sometimes, I swear she had an opinion.

I let the dog out for a few minutes and went back to

the screen. The sound of distant helicopter blades hacked into the silence. It came closer and passed noisily overhead. The postcard was still balanced on my keyboard beside the invitation. I'd not moved but the afternoon had not been uneventful. The news had come to me. I had watched something happen online. The clues had been there for me to act upon right at the beginning, but I had chosen not to, and there I sat, a hyperlink away from a story that I should have got myself.

> BOMB BLAST KILLS GECKO BOSS
> Games software millionaire Douglas 'Gecko' Samuels, 36, has been killed in an explosion at his London home. A journalist from an online news service, Technology Week, has been taken to hospital with serious injuries.

I called Richard, but his phone was engaged.

I called his mobile.

'Yeah.'

'Richard.'

'I know. I'm on the other line.' He cut me off.

I rang the office.

'This is Technology Online, how can I help you?'

'Cath. It's Georgina Powers. What's going on?'

'I don't know.'

'Who was it?'

'Jo Casey.'

'Is she OK?'

'We haven't heard.'

'Put me through to Max.'

'He's not taking calls. The police are here. I'm sorry, Georgina, I've got to go. I'll tell him you called.'

The phone went dead, and rang the instant I replaced the receiver. It was Richard.

'Max wants you to cover it.'

My mouth dried and my heartbeat accelerated.

'What's wrong with Mary?'

'She's leaving the company for the nationals.'

I sighed. Mary'd been on the staff for ten years, and it looked like she was going in glory. I'd taken a more ignominious route to an intermittently successful freelance career. I'd resigned before Max could sack me.

'Max has an office full of computer-assisted reporters. He can send one of them,' I said.

'He wants experience.'

'Is Jo Casey all right?'

'She's dead, George.' I clicked the cursor pointlessly around the screen.

'George?'

'I can't, Richard. You know I can't.'

I heard him take a long breath in and out. The sound dissolved into silence.

'They were killed inside the house, George. Do you understand? *Inside* the house.'

I tried to salvage some pride by making a few calls. I spoke to Max, who gave me the name of the detective superintendent who was covering the case, a guy called Daniel Spencer.

'What was Jo Casey doing at Gecko Samuels' place when everyone else had been invited to a press conference in town?' I said.

I could hear a slight gasp as Max dragged on one of the small cigars that he preferred. It would have been the tenth of the day. He was a moderate man.

'Exactly.'

'What about Danny Morgan? Have you spoken to him?' I said.

'Only to tell him to calm down. He got all hairy-chested about who was going to do the story. He and Jo were close. He assumed he had a right. I disabused him of that notion.'

'So what did he do?'

'He resigned.'

'Home number?'

There was a pause as Max touched the keyboard and brought up the file. He gave me the number, a mobile and an email address. I wrote them down.

'I suppose, technically, I'm in breach of the Data Protection Act,' he said, and then he surprised me by asking how I was. I lied and said I was OK.

'You're recovered then?'

'Yes.'

I could hear another gasp as he inhaled and a pause as the smoke flowed out of his mouth.

'Jo Casey showed a lot of promise, Georgina. No one's going to forget that she worked for us.'

It was as close to raw emotion as I had heard in the ten years I had worked for him. I let the moment breathe.

'There are no details online,' I said.

'It was a nail bomb. Get *off* line and tell me the rest,' he said, and put the phone down before I could negotiate my fee.

CHAPTER THREE

# EVERY PICTURE TELLS A STORY

Detective Superintendent Daniel Spencer was a tall, handsome black policeman. He looked fit and sharp, the sort who might work out, who read a broadsheet newspaper, who was sensitive to issues and could pass psychometric tests. He made my overweight friend, DI Robert Falk, who was lurking in the background in his cheap suit, look a little shabby and old-fashioned, like an embarrassing remnant of the fry-up-and-a-Rothmans generation of British policemen. But appearances, as they say, can deceive, and I for one wasn't surprised to see Robert at the police press conference the day after. He'd been with the National Criminal Intelligence Service for three years now, and I'd seen him taking up the space of at least two back seats at the press conferences of a couple of high-profile investigations that year.

Robert's specialist subjects were computer security and Chinese food, and for all I knew, Spencer's smooth looks might also have disguised an entirely different nature. There were traces of an east London accent, and a careful, methodical way of speaking such as criminals use when they want your attention. The TV camera moved closer to his face.

'On December 1st, 11.47 a.m., a 999 call alerted the

police to an explosion at thirty-five Market Road, Hackney,' he began. 'What was, at first, feared to be a gas explosion, was in fact quickly ascertained to have been a bomb blast.

'There were two victims: Douglas Raymond Samuels, whose home it was, and Joanna Sarah Casey. Mr Samuels, aged thirty-six, was the joint managing director of a prominent computer software company, Gecko Games PLC. He was pronounced dead at the scene. Jo Casey, a twenty-four-year-old journalist with a computer industry news service called Technology Online, was taken by air ambulance to the Royal London Hospital, where she was pronounced dead at 13.29 p.m. Both Mr Samuels and Ms Casey died as a result of severe head and chest injuries. Ms Casey was six weeks pregnant.'

I sat in the front room and chewed the knuckle of my thumb as the journalists' questions came thick and fast. Spencer held up his hand for quiet and got it.

'We need to establish when Jo Casey arrived at the house and her purpose for being there. It appears that her arrival delayed Mr Samuels' departure for a press conference at midday at the White House Club for which Mr Samuels' co-director and partner, Ms Cherry Shankar, had already left an hour before.

'This murder investigation is still in its very early stages, but so far we have this piece of information. A witness heard a motorbike in Market Road some minutes before the blast. Another witness saw a motorbike turning into Mare Street a few minutes after the blast and taking the route north and west.

'Who was that motorcyclist? Was he, or she, a messenger? If so, which courier service did he, or she, work for? The package may have been delivered to

Mr Samuels' home quite innocently. That messenger has valuable evidence to impart. It may be that the motorcyclist seen by our witnesses was not delivering the package at all and was simply driving through the area. If so, then he, or she, may have seen something important. We need to trace this person.'

Spencer then gave out a freephone Crimestoppers number and an Area Murder Investigation Pool number where he, or a member of his team, could be contacted by anyone with any information.

The news programme cut to a shot of Cherry Shankar, who looked chic, shocked and harassed as her aides hurried her away from the cameras. Her blood-red hair swung across her pale Asian face. She didn't push it away from her eyes and she said nothing.

A potted history of Gecko Games that followed described its rise from a middling eighties distribution firm to the nineties games creation giant. Gecko's top-selling character, Creature, roared at the screen and explosive flashes throbbed from its twenty-four mud-coloured fingers. A colourful computer-generated pie chart showed the world games market and the UK games market, and the biggest slices had Gecko's name on them. Another multicoloured chart showed Gecko's UK market profile. Teenage boys were the bedrock of its sales figures, and it was for precisely that reason that the company had chosen to give a £2 million donation towards a campaign by the National Family Advice Bureau to reduce the rate of teenage pregnancies in the United Kingdom. Controversially, the company had been supplying Creature multicoloured condoms with its games for more than a year.

Max looked smaller and frailer than he did in reality, and you couldn't see his wheelchair. His beard was grey and his gingery hair had receded in two deep crescents as far back as the crown of his head. In a few minutes, as the TV's chosen talking head for the technology industry, he said more to an audience of six million than he'd said to an individual person in twenty years.

When asked how Samuels' death might affect Gecko Games, he said that 'Gecko' Samuels was the first of the global games moguls but his company was frankly too big and multinational now for his death to make much of an impact on its future. If he had said, as I suspected he would have, that Cherry would have been a greater loss, it was edited out.

When asked about his employee, Jo Casey, he said that Jo was a hard-working young journalist with a great career ahead of her. He couldn't explain what she had being doing at Douglas Samuels' home that day except to say that given that she was a technology journalist and Samuels was a key industry figure, he wasn't surprised or shocked that she had been there, just sorry. He hadn't known that she was pregnant. He said that his staff did not confide in him.

He'd got that right.

I switched off the television and lit a cigarette. The sound of the helicopter blades whirring in the winter sky above the houses and tower blocks came back to me. What I had assumed to be a police gunship circling over east London had been the air ambulance flying Jo Casey and her unborn child to A&E. I had to wonder, like everyone else was wondering: whose kid was it?

I made two calls: one to Danny Morgan's mobile and one to Robert Falk's. Both told me to leave a message. As I turned the pages of my ageing contact book, I found two numbers for Cherry Shankar, a mobile and her home number. I doubted if she'd be at home, whatever was left of it, and I hesitated to call her mobile even though I had a right to phone her, an obligation even. We went back a long way and I would have been expected to offer my condolences. Anyone would buy that, buy zircons for diamonds, but I knew what was really going on and I didn't want her to see through me. It wouldn't stop at condolences. She was big news now. Five minutes after I'd seen the headline, I could feel a stirring in my guts like I'd swallowed a speed bomber with my beer. That Cherry Shankar might talk to me was my *edge*. She was my inside track on this story. I had something that Danny Morgan wouldn't have. The joy bubbling inside me was enough to make my hands tremble as I held the page on which her number was written. Yes, I said to myself, you've got an edge, and I sent her an email instead. I told her that I was sorry and if she wanted to talk, I'd listen.

I hate myself sometimes.

The computer was on, like always. It was never turned off, not even at night, when the noise of its cooling fan sometimes kept me awake. I was a light sleeper, even when I'd had a drink. Half dead with exhaustion or half cut, I'd wake up to a false dawn and hear the fan spinning and I'd start thinking about how I was going to open the doors to the house and walk out. I was thinking about it now, on a gloomy winter afternoon, with the postcard resting on the bottom edge of the screen, a blank presence in the corner of my eye.

I picked it up. I didn't get much post, but here it was. Maybe Richard was right about my weird boyfriends. Maybe one of them would try to run me over and then send me a strangely threatening card. Maybe I did have reason to be afraid. I flicked at the card with my fingers.

And if I had reason to be afraid, the thing that gave me *a reason to be afraid* had gone to *the wrong house*.

It couldn't be Tony, then. Tony, my ex, knew where I lived. But Tony didn't hate me like that, I told myself, did he? I searched for the business card of the young detective constable who had taken my statement on the night Richard and I had been knocked down. When I found the card, I started to tap out his number, but stopped and called Richard instead. I didn't know whether I was calling him to be reassured or rebuked.

'Do you think this postcard, you know, the weird boyfriend one, is some sort of publicity stunt?' I said.

'What?'

'You know, you get the card and then a week later you get some sort of multimedia marketing explanation for the mystery? Muggers.com or something?'

'You mean you think it's a teaser?'

'It's certainly that.'

Richard was silent.

'Well?' I said.

'George, what story are you working on?'

'I don't know.'

'You don't know.'

He was talking to me like I was eight years old.

'You are working on *the* story,' he continued. 'You are working on *the big* story. What happened to us is a *little* story. No one is interested in what happened to us. We are not worth millions of quid. We do not affect a share price or move a market. We are little people. We are journalists. We are not even important journalists. We do not have a hotline to Number Ten. We have not been injured while covering some exotic skirmish abroad. We do not front *Crimewatch*. We were knocked over on the way home from the pub. Get a fucking grip.'

I lit another cigarette and listened to the slight wheeze of his breathing.

'So,' I said, 'what do you think?'

He cut me off.

I replaced the receiver and logged on to the Net, and entered my name on a People Searcher. Richard's address and his telephone number appeared. The People Searcher was out of date but the exact location of the house, in a terrace between the canal and the park, was marked on a handy nationwide map linked to the site.

I entered Cherry's name, and Gecko's, and Jo's. Cherry and Gecko had the same address and an ex-directory phone number. Jo was listed as living in Plymouth.

It was childishly easy to find out where someone lived, except if, like me, or like Jo, the records had yet to be updated from the phone directories and the electoral registers. She hadn't been in London long and I hadn't been in my new home that long either.

That was why the card had gone to Richard's. It was my old address. Whoever had sent it either knew me when I lived there, or was using out-of-date records. I figured too that whoever took the package to Gecko Samuels' house must have addressed it to Gecko or to Cherry. The package had to be for them. If it had been for Jo, that someone would have had to have known that she'd be there.

I picked up the card and put it back down, reaching up to the books on my shelf. I found what I wanted, dusty and unloved, tucked in next to *Newsman's English*.

*The Hidden Language of Your Handwriting* by James

Green and David Lewis. 'Health, Job Prospects, Sexual Attraction, Personality and Emotions . . . Revealed at the Stroke of a Pen!'

I turned the postcard over.

*Be seeing you.*

The quasi-scientific guide to graphology had a handy dictionary based on the Funnel Method of Analysis set out at the back.

*Black ink:* an overconcern with precision in communications; a desire to be clearly understood.
*Long, straight upstrokes:* aggression
*Long, straight downstrokes:* aggression.
*Rigid; angular:* directly or indirectly expressed aggression.
*Forward slant:* sociable, outgoing.

I slung the book on to the desk. Obsessive, aggressive and sociable. Unfortunately, I could think of someone who fitted that description, and Richard was right, he *was* an ex-boyfriend. His name was Pal Kuthy.

It was stretching it to call him a boyfriend. I'd two-timed the man I *thought* was my boyfriend by sleeping with him, and to my mind, Pal wasn't so much weird as ruthless. He was the kind of guy who always seemed to be smiling, like he always knew something you didn't. He was always grinning at his own private, cruel joke. I'd had the last laugh, until now, at least. I'd fingered him for trading in stolen computer chips. He'd learned how to deal in illicit technology when trade with Eastern Europe was strictly controlled. When the Wall had come down, he'd discovered that Western organisations needed his skills, but when he got caught, not even his friends in secret places could save him from jail. I reckoned he'd be out about now, and knowing him like I did, I was right to be afraid.

The dog pushed the door wide open and came into the room. She gave me a moist, reproachful look.

'Oh, all right,' I said, and led the way to the kitchen, which was a long, narrow affair with the usual fitted melamine boxes on the wall. The dog's bowl was by the cupboard under the steel sink, and she sat patiently by as I shovelled a scoop into a sack of dry mixture that looked like rabbit droppings and filled the dish.

'There,' I said.

She looked at the khaki-coloured food and then at me. I was with her. It didn't seem right to feed her little round pellets of desiccated lamb instead of a bloody bone.

'Eat,' I said.

She turned away from the dish and loped through the house towards the front door, where she sat by the coat stand and waited, eternal hope dancing like a flame in her charcoal-coloured eyes.

'No deal,' I said, and opened the back door instead. In a spirit of compromise, the dog ran past me and out, barking. Her joyful yelps demanded answers, and soon the background hum of the rush-hour traffic was punctuated with ululating calls of the domesticated wild. I stood with the light behind me, looking out on my strip of scrubby lawn, where there were no colours, just pools of black and the pale light from the kitchen casting my long dark shadow to the edge of the canal.

The early winter darkness meant that the lights were already on in the windows of the three-storey houses on the far side, but the blinds had yet to be drawn. There were lights too in the tall high-rise beyond, with an occasional bloodshot square of festive red. Upstairs,

Richard's bedroom light was on, but where I used to sleep, the room was dark. It was going to be their baby's room, but there never was a baby for Mary, and Richard used it as an office.

The cold air that smelled of still water and damp grass felt fresh against my dry skin, and I thought now might be the right time. My brain told my heart, which began to race, and my body seized, unable to move through the clear membrane that seemed to have formed between the doorway and the outside. The dog's eyes glowed green in the far corner of the garden and I could just make out the burnished colour of her coat. She padded quietly towards me as I tried to steady my shallow breathing. She was almost upon me when I looked up and saw a figure standing at the window of a flat on one of the upper floors of the tower block. It was a man, I was sure of that, but it wasn't clear if he had his back to me or if he was facing me.

I could hear my own blood pumping like an engine until the sound of the television, the voices telling me the news, the muffled helicopter blades and a paw scratching at the door brought a reality to the panic. I had stepped back and shut the door in the dog's face. I lit a cigarette with shaking hands, and when I opened the door, the man at the window had gone and the dog was sitting waiting for me, her ears pricked and her brow knotted into a furrow of curiosity.

'In,' I said, and as I shut the door behind her, the telephone rang.

It was a man's voice.

'Georgina?'

'Who's this?'

'I'm ringing to ask if you're OK.'

His question threw me. I didn't recognise the voice, which had a trace of a West Country accent.

'I'm sorry. I didn't quite catch your name,' I said.

'Dr Lane.' I sucked on my cigarette, waiting for an explanation.

'You didn't attend your follow-up appointment at the hospital,' he said.

'So?'

'So, are you OK?'

I tried to put a face to the name.

'After the accident,' he repeated. 'You had concussion.'

'That's right.'

'But you didn't attend the follow-up consultation.'

'Do I get fined?'

'No. Though we would have liked forty-eight hours' notice.'

'OK. What now?'

'I wondered if you'd like to come out for a drink?'

That stalled me. I mentioned something about ethics and he laughed. I suddenly had a picture of him in my head. It was the doctor who'd treated us that night. He'd told me to put my cigarette out. He'd looked like a student in a lab coat. He'd shone a light in my eyes and said they were an interesting blue.

'You're the guy with the blond hair, dark roots, right?' I said.

'You're the girl with the red hair, dark roots, right?'

'Right,' I said, calmer now, my heartbeat slowing to a lazy groove. I remembered thinking at the time that here was someone who was exactly my type. A doctor, Richard, I said to myself. What do you think about that? Nothing weird about a doctor, a fine, upstanding young man working for the community. Less weird than a journalist, even, I'd say.

'Concussion,' the doctor said.

'I don't remember.'

'I do.'

'That was a joke.'

He laughed again, a soft chuckle.

'So, how about it, Georgina? You and me. Let's meet somewhere.'

I said I'd give it some thought, but the truth was, the thought was blurred by fear.

'Come on.'

'I've had some bad news,' I said, and as I put down the phone, the dog growled and I turned to see a man walking past the window. I glimpsed dark trousers, a beige raincoat with a yellowish tartan lining and the belt hanging loose. A brown paper bag with handles dangled from his large banana-shaped fingers, and a little wisp of steam drifted out of the bag, trailing behind him and turning to the colour of Scotch in the lamplight. He opened the iron gate and trod lightly down the mossy stone steps to my flat. I held the dog's collar tightly as the doorbell rang and she began to bark.

'Mrs Powers,' he said, when I opened the door.

'DI Falk,' I replied.

He held up the bag of Chinese food for my formal inspection.

'Supper?'

The front room and the dining room were one long living area that could be closed off by dividing doors. The dining room was tagged on to the kitchen and looked out over the garden. We sat there at the table with the doors to the living room open. The wallpaper in one room clashed with the other.

'It's coming along,' Robert said, looking around.

'Yeah.'

'I thought you were going to knock the wall down into the kitchen.'

'No.'

'Make it an L-shaped kitchen-diner.'

'No.'

'Best to keep the integrity of the room, eh?'

'If you say so, Robert.'

He dished out several scoops of steaming saffron-coloured noodles and laid out some twenty quid's worth of spare ribs, sweet and sour pork, beef chilli, and vegetable curry. It was standard takeaway fare, but good quality. When I said Robert was an expert in Chinese food, I meant within the narrow range of local availability.

'I was going to ask if you wanted to eat out, but I thought perhaps it was too early,' he said.

'Seven is not too early to eat.'

'Too early after the accident.'

I stuck my white plastic fork into the noodles and wound them around and around.

'It's been a month.'

Robert wiped orange-coloured sauce from his cherry lips with a white paper napkin.

'You need a holiday, that's all.'

'I need to work.'

He took a sip of beer.

'Did you know Jo Casey?' he said.

'No, but apparently she was a bit like me.'

'As if.'

I gave him a cheesy smile. It was a shameless piece of flattery, but I expected it from my friends.

'Do you know what she was working on?' he asked.

'No, but her boyfriend Danny Morgan might. Has he been on to you?'

He thought for a moment and then remembered the name.

'He represented Technology Online at the press conference, yes?'

'No, he wasn't representing them,' I said. 'He'd just got fired.'

'Why?'

'He and Jo were an item. He wanted to do the story.'

'And?'

'And Max didn't want him to.'

Robert leaned back. A couple of drops of sticky red sauce had dripped from a spare rib and landed on his shirt.

'You look like you've been shot,' I said.

He kept his eyes on me and brushed the napkin half-heartedly against his ample chest.

'Why didn't he want him to?'

'Too big a story. He insisted. Max told him to bugger off.'

Robert filled his mouth with beef chilli. His cheeks shook as he swallowed, and the mole high on his cheekbone bobbed about like a bead in a belly dancer's navel.

'We're thinking that maybe Jo Casey and Gecko Samuels were an item,' he said.

I pushed away my paper plate and picked up my packet of cigarettes.

'Mind if I smoke?' I said.

He never did mind, and while he ate the remains of

our meal, I blew clouds above his head. We were quiet for a while until I asked him: 'What does Cherry say?'

'She says she has no idea.'

'Would it have mattered to her?'

He said nothing.

'If it did, you think she had something to do with it?' I said.

Robert focused on a stray noodle that had stuck to his plate and picked at it with his finger.

'Intuitively?' he said.

Robert valued intuition in crime investigation. Leaps of imagination, he argued, were responsible for the most significant advances in science – intuition first, and then systematic proof. On the other hand, intuition, being regarded as a feminine quality rather than a fundamental human one, was such a degraded talent that if he divulged anything to me based on intuition rather than fact, no one could touch him for it.

'I don't think so,' he said.

'How is she?'

'OK. Under the circumstances.'

'She's a friend of mine.'

That interested him, so I said, 'Sort of,' and then, 'How did it play out?'

'It looks like Samuels accepted the parcel and took it into the house.'

'Where was Jo Casey?'

'She was by the window.'

I caught my own reflection in the French windows and was surprised to see that it was snowing outside. Small, insignificant flakes that would never settle fell from the dark sky and brightened the air so that it seemed like morning. I remembered Jo Casey looking at me. Her eyes had glanced quickly around the room, and seeing me, she had held my gaze for that curious moment just before Richard had waved his fingers in front of my face and she had smiled at him. Richard had said she was a bit like me. I wondered if she had had my taste in men.

'When does Pal Kuthy get out of jail?' I said.

'Six months ago.'

The inside of my mouth felt as dry as cotton. I sucked in the last of my cigarette and ground the end into my paper plate.

'Any idea where he is?'

'He flew to Switzerland.'

'Why didn't you tell me?'

'The man's gone. He stuck around for a while but now he's gone. Don't worry about it.'

'He could have run us down. I think he could have done that.'

I lit another cigarette and he said nothing.

'Richard mentioned my weird ex-boyfriends. Pal was kind of weird, don't you think?'

Robert cleared the tin-foil trays and scraps of food from the table and tipped them back into the paper bag. He left me my paper-plate ashtray and took the leftovers into the kitchen. When he returned, he popped open another bottle of beer and shared it with me.

'Mary been round much?' he said.

'Like a flea on a dog's tail.'

I sipped the drink and spat it out. We started to laugh, and then it built and built until the tears squeezed out of our eyes as we roared at the hilarity of my former landlord's picaresque interlude with Mary Stow, who had conned him into an engagement and me out of a home.

'She's leaving anyway,' I said at last.

'Him?'

'I don't know about that. *Technology Week*, sorry, Online.'

'What about you?'

'I'm still working for them,' I said.

'On this?'

'Max's asked me, but . . .'

'. . . but you've got other things on your mind.'

Robert reached over and patted my arm with his warm plate-sized paw.

'Kuthy left the country. I made sure.'

'I put him in jail, Robert.'

'Not you, me, the police, the courts.'

'You couldn't have done it without me. He said he'd make me pay.'

He sighed and drew his hand back.

'He wouldn't hurt you. He's the philosophical type.'

I remembered two shots popped into the pillow that my head had been resting on. Pal could have killed me then but he didn't. I could have taken some comfort from that, except that that was before I put him in jail.

'He did that guy in the bath. Broke both his legs and left a Braun electric on a timer in the water with him. Guy waited two hours for the switch to flick. Philosophical, as in what?'

Robert cleared his throat.

'That was different. In his own way, he was rather fond of you.'

I got up and left the room. Robert was still sitting at the table, folding and refolding a paper napkin, when I came back and placed the postcard in front of him.

He stared at it for a long time, and then flipped it over with a fingernail.

*Be seeing you.*

He sucked and chewed at his lips.
'When did you receive this?'
'Yesterday.'
He checked out the address.
'Old address.'
'Yes.'
'West End postmark.'
'Yes.'
'Have you showed it to the officer on your case?'
'Not yet.'
'Like me to do it?'
'I can do it.'
Robert pushed his steel-rimmed glasses back on to the bridge of his fleshy nose.
'I'd like to do it,' he said.
'And get involved?'
He blinked behind the lozenges of glass, and his eyes looked smaller, harder and very blue.
'Could you find me an envelope?' he said.

CHAPTER FOUR

# MONKEY BOY

In his own way, Pal Kuthy, a poker-playing, psychopathic Hungarian technology smuggler and redundant spy, was rather fond of me. Not weird, like Richard said, just extreme. I'd met him on a plane leaving Las Vegas, on my way home with petty revenge in my heart and a story about a million dollars' worth of memory chips in my head. I hadn't realised that he was looking for them.

I'd been sleeping with a Japanese ex-pat businessman called Shinichiro Saito. I was pregnant by him and not that happy with the situation. Pal was very happy. He said it turned him on. He turned me on too, at first, but I shopped him in the end for two reasons: I was on to a big, big story; and I was afraid of him. He'd send me a postcard like that all right, just to rattle my cage. Switzerland. Zurich, I reckoned, picking up what he was owed, and only a couple of hours or so away from a West End postmark.

I lost that baby, my second. I dream of them sometimes, not just the ones that might have been, but thousands of others. In my dream, their eyes are shut and their hands are the colour of the sunrise. Fleshy lifelines anchor their bodies in a silent floating world, while their faces bob and press against a soft, membranous window through which I can see them all. The only sound is a low drumming, like the chanting of priests. I think it is just one heartbeat, but when I look for the child, my child, whose heart is beating, every one opens its eyes and sees me.

Sometimes I try to manufacture my dreams so that I get what I want. After the accident, I tried to think about what had happened to Richard and me so that I could dream about that. I tried to force my mind's eye open wide to take in a three-hundred-and-sixty-degree perspective on the events as they occurred, to rerun the flickering images, force myself to glimpse the driver in the hope that maybe I *had* seen him. I saw things that I couldn't possibly have seen: I saw myself stepping out on to the crossing, the car accelerating towards us, Richard shoving me in the back. When I saw my head hit the ground, I felt an ache deep inside and I lay there wishing that I had a broken leg or a broken arm that someone could see and nurse.

This time, nothing came of my efforts to rebuild those few unresolved minutes of my life. I lay in bed with the sidelight on and my eyes closed, listening to the dog breathing, the computer's fan spinning, and thinking of nothing. I tried to paste people that I knew on to the scene of the crime, but no one seemed to fit as well as Pal Kuthy.

And the others? No. Richard was wrong. My weird boyfriends were nothing special. Just the type of bastard that a girl gets to tangle with if she's easily bored.

Take the first heartbreaker, my ex-husband, Eddie Powers, a duplicitous American charmer whose motto was 'Follow the Money'. He'd slept with my best friend but he blamed me for my unforgiving nature when I divorced him. If anything, I should have run *him* over. He was a hustler, but he wasn't the violent type. He was long gone anyway, too, probably in Hawaii, having his back rubbed and scamming some other sucker.

Warren Graham was my best friend and altogether different. He was my soul mate, a good-looking black man who cared for me but let me down. When I knew him, he was a cab driver and a hacker. He used to hack for fun but he had followed the money just like Eddie. It wasn't all bad. I wouldn't have the flat if it hadn't been for his 'loan'. He thought I had an unforgiving nature too. Run me over? For not telling him how much I cared? For hating him in the end? I didn't buy it. He didn't want me dead, just like I didn't want him dead, because then it would be over.

Tony Levi I had never really loved, because he tried to make me his doll. He was an ex-boxer, world class, and East End businessman, and was as straight as any wide boy could be. He had a good body, a nice technique, a bad temper and a jealous heart. He'd slapped me a couple of times, but basically, he was an old-fashioned London boy and, like they say, wouldn't really hurt a lady. If he had wanted to kill me, he'd have shot me. He did owe me a favour; that was always dangerous. It was the sort of debt that a nervous kind of person would wipe someone out for rather than have it hanging over them. But Tony Levi wasn't a nervous kind of person. In any case, I was looking after his dog, and he knew where I lived.

Love was too strong a word for what I felt for Shinichiro Saito, but he was the only straight that I had enjoyed in a long line of shady sorts. He was an amateur sumo wrestler, and *sarariman* for a major Japanese chip firm, an innocent abroad who had wanted a white girl for a change. When I was pregnant with his baby, he had tried to do the honourable thing, Japanese style, and pay for my abortion. He got to keep his money because I'd lost the baby anyway. He was probably married with a couple of kids. I couldn't see him bothering to come looking for trouble. I hadn't hurt him, much.

Abdul Malik, the East End boy who played with phones, was buried in a graveyard off the Romford Road. His death had caused major problems hereabouts for a local Bengali gang who used him for their telecomms frauds. Cracking that was a big story for me, although the others who followed up on it seemed to think it was a really big deal that I had been his girlfriend, being that he was a teenager and black. The other insignificants, whose names I had forgotten and who had probably forgotten me, didn't add up to a musty box of love letters. Richard had a real nerve pointing a fault-finding finger at me. I couldn't think of one woman of his who hadn't tried to use him. Only Mary had cared enough to make a fool of herself over him, and it's never wise to make a fool of anyone.

I swung my legs off the bed and rolled myself a joint. It was a harmless little habit that I found hard to break, since grass was easier on me than alcohol, and tax-free. As I was lighting up, the phone rang and I listened to my voice on the answer phone.

'This is Georgina Powers. Leave a message or call this number.'

The number was my mobile phone. No one left a message, but a minute later my mobile rang.

It was Danny Morgan.

'You called me,' he said.

The bloke was wired. He was talking fast and I could

hear him sucking on his cigarette like the filter was blocked.

'I knew you and Jo were friends,' I said.

'You got anything?'

'Have you?'

'I got fired. I don't work for Technology Online. I'm a freelance now.'

I spared him my opinion on the wisdom of his choice.

'A friend of mine saw you at the police press conference making out you were staff,' I said.

'So?'

'So, he asked me what the deal was. You've got to be careful, Danny boy.'

'Don't call me that.'

'I told him you and Jo were friends.'

I could hear the sound of traffic. Other people's passing conversations and laughter ebbed and flowed in the thunder of heavy-duty wheels and gear changes, but Danny didn't speak.

'Danny?'

'We were friends,' he said.

I thought about how drunk he was and how I might push it a little, milk him while he was vulnerable.

'Did you know she was pregnant, Danny?'

I couldn't hear. His answer was muffled.

'Danny? Are you OK?'

'I'm OK.'

'Was it your baby, Danny?'

'I don't know, OK? Now what have *you* got?'

'I've got a bottle of Scotch, a spliff, and I'm on my own.'

He was crying, I knew it, and comfort was just a cab ride away.

'Perfect,' he said. 'Fucking perfect.'

*

It was three in the morning when the tick-tock engine of a taxi and a dog bark told me he'd arrived. I got out of bed and went to the door. He stood there in his oversized leather jacket, with snowflakes melting in his hair, and letting the cold night air into my hall. He squinted at me through the smoke and the steamy vapour of his breath, a cigarette hanging from his lips and a bony hand resting on the door to steady himself. He took the cigarette from his mouth with a lazy motion of his long fingers and exhaled. The dog moved her muzzle an inch away from his crotch and made a sawing noise with her throat. I swear sometimes it was like living with your dad.

'You started without me,' I said, and Danny Morgan, drunk as a sailor on shore leave, fell through the door into my arms.

I dragged him with difficulty into the front room. I was tall enough but a bit lightweight, and he was a big-boned lad, and young, like a gangly-legged colt. The dog got in the way and nearly had us both over, but I managed to manoeuvre my drunken diabolo through the door and on to the floor. At one point I was astride him, but there was nothing in it for either of us. I had to go and get a bucket. It was plain that he'd eaten nothing all day, and when he'd finished heaving up his liquid supper, I covered him with a throw and went back to bed.

At about four-thirty, I heard him get up and stumble around for the toilet. The chain flushed, water ran into the sink, and a few minutes later the door to my bedroom opened and he got into bed with me, fully clothed.

I awoke at six and Danny Morgan at ten. He walked

into my office hunting for a cigarette. When he found my pack, he lifted one before following the smell of coffee into the kitchen. He was back a few seconds later.

'That dog of yours . . .'

I called her. She sat by me and Danny started off towards the kitchen again.

'Good girl,' I said.

When he came back a few moments later, he had two cups clasped in his shaky hands and the cigarette clamped between his teeth.

'I didn't know if you took milk and sugar so I gave you both,' he said, and swung his legs across a spare chair in the corner. We said nothing for about ten minutes while we sucked on the twin stars of the junkie firmament: caffeine and nicotine.

'I was dreaming of Jo,' he said, eventually.

'I doubt it,' I said.

'Well, I . . .'

'Gimme a break. You didn't move enough for me to notice. I had to hold a mirror to your face just to be sure you weren't dead,' I said.

He looked neither relieved nor disappointed.

'How are you feeling?' I said after a while.

'My head hurts like a bastard.'

'I didn't mean that.'

He said nothing.

'It must be tough for you right now.'

'Nice place. Good spot by the canal.'

'Where do you live?'

'Other side of the park.'

'Did you live with Jo?'

He looked me in the eye. He knew what I was getting at. 'We don't live together. There are four bedsits in the place. I have one, she has one, girl works for Marks and Spencer has one and a weightlifter has another.'

He talked about her in the present tense like he couldn't quite believe that she was dead. He was trying to keep her alive by telling me that she was still here. I didn't want to look at him while he struggled with the pain of placing Jo Casey in the past. It would make it harder for me. I stroked the dog's massive head and watched the drool drip from her black lips.

'She *had* one,' I said.

His eyes showed his confusion.

'Yeah. That's right. She had one,' he said.

'How long had you known her, Danny?'

'I've known her . . . Fuck it. I *knew*. I *knew*. I *knew* Jo. That's it. I *knew* Jo at college.'

'Did you know that she was pregnant?'

He was choked up but I didn't want him to stop talking. I wanted to know what he knew.

'I didn't know.'

'Was it yours?'

'It could have been. I don't know. There were others.'

He pulled hard on his cigarette and squinted, like he was trying to make the tears back up. I waited as he closed his eyes and squeezed the bridge of his nose with his fingers. I wanted to tell him to cry and get it over with, but people have all sorts of hidden rules about self-control. When he finally looked up, his eyes were dry and he was staring at the screen.

'Are you online?' he said.

'Always,' I said, without looking back. 'It's a ten-quid-a-day habit.'

'Expenses.'

I nodded.

'Expenses.'

'So you're working.'

'I'm working.'

'On me?'

I said nothing.

'Jo would have done that. Used people.'

'I could have shut the door in your face.'

He pushed the chair away and got up.

'I don't care if you get the story or if I get the story. I want to know why this happened. I want to know who blew them to fucking kingdom come, and why.'

I turned to the screen and logged off.

'That *is* the story, Danny.'

'You're doing this for money. I'm not doing it for money.'

I stood up.

'Money's just a measure of how good the story is, but it only gets to be part of the buzz if there is a lot of it to be made. You could make a great deal just by saying you were the father of the child.'

He stood there for a bit. I thought he was mulling it over, but he said, 'I'm gay.'

*The grieving gay father of bomb victim's child.*

'Think of a number and double it,' I said.

I stood by the kitchen door, which I had opened to let the dog out, and some air in. It was cold and bright, as if the greyness had been filtered from the sky by the snow that had fallen and melted as soon as it touched the ground. The water of the Grand Union was brown and still as a mud flat at the end of my garden.

The perfect intro ran through my head, as I tried to bury my weasel words about what was and wasn't a story, and the role money played in it all. They were worth a considerable amount, Jo, her dead baby and

Danny Morgan. He said he didn't know if it was his, but that didn't matter; it could be, which meant everything. I didn't have to hit the streets because the story was right here. All I had to do was make a phone call.

The dog's ears pricked up and she faced me, standing alert in the chilly sunlight by the lime-green trunk of an old tree. I could feel his presence behind me.

'Was she seeing Gecko Samuels?' I said, turning.

He said nothing.

'That would have been interesting,' I said. I thought of Cherry. I hadn't known Jo Casey, but I'd known Gecko Samuels, and the fact that he might have had a mistress didn't surprise me. It wouldn't surprise me if they found more than one.

'Why?' he said.

'It might have been Gecko's baby. You said there were others.'

'Does that make it a better story than if it had been mine?'

'For sure.'

'Ask me who I was seeing.'

I hesitated. He'd wrong-footed me.

'Who are you seeing?' I said.

'Not are. *Were*. Ask me. Danny, who *were* you seeing?'

I saw the picture then, in a glorious instant of intuition. I didn't have to ask, but I did.

'OK. Danny, who *were* you seeing?'

'Gecko,' he said, 'I was seeing Gecko Samuels.'

He looked directly at me. His eyes full of pain. I took my time. I didn't want to hurry him, so I waited until I thought we both understood each other, and I said,

'With world syndication, that's worth six figures, Danny.'

Big tearless sobs contorted his face as his body heaved. I should have put my arms around him but I couldn't. I didn't want to touch him. I didn't want his silent grief pouring over me and making a difference. I hadn't known that Gecko was gay, and if I hadn't known, then no one, outside of the discreet people who were sleeping with him, had. It wasn't public knowledge, and the story had just become bigger than I could have dreamed of.

'I slept with Jo and I slept with him. It could have been my baby. I've lost everything. Everything.'

I waited as long as I could bear to, but when I looked back it wasn't long enough.

'Do we have a deal?' I asked.

His face was wet but his eyes were deadened of all expression except disgust.

'What do I need you for?' he said, and he walked out of my house taking my packet of cigarettes with him.

CHAPTER FIVE

# SELLING YOUR SOUL

It was like I hadn't eaten in a week and someone had walked out with my lunch. I had a story to die for that had landed in my lap, and I had lost it. To bloody die for.

It was the Deadly Triangle of Love angle, worth a small fortune in syndication because Gecko Samuels had been a big-time international businessman with added software charisma. Any red-blooded tabloid would have splashed it on the front page and coupled it with an inside double-page spread with photos of Danny Morgan cornered in a studio looking moody and fey at one and the same time.

I thought he could do it. His career as a journalist would have been technically over, but he would have a bright future in male modelling, selling memoirs and flash-bulb celebrity parties.

If the boy made the call before I did, I could kiss the cash goodbye. He was right. He didn't need me. I had to get in first. I had played it all wrong by needing it too much. I knew that the real story, the *honest* story, was *why* Jo and Gecko had died, but no one had that yet and I had this. I hadn't worked in weeks. I was marooned on a subterranean island and the only way out was via a telephone line.

I called Diane Shine, a journalist I had known for a long time. We'd worked together when Technology Online was *Technology Week*, but now she worked at the biggest news agency in Britain. I wanted her to do the deal. It wasn't that I trusted her, but I knew that even minus ten per cent she'd get more than I could.

'Girl,' she said when she heard my voice. She sounded like a cat settling into a spot in the sun. 'We haven't heard from you in a while. How are you doing?'

I said I was working, you know, doing OK.

'How's Richard?'

The sly smile she was wearing eased down the line like silk over nylon. We both knew what she was at. Richard still had the imprint of her kitten heel on his heart.

'We got hit by a car.'

'Shit.'

'We're OK, though.'

'Well, give him my love, won't you? Now, what have you got?'

I told her.

'Baby, get me a police quote and book a cruise,' she said.

I asked to speak to Detective Superintendent Daniel Spencer and was offered a two-rank drop from the top, so I said I had information and two minutes later he was on the line. He said his name briskly and with more of an East End accent than he had had when he had spoken at the televised press conference. I told him I was working for Technology Online, which wasn't the truth but it wasn't a lie either. I was working for Diane's agency, but I wasn't sure how co-operative he'd be if I told him that.

I told him about Danny Morgan and Gecko, and about Jo Casey's baby. He said he knew all about it, which meant he was more than one step ahead of me. I was surprised but not too disappointed, because I wasn't actually phoning to break the case but to get a line.

'It must explain why she was there,' I said.

'It might do,' he said.

I was happy with that. I could craft those three words into an indirect quote.

*Detective Superintendent Daniel Spencer confirmed that it might explain Jo Casey's presence at the house.*

I had what I wanted and my stomach began to churn. I could lose my edge any time soon. I had started to run for the line, and Spencer could overtake me if he wanted to. Now he knew it was out, he could release the information so as to control it, and I would have nothing. I wanted to get off the phone and call Diane, but he slowed everything right up, even the way he spoke. I imagined him clicking his fingers above his head and a press officer running to get a hastily scribbled note.

'What isn't a "might", Georgina – may I call you Georgina?'

'Please do.'

'What isn't a might is that Jo Casey was there when a bomb arrived, and it killed her and Gecko Samuels.'

Who killed them and why? The real story wouldn't go away. I felt tired suddenly. There was a time when I would have worked towards getting an answer to those questions. This time I just wanted a fast story. I just wanted a break. I felt as if I was sinking.

'But the bomb was for Gecko, wasn't it?' I said.

'How do you know that?'

I could have shot myself. I shouldn't have been doing this. I should have been saying my thanks and goodbyes. He was keeping me online and I was helping him.

'Jo didn't live there, so I assume it was addressed to him or to Cherry. It could have been for Cherry. Was it?'

'I can't comment,' he said.

'Thank you, Detective. I'll be in touch if I need more information.' I'd made a grab for that little extra. Now I wanted out, but he wasn't letting me go.

'We are considering the possibility that this was a hate crime,' he said. 'The gay angle could be very important.'

'Has anyone claimed responsibility?' I asked.

'Not yet.'

I had more than enough, a quote from Spencer and a new angle. I should have gone off line then, but the old me wasn't shifting.

'I can't see it,' I said. 'I never knew Gecko Samuels was gay, and I knew him pretty well.'

'How well?'

I kept cool.

'I've been in the industry ten years and I never heard a whisper. If he had a reputation, it was as a womaniser.'

'That doesn't mean he didn't sleep with men.'

'No. But if he did, he was very, very discreet.'

'Somebody must have known.'

I thought about Danny Morgan. He was a journalist, and he hadn't exactly spread the news that he and Gecko were lovers. God damn. It must have been love.

'Like I said, there was never any industry gossip about that,' I said.

'About what then?' Spencer enquired.

'The usual. Coke.'

'That's quite a claim.'

'It's rife in this business.'

'What about Cherry Shankar?'

'No.'

'But the industry gossip was that he was involved in drugs?'

'He took them, if that's what you mean by involved.'

'Involved means involved: user, dealer, distributor.'

I laughed. 'The guy was worth zillions, why would he bother making a business of it?'

'How well do you know Cherry Shankar?'

'She's a friend, Superintendent.'

'More than just an industry contact.'

'Yes.'

'Does she take drugs?'

'I have no idea.'

'No industry gossip about her?'

'No. This is a why, right?'

'Drugs, sex, money, power are four sure routes to murder.'

'You forgot madness, Detective Superintendent, and hate.'

I heard a motorcycle slow in the road and stop outside. I left the phone hanging by its cord and hurried into the front room, making sure I kept close to the walls so that no one outside could see me. I stood to the side of the bay window and just far enough back to see out and not be seen.

There was a maroon-coloured bike parked close to the pavement, and I could see a person in black leathers and a full-face helmet. It looked like a man, not too tall or too broad. He had a khaki-coloured courier bag slung over his shoulders, but I couldn't see a logo. I saw his booted legs through the iron railings, belted with straps of steel, as he dismounted and walked towards the outside gate. He stopped, as if he was checking the house numbers, and pushed the gate open. The dog began to bark. He put a gloved hand on the gate that led to my basement, hesitated, and then went up the stairs to Richard's. I heard him ring the bell and it occurred to me that Richard wouldn't be able to answer in time.

I went back and picked up the phone.

'I'm sorry. I have to go now. There's someone at the door. Thank you for talking to me,' I said, and hung up. I told the dog to shut up, and went back to the window. Richard's front door bell rang intermittently and the dog started up again. My phone rang. It was Richard on his mobile.

'Georgina, for God's sake, see who it is, will you? I'm having a crap.'

'It's a courier.'

'Well, could you sign for whatever he has for me and take it in?'

'It's a courier with a package.'

'Sign for it.'

'Are you expecting anything?'

'Yes.'

'I don't want to.'

'Georgina, please. What's the fucking problem?'

'I can't see a logo.'

'So?'

'I don't know who it is.'

'Oh, fucking leave it.'

I went back into the front room, but this time I went right up to the window and peered through the dirty glass.

As soon as I saw the courier come down the stairs, I

ran towards the door, then stopped. I was going nowhere. I stood staring at its black oblong mass, telling myself that my intuition was unreasonable. It had been thrown off course by a knock to the head and an injection of fear, but I might as well have been teetering on the edge of a fathomless abyss. I couldn't open the door. I stood instead with clammy hands gripped in tight fists, the agitated dog pacing around me, until I heard an engine fire, a throttle whine, and the motorbike pulled away.

The phone started ringing almost as soon as it had gone. I picked it up, cleared the line and dialled Diane's number.

'We just got a spoiler,' she said. 'Double whammy. Sorry.'

'Don't tell me. The police.'

'And Danny Morgan.'

I told Richard.

He was sitting at the kitchen table peeling potatoes in a pair of torn shorts with his stiff plaster-encased leg at a right angle.

'How far have you got on the rest of it?'

'The rest?'

'They died, remember? You think this is about love?'

'Diane sends hers.'

He tossed the potato into the saucepan and it made a splash. We didn't speak until the potatoes were mashed and on my plate with an organic Cumberland sausage and some gamy gravy.

'It wasn't public knowledge that Gecko was gay, or that he swung both ways, so why would he be a target?' I said. 'The only thing he was open about was women and money. He was a flash bastard.'

'He lived in Hackney, George.'

'Three-storey Georgian Hackney with private walled garden overlooking a nice tidy tree-lined square, as opposed to two-room maisonette with communal shit-strewn walkway overlooking nasty one-way system. Yes, he lived in Hackney.'

'Hardly flash, with what he earned.'

'Cherry wanted to live there. He agreed because it looked street. He just knew how to slum.'

'You didn't like him.'

'Cherry made him.'

'And he cheated on her.'

I didn't answer. I picked at my food and pushed the plate away.

'Well, you can't say he hasn't paid for it,' Richard said.

He was right. Gecko had paid for it, and I should give the guy a break. As I got up to leave, Richard placed his knife and fork on his plate. He hadn't finished but he was going to offer to limp to the door with me. I raised my hand to put him off, and left.

When I got home I had mail. Forty-nine items I didn't want to read and one that I did. It was from Cherry Shankar, and all it said was: *Call me.*

She brushed aside the regrets I voiced at having left it so long. She said it was as much her fault as mine. I said that I was really sorry about Gecko and she told me what had happened that day. I listened and said what I hoped were the right things, but the worst part was that I had to get answers and she just kept asking questions. Why Gecko? Why us? Who could have done this? In the end, I asked her what I had been putting off. I asked her if she knew about Gecko and Danny Morgan.

'What do you think?' she said.
I said nothing.
'I'm curious about that Jo Casey, though,' she said.
'Why?'
'What was she doing there? If it was business, why didn't she go to the conference?'
'Did you know she was pregnant?' I said.
'How would I have known that?'
'Do you think she went to the house to confront him?'
'Was she pregnant by him?'
'I don't know.'
'By the other guy? Danny?'
'Maybe, but I asked him and he didn't really know. He said there were others. It could have been his, though. If it was, maybe she found out about him and Gecko.'
'They're doing tests,' she said.
'DNA?'
'Yes.'
A picture of a post-mortem flashed into my head. It was not complete, just a morbid fragment of a whole, a sliver of bloody tissue and the steel point of an instrument. I wrote down what she said and drew two lines by it. I had to check up on that.
There was silence between us.
'I heard you had an accident,' she said. 'I'm sorry I didn't call.'
I told her it was OK, water under the bridge.
'It was a hit-and-run.'
'They get them?'
'No.'
'Scary.'
I wanted to change the subject, so I told her that the

story about Danny Morgan and Gecko would probably be in the tabloids the next day and that she wasn't to upset herself. We were all on to it. Danny had just got there first. He had an inside track, but at the end of the day, it was just business. She said she understood, and she asked me if I was going to be at the Gecko Games press conference the next day. I said that I couldn't make it, and she told me to try, because it would be good to see me, a friendly face and all that.

'I loved Gecko, really loved him, you know?' she said.

It was some kind of love. I remembered her telling me once that Gecko believed that you could be mentally faithful to someone when you were fucking someone else. At the time, I couldn't believe that someone so smart could be so stupid. She told me that they were soul mates. They valued spiritual love and friendship above all else. Jealousy was self-love. Sleeping around wasn't important. It was just sex, just satisfying a bodily need. It wasn't about true love. Well, hell, I knew *that*.

She'd made him sound so connected, almost holy, like he'd discovered the key to the lock of the invisible door that led to eternal happiness. The dispossessed possessives meanwhile were doomed to sweat at the perilous coalface of human relationships because we had the green-eyed monkey pulling at our ears while we made the beast with two backs.

'Gecko just isn't jealous, of anything. He's my best friend and I am his. It's the purest form of love, you know? Jealousy is a power thing, a control thing. It's so negative,' she'd said.

'Does he lie to you?'

'He doesn't need to.'

'How about you? Do you lie to him?'

Cherry had laughed at that, but just with her mouth, not her coffee-coloured eyes. Her eyes were hating me.

'Of course not.'

I should have left it at that, but I didn't. I said, 'Because you don't have to, do you, Cherry?' She didn't answer me, and I knew why. Gecko was the only one. What she did say was, 'I know about you two, if that's what you mean.'

'Cherry, I met him before you did, and I was drunk. Very drunk,' I said. She had looked too smug in her own blamelessness for me to stop myself. 'What does Gecko do anyway? Keep a database of us all for you?'

She'd paid the bill and left.

They'd never married, but that was no big deal. She was a bit older than him, five years, not enough to make the difference show. They looked about the same age. He appeared older if anything. He had the optimistic, confident swagger of someone who knew the rules and broke them when it suited him. She was quieter, but wackier, someone who appeared never to understand rules in the first place. She did things very much her own way. She'd be thinking while he talked and then she'd come in with something, an idea, a feeling, and his mind would almost pop with possibilities. Gecko never had an original idea in his life, but he knew one when he saw one, and he knew what to do with it, and that's as important a talent as thinking of them, more in his business.

'Did you two never want children, Cherry?' I asked now.

Cherry sighed. I think she was a little high.

'I did, but Gecko didn't. He didn't want children at all.'

I didn't like to ask her if she dreamed of them, like I

did, so instead I asked her where she was living. She said that she couldn't tell me. The police had put her up in a safe house.

'I'm going to have to rent somewhere for a while,' she said. 'We've got the place in France, the one in New York and the one in LA, but they're not very practical right now.'

'What about your folks?'

Cherry's family had moved out of the East End proper to a property the size of a small hotel in South Woodford, a popular stopping-off point en route to Chigwell for East End business folk and geezers who had made good, one way or another, in the rapacious and munificent City. The Shankars' source of wealth had been a traditional East End occupation, the rag trade. They had made their money before she had, and Cherry had gone to a private girls' school.

'I'm afraid for them,' she said.

In the knotted ball of possibilities that was the story I was tracking, I hadn't teased out that one. It was not something Spencer had mentioned either. It made me think how he had been using me more than I had used him. Cherry was as British as I was, but if the bomb was a hate crime, then the fact that she was of Asian origin was going to be as much of a factor as the fact that Gecko was gay. More so, because Gecko was a closet gay, but nothing could disguise Cherry's authentic ethnic looks, not the crimson hair dye or the cool clubwear.

'When's the funeral?' I said.

'Next week. Gecko's family are sorting it out. I wanted something quiet, simple, you know?'

Her voice faded away as she gave up on it; whatever she had wanted, she was not going to get.

'What do you think?' she said.

I hesitated. The conversation had become personal and two-way. We were friends but I hadn't taken off my hack's hat all the time we had been talking together. Hacks ask the questions always, and their opinions are really questions in disguise.

'Quiet and simple,' I said.

'Not the funeral. The bomb. What do you think about the bomb? Do you think it could be a race thing?'

I didn't want to tell her that I hadn't got as far as thinking about the 'who' and the 'why', because I had been waylaid by 'how much'.

'I don't know. What do you think?' I said.

I heard the sound of a glass being filled and the bell-like ring of ice close to her mouth.

'I think there'll be a second, don't you? It doesn't make sense that someone wanted to kill Gecko or that girl.'

'How can you be sure, Cherry? How well did you know him, or her, or anyone that knew them?' I said.

Her voice dropped to a whisper.

'I know something, but I'm not supposed to tell.'

The hair at the back of my neck prickled. I felt a slight rush of anticipation. I didn't want to speak in case I said the wrong thing.

'Who said you weren't supposed to tell?'

'The police.'

'Spencer?'

'A fat man. Falk.'

'I know him.'

There was silence.

'I'm not supposed to tell. We have to wait, you see.'

I didn't answer, and we were silent for a little while until she said, 'That Danny, how could he just sell his soul like that?' and I said that I just didn't know.

CHAPTER SIX

# A MANY-SPLENDOURED THING

The story had hit the wires before it had hit the streets. All the news hubs had the bare bones of it, but for the graphic thrill of Danny Morgan's tale of love and grief the world had to wait for the print tabloids. As I laid them out on the kitchen table, Danny's portrait reminded me that he had taken my cigarettes. I picked up the phone and called a cab. A man with a Cockney Asian accent replied.

'Hi, can you get me sixty Marlboro?' I said.

'Where to, madam?'

I told him, made sure he understood I was the basement flat. He said he knew it and that he'd be five minutes.

'And a bottle of milk.'

'Bottle of milk. Yes, madam.'

The cab was on time. A rheumy-eyed old boy in a beige shalwar kameez under a grey anorak and wearing a round white hat handed me the goods and gave me a couple of quid change from a twenty.

'Terrible cold weather,' he said, and I said it was and thanked him before shutting the door quickly.

I turned the heating up and read the news over a breakfast of tea and nicotine. I checked the front page and pulled out the spread as much as to estimate how much I had lost on the day as to read the sorry facts. I reckoned twenty easy. Danny Morgan had cleaned up on a dirty story.

The tabloids asked the big questions, of course. Had tragic Jo Casey get caught up in a gay hate campaign? Had she gone to the house for a showdown with Gecko Samuels? Was he her lover? Or was he her love rival? Danny 'I loved them both' Morgan exposed his bony chest and his duplicity. Jo was his best friend. They had slept together for companionship but he had never told Jo about his affair with Gecko. She must have found out. Just in case we couldn't imagine the scene between Gecko and Jo, there was a photo casebook of black-and-white stills showing the action as it might have happened, played out by an actor and actress who looked like them. 'Jo' was wearing a tight top and combat trousers. 'Gecko' was wearing a high-value, loose black sweatshirt with a slight V-neck, and dark, relaxed trousers. Bubble speak came out of their mouths.

'*Gecko, Danny says you're sleeping with him.*'

'*So?*'

'*So? I'm pregnant.*'

His hands rest on his hips and his brow is furrowed.

'*Am I the father?*'

'*I don't know. It could be Danny.*'

She cocks her head.

'*Is that the doorbell?*'

'*Stay here. I'll go.*'

The final scene was missing. They had to draw the line somewhere.

I knew Gecko of old. He had the sexual appetite of a pondful of frogs in springtime. He would have gone for

Jo, and if he liked men too, why not Danny? Danny was hinting that either of them could have been the father of Jo's child, but Jo wasn't around to tell us if she had so much as kissed Gecko Samuels, and he wasn't either. Nor was the child, to become the wise man that knew its own father.

I shuffled the newspaper back together and ignored the dog, which had spied an impudent cat in the garden and was huffing and puffing about it by the back door. The police must have added *jealous revenge* to the list of motives. Danny would be in the frame. And Cherry Shankar, of course.

It seemed to me that there was room for someone else in the picture. Gecko had been the lover of many and therefore the rival of more than a few. He could have been the light of someone else's life, or the bane. Whoever it was, they would have seen the same pages of the same newspaper that morning and felt either rage or satisfaction. The bomb could have been about love, jealous love. I glanced at my watch. It was almost eleven a.m., and I didn't want to miss the press conference that Gecko Games had gone ahead and rescheduled for that day. The news of the sponsorship had been swept away by the death of Gecko Samuels, but the aim of the conference wasn't publicity any more, rather reassurance about the future of the company. I had planned to sit in my front room and watch it on CNN.

Cherry took to the stage looking brave and slight in the spotlight in front of a huge graphic of Creature in its role as contraceptive dealer for the E-generation. In the palm of one repto-simian hand it offered a day-glo condom, while a slogan exploded from a preposterous multiplexed weapon that it gripped in the other. It said simply: *Love.*

She stepped up to the mike and read the statistics in her almost childlike voice. From time to time she added 'you know?' at the end of her statements, the perennial, non-threatening, hip question that had the effect of personalising what she was saying. The UK had the highest rate of teenage births in Europe, you know? A quarter of boys and a fifth of girls had had sex before reaching the age of consent. And girls regretted it more. Question mark.

She paused, gripping the lectern, as the Creature dissolved into a grainy black-and-white photograph of a teenage girl. The voice of a twelve-year-old spoke from the darkness.

'*It was just one of those things. I wish I'd never done it actually. When you imagine it, you don't imagine it like that. It was all really rushed. It was over and done with. I did not really speak to him after, I just felt stupid, so I walked out of the room, and that was that.*'

Oh baby, I thought, have we been there and done that.

Cherry allowed the girl's words to resonate in the black emptiness before her, then said that having sex young might not be a good idea but, whatever happened, it was important that teenagers, boys and girls, took care of themselves. That was why Gecko Games, despite the initial controversy, continued to give away free condoms with its games.

The girl's unsmiling face gave way to a still of her standing with a black boy, surly and cool, beside her. They did not touch.

'Our main customers are teenage boys,' Cherry said. 'Girls know they should take care of themselves but statistics also show that they don't like to carry condoms, they expect their boyfriends to. Fact, kids talk about sex among themselves; fact, they need good, accurate information. We at Gecko Games thought we'd help out.'

The girl and boy now stood in a multicultural crowd of their peers, and Cherry didn't sound flaky any more. She told the hidden crowd of media personnel that Gecko Games, in conjunction with the National Family Advice Bureau, would be running a national advertising campaign worth £2 million aimed directly at teenage boys and featuring Creature, with the simple slogan, *Love.*

There was silence.

Cherry squinted into the bright lights, and I felt the tension rise in the hidden audience, and in myself, in the expectation that she might speak off message, break down even. An aide hurried to her side, but she raised her hand to stop her. Her voice trembled slightly.

'It's not just about girls and boys, you know? It's about loving our children. All our children. Our children don't just grow up to be heterosexual. They grow up to be bisexual. They grow up to be homosexual. They need to take care of themselves too, each and every one of them. Thank you.'

The questions came like Stukas out of the sun, but the aide stepped smartly forward and removed Cherry from the line of fire. She would not, the woman said, be answering any questions concerning the death of Gecko Samuels and its effect on the company. Instead – the woman held up a single piece of paper – she would read a prepared statement. It was what everyone had been waiting for.

It may have been a page long, but the short of it was Business As Usual.

I switched off the TV and left the room with the word 'controversy' stuck in my mind. As I recalled, there hadn't been that much, a little light protest from the usual suspects of the religious right and other groups concerned with family morals and the promotion of teenage sex as a lifestyle choice. Their protestations hardly rated the pole position they had had in her statement, unless the corporate flaks had considered that by making Cherry and the company appear braver, the business survival message Gecko Games wanted to get over would be stronger. They had a share price to think about.

Thinking about the moral minority made me start wondering about *my* lifestyle choice, which, at that moment, wasn't serving me too well in that department. I'd never actually met anyone by chance within the confines of my own home, and I was frankly tiring of playing the part of my own weird boyfriend. I don't know, what with Christmas passing me by in the local pubs and the clubs up West, I felt lonely. I just had Richard for company, and I was as tired of him as he was of me. I thought of Cherry and Gecko, Jo Casey and Danny, and decided that I was sick of death and pain. I wanted some laughs. I wanted someone to kiss me and I wanted to kiss them back. I thought of Tony but my pride wouldn't let me, and in any case, it was the doctor with the blond hair and the dark roots that I wanted. He'd had a nerve to ring me up like he did, but he had judged it right. We had definitely connected. If I'd met him anywhere else but A&E, the game would definitely have been on.

The angel on my shoulder wagged his pale finger.

This is how you get into all that trouble, he whispered. You can't trust your judgement with men. You take too many risks. You don't think things through. They just have to press the right button in your head and you're off. I told the angel flat that no quickfire button had been pressed. I just wanted company and I didn't want it to be Richard or Robert Falk or the damned dog that wasn't mine.

Somewhere in my office was my hospital appointments card. It had also been sent to Richard's house. I presumed it was because, in the state that I was in, I had not said the key words 'Basement Flat' before the number and the road. I concocted a little plan that would make me sound a little less desperate. I'd tell him I needed a prescription, something to make me sleep, that I wasn't on a doctor's list, something like that, and then I made the call.

'I'd like to speak to Dr Lane. I'm returning his call,' I said.

'Department?'

'A and E.'

'One moment, please.'

I waited.

'A and E admin, can I help you?'

It was a woman's voice.

'Could I speak to Dr Lane, please?'

'One moment. We're very busy.'

I waited for at least five minutes, and then I heard another woman's hurried voice.

'Dr Lane speaking.'

I was too surprised to answer right away.

'Hello?' she said.

'I'm sorry, I must have the wrong person. The Dr Lane I want to speak to is a man.'

'Do you have the right department?'

'I think so. He's young, with blond hair and dark roots.'

'That's Dr Walker. He's not here at the moment. Do you want to leave a message?'

'No. I must be confused. I'm sure it was a Dr Lane that called me.'

'Can you tell me what it was about?'

I hesitated.

'A missed appointment.'

'Unlikely. Let me transfer you to patient administration. They should be able to sort it out.'

Her voice cut out as she tried to transfer me. I put the phone down. Someone was jerking my chain.

I called the hospital switchboard.

'Could I speak to Dr Walker, please?'

'Department?'

'A and E.'

I waited.

'A and E, can I help you?'

'Could I leave a message for Dr Walker, please?'

I left my name and number.

'Say I'm returning his call.'

The cheap little shit.

I was so angry that I walked to the front door and grabbed my coat, a three-quarter black leather number. The dog was at my heels. If it looked like a possibility that I might open the door, she wasn't about to miss out.

I actually had the coat on and my fingers on the door handle when I became conscious of what I was about to do. The moment that happened I knew I wasn't going to make it. The rush of anger that had overridden the fear subsided, and I was alone again with the pudding-faced god of homebodies, my palms sweating and a sick feeling in my stomach.

I took off my coat and went back into the front room. It wasn't so bad, I told myself. There was always daytime television.

Dr Walker called me at around five. I was ready for a fight, but I wasn't sure that I had the right man. The voice on the phone claiming to be Dr Lane's had had an accent, West Country or Norfolk. It was so slight that it was hard to tell which, but Dr Walker had neither. If I had to guess, I'd say he was a Camden boy with a voice as soft as butter.

'Thanks for calling back,' I said, 'but I think I've made a mistake. I'm sorry to waste your time.'

I was out of there but he said, 'Wait a minute,' and I hesitated.

'Georgina Powers. Red hair. Dark roots. Blue eyes.'

I paused. He must have seen a thousand people since we'd stumbled in that night. I wasn't wrong. We'd connected all right.

'Memorably bad hair, clearly,' I said.

'No, just memorable.'

The sweet talk hit me like a bullet in slow motion.

'Concussion, yes?' he said.

'That's right.'

'How are you feeling now?' he said.

I wanted to say 'fine' but the word stuck in my throat. The sudden stop in our conversation created a vacuum that he didn't fill. I tried something close to the truth.

'I'm not sure how I feel. I haven't been myself. I can't sleep. I was wondering if you could give me a prescription.'

'Don't you have a GP?'

'No.'

'You should come back in, let me have a look at you.'

I wanted to tell him that if I could have opened the damned door to the outside world I'd have been there in less than half an hour. Instead, I told him about the call I'd got from the hospital.

'Someone who said he was Dr Lane. I thought it was you.'

'I'm Dr Walker.'

'I know that now.'

'Why did you think it was me?'

This was the man *inside* the white coat speaking, wanting me to tell him that I had remembered him like he had remembered me. I should have ended it there.

'I thought it was you because he asked me out for a drink. Someone's been having me on. I won't waste any more of your time,' I said. I felt stupidly self-conscious.

'You've made up your mind, then?'

'About what?'

'About the drink.'

'Was it you?' I said.

'No.'

'Did you set it up?'

'No.'

'It's just that he knew what I looked like, and he said . . .'

I stopped and tried to remember. There was doubt in my mind. I had wanted Dr Lane to be the blond boy with the dark roots, but I couldn't remember if he had said that he was or if I had simply assumed it.

'He had my phone number. He knew that I'd had concussion. He knew that I had missed an appointment.'

'I'll look into it.'

'Thank you.'

'If I asked you out for a drink, what would you say?'

I took a moment. The angel was at my shoulder.

'I'd say I'd have to think about it,' I said.

It was three a.m. when the doorbell rang and Girl's bulk hurried past my door, her growl escalating into a wolfish snarl. I wasn't asleep, but I wasn't awake either. I was trying to fix my dreams so I could see the car driver but I was getting ghosting from an image of Dr Walker leaning his face towards mine and shining a light in my eyes. I opened my eyes and pulled on my jeans under the old sweatshirt I wore to bed. Dragging the dog back by her collar, I checked who it was through the security lens in the door. It could have been relief tinged with disappointment or disappointment tinged with relief that I felt when I saw who it was. I was too numb to tell. Danny Morgan was outside, swaying in the wind, as drunk as he had been before. I opened the door very slightly and kept the chain on.

'Can't you phone a friend?' I said, and very slowly and carefully he replied:

'My name is Michael Caine.'

I gripped the dog's collar while Danny drew out a box of matches and tried to light the cigarette that drooped from his lips. He bent his unsteady body over his cupped hands, but the tearing wind blew out the flame. He was still working at it when I shut the door.

I went into the kitchen. The cold floor chilled my feet, and little clouds of vapour formed by my breath condensed on the windowpanes. The branches of the trees in the garden whipped back and forth as I filled the kettle and placed it on the stove. I looked outside as I waited for it to boil. The lights were out in the houses across the canal, but in the tower block the red light shone and six windows formed a geometric pattern of insomnia against the sky. I could webcam the tower block, I thought, and create a home page for bad sleepers. They could bet on the last light out or on the final pattern of wakefulness that remained on the building at daybreak. I could run banner ads for Temazepam and Night Nurse. While I was thinking up e-names that would guarantee commercial success, the doorbell rang as the kettle boiled and blew a whistle on my dreams.

Danny Morgan was still there, but he had somehow defeated the wind and lit his cigarette. He leaned one hand on the doorframe and the front of his jacket bowed open to reveal an open-necked Hawaiian shirt and a strangely hairless chest.

I opened the door.

'Gonna let me in?'

'Go away. Go home. Jesus.'

'I can't go home.'

'Why not?'

'Too many memories. Bad memories.'

'Staked out?'

He licked his cracked lips.

'In this weather?' I said.

He squinted at me.

'Bastards,' he said.

'So book into a hotel. You got money.'

I made to shut the door again, but he had propped his boot against it. I pushed back hard. He overbalanced and took the dustbin with him. They hit the floor together and he slung an arm over it like a man overboard might grasp at a passing barrel. As he struggled to right himself, the rolling bin spun him back to where he had started, and so it went on. He was persistent, but when he wasn't trying to get off his back, he was lying on it, and the period between grew longer and longer. During prolonged breaks in the action, he lay on the ground with his cigarette in his mouth and his legs splayed.

I couldn't close the door and I couldn't leave him. If I left him where he was, he'd freeze to death. The problem was, I'd have to step outside the door to help him. In my mind it was no small problem, because the situation outside was unpredictable. I had only ever planned for the expected, the way upstairs to Richard's. I couldn't even call Richard because Richard couldn't help.

'Get out. Out,' I said to the dog.

The look she gave me betrayed her confusion.

'Out.'

Her ears lay back.

'Out.'

She slunk out of the door and stepped over Danny, who was making yet another pointless attempt at righting himself. Once she was blocking the route from the steps up to the gate, the little basement yard felt more enclosed, and I felt more confident that I could step into it. I opened the door wide and the storm blasted into my body. It was like jumping from a plane. I was in freefall. I tried not to look at anything beyond the space directly in front of me as I pushed myself forward into the void and grabbed Danny's arms. His fingers gripped my shoulders as I bent my knees and hauled him up towards me. I struggled to lift him, but he was too big, too heavy and too drunk. He loosed an arm from my grasp and leaned yet again on the dustbin for support, but it spun like a cue ball and I fell forward on to him.

I thought I was screaming. Inside my head I was, but my mouth was tight shut as I scrambled over his body and got behind him so that I could push against him. The sweat was pouring down my body, and as he began to laugh, I hit the back of his head over and over. He bore the pain of the blows like an old mule.

'You fucker. You fucker. Fucking move. Move,' I screamed.

Once again, he slowly bent his knees while I pushed against his back. He half stood, staggered and fell, forward this time, against the door and into the house. As he lurched forward into the hall, I went backwards and sat down hard on the freezing paving. The wind blew around me as I watched him get to his feet, turn and begin to close the door on me. He had the quiet, responsible look of someone who had dutifully put the milk bottles out and was turning in for the night.

His stupefied eyes seemed not to see me, but I had focused on the narrow light that was disappearing as the door closed. My heart hammered against my chest like a fist at the locked door of a burning house, and I threw myself at the door. The force knocked him off balance, his eyes widening in confusion as he saw me. I pushed harder and he stumbled backwards, taking the hall table and the phone with him. I kicked his legs out of the way and pushed inside, and somehow, the dog got in without losing her tail as I slammed the door behind me.

The storm was locked outside and the house was silent but for the monotonous tone of the telephone,

Danny's laboured breathing and my own. Girl looked down at Danny spread-eagled in the hallway, then back at me. Her eyes said it all.

CHAPTER SEVEN

# MY SHIP IS COMING IN

He was still blocking the hall the next morning. I had made no attempt to move him. I'd cleared the splintered table, my notebook, the junk mail, unopened Christmas cards, bills and Post-it pads from around his body, put the phone back on the hook and covered him with the throw I'd used the last time he'd paid me a visit. I didn't sleep. I spent the night watching the six windows in the tower block and thinking that I could kill Danny Morgan for what he had put me through.

The lights were constant in the blackness of the storm. I saw one person, on the seventh floor. He stood at the window, his solid form dark and naked against the dim red light. He was smoking a cigarette, and I wondered if he had finished making love, or if he were waiting for someone, or if he was simply imprisoned like I was and the nights felt longer than the days for him too. He turned and looked down towards my kitchen light. He seemed to be able to see me too. There was a time when I would have stood my ground, but not now. I stepped back instinctively and it took a moment or two before I was calm enough to step forward again. I looked up at the block for my sleepless companion, but he had gone, and the wind whipped at the trees and sleety rain peppered the pane.

Danny's hands were cold. There was a slime of vomit on the floor, on his Hawaiian shirt and around his dry mouth. The rancid smell of it and fermented alcohol lingered over him.

'Danny?'

There was no reply. I touched his mask-like face. It was as cold and clammy as his hands. 'Danny?'

I tried to lift him but I couldn't manage it. His hand clung to his jacket, but as his arm fell loosely to the floor, his heavy jacket gaped open. Tucked into the inside pocket was a mobile phone and a spiral-bound reporter's notebook. I took the notebook and the phone and placed them on the floor behind me with the debris from the night before. His top pocket held his cigarettes and lighter. In his trouser pockets were some house keys and some loose change. I rolled him over. In the back pocket he had a wallet containing five pounds, some credit and debit cards and a membership card to a Soho drinking club.

'Danny?'

I said it a bit louder this time. He didn't stir, not even when the telephone rang.

I had to stretch over him to answer it.

'Hello,' I said.

'Hi, Georgina, it's me, John Walker.'

I caught my breath.

'Hello?' he said.

'Did you find out who called me?' I said.

'I don't know if I should tell you.'

'Why not?'

'You being a journalist and all.'

'That bad?'

'I'm annoyed about it. Put it that way.'

'You don't deal with the press often, do you?' I said.

'No. Why?'

'You've said enough already. You should have said nothing. From now on, it's just hassle.'

I looked down at Danny. His head was back and his mouth was open. He'd had a molar pulled and it left a large gap where the tip of his furred tongue rested.

'You wouldn't hassle me, would you?'

'It's my given name.'

He seemed to hesitate, and then he said, 'Dr Lane leaves her password on the underside of department keyboards.'

'I bet she isn't the only one.'

'No, she's not. Someone must have seen you and liked the look of you. Not that I blame him.'

'He used the password to do what?'

'To get your name and address from the records. Maybe you should come up to the hospital, make an official complaint.'

The right name and address, I said to myself, like the appointment card. I sat back on my heels and dried my hands on my jeans. My body was coated with perspiration and my heart was racing. Just the thought of trying to make it to the hospital made me feel weak.

'No. I can't do that.'

'OK. I'll handle it if you like.'

'Forget about it.'

'That's very good of you.'

No one said anything for a while after that, but no one thought of ending it either.

'You're working a long shift,' I said, finally.

'I'm at home. I go back in a couple of hours.'

'Shouldn't you be asleep?'

'Sometimes you just can't sleep, even when you should.'

I knew what he meant but I said nothing.

'I could arrange that prescription for you, but I'd have to see you,' he said.

He was chancing it now as much as I had been, but I was losing my nerve. I didn't want to think about how I was going to get to see him. I thanked him and said I couldn't get to the hospital. I was really busy.

'What about that drink?' he said.

'I'll make an appointment.'

'Is that a yes?'

The dog was sniffing around Danny's face, her nose against his lips. I pushed her away.

'What do I get to call you now?' I said.

'John.'

'Johnny Walker. Like the Scotch.'

'No. John. Like the brother. You know.'

I laughed as I remembered the song that went '*The sun ain't going to shine any more. The moon ain't going to rise in the sky.*' I saw my hands stretched out as I hit the pavement and the laughter died in my throat.

'Come on, when do I get to see you?' he said.

'Like I said, I'll think about it.'

I put the receiver down like it had burned me.

I stared at Danny in my hallway and I'd never felt lonelier. I was sealed in this place. I might as well have been buried alive, a potential museum piece, drifting into the afterlife with my dog and supplies of food, booze and dope to see me across the river of hate. I laughed to myself. Yeah. Some future archaeologist would find me and wonder what purpose the geezer in the Hawaiian shirt had served.

'Danny, wake up,' I said.

But Danny didn't wake up, because Danny was dead.

*

The police had arrived with the ambulance, but they waited twenty minutes for the police surgeon, a petite, light-skinned Asian woman, who donned her latex gloves and got to work briskly. She said that if Danny had been alive at three, then he had died shortly afterwards, because rigor mortis had already frozen his eyelids and his jaw. She slipped a thermometer into his rectum and took his body temperature. I heard her say something about the coroner. That was what stuck in my mind, because I would have to go to the inquest.

The number of people that had to come into my home to see the body and finally take it away had set my teeth on edge. I wanted to be in control but I wasn't. They took over and made the inside of my house like the outside. I felt as if I had been flung into the open. Richard talked to me on the phone, but it was only when Robert Falk arrived that I finally relaxed. He was the first person I had called after the ambulance, but he didn't ask the questions. The local detective constable who had been handling the hit-and-run turned up, and he did. I found it difficult to talk to him.

'It's been a month,' I said, and he said he knew that.

'You must have something,' I said.

He exercised his right to remain silent and changed the subject.

'What happened here?' he said.

'He was slaughtered when he got here. He said he had nowhere to go,' I explained. 'I told him no deal, but he wouldn't let me shut the door. His foot got caught as I was trying to keep him out. He fell over. I couldn't leave him. The weather was too bad. So I tried to get him in. He fell over again inside. I decided to let him sleep it off and I went back to bed.'

The last bit was a lie. I didn't want them to think that

I had been sitting up awake while a man was dying in my hall. It all seemed reasonable enough to the DC, but Robert prolonged the interview. He asked me why Danny had come to me of all people. I said I didn't know. It was true, but somehow he had made me feel guilty. He was a cop. You know how it is.

I explained that Max had wanted me to cover the Gecko story, but that Danny had resigned so that he could do it freelance.

'He wanted to find out, for Jo. I'd called him to find out what he'd got. He turned up at my place at three in the morning, too drunk to stand. It was the day before the story broke about him and Gecko. He left here, did the deal. Got his chest waxed and oiled for the shoot, took the thirty pieces of silver. He turned up again last night, out of the blue. He said the press were camped outside his flat.'

'He could have gone to a hotel. He had money,' Robert said.

'I told him that myself, Robert. I hardly knew the guy.'

The DC was surprised that we were on first-name terms. He sat back from the table and looked at us, from one to the other.

'Just good friends,' I said, and lit a cigarette.

When the DC left and we were alone, Robert let the dog out in the garden and made the tea.

'You should get leaf tea,' he called out from the kitchen. 'Tea bags are just not the same.'

I sat at the dining table and watched the dog sniffing about outside. Robert let her in and handed me a clumsy, thick-rimmed mug that had some slogan about e-business around its middle. The tea was hot and sweet.

'I don't take sugar,' I said.

'Drink it,' he replied.

I took a couple of sips and felt a little better. If Robert hadn't stayed, I would have had a Scotch. My motto is you have Scotch for shock and gin for sin.

'Was that the truth, Georgina?'

'What do you mean?'

'He came here out of the blue?'

'I don't get you.'

'Were you working together?'

I pushed the chair back, got up and went into the kitchen. My chest felt tight and tense. I took a mop and bucket from a cupboard and began to fill the bucket with hot water and disinfectant. I went into the hall and stared at the mess. 'Let me do that,' Robert said. He was standing behind me.

'No. This is your chance of a lifetime. Georgina Powers cleans up. Now *that's* a story. She poses with a mop and bucket. Get it? Take a picture. Sell it. She can show you how.'

I stuck the mop into the steaming water and slopped it about the floor. There wasn't that much spew. Most of it had run back down his throat and choked him.

'You think we split it, don't you?' I said.

Robert said nothing, and I turned on him.

'I don't need your fucking approval. The story landed in my lap. I wanted it and I had it. I know I should have been looking for something more fucking noble than a "who slept with who" but that's life. My life right now. Danny Morgan gave me the finger and walked out of here. He stiffed me. Him and Detective Superintendent bloody Spencer. I don't know why he came back here. I didn't want him. Nobody did.'

Robert took the mop, leaned it against the wall and took my hand. It was suddenly very easy. I just gave in, closed my eyes and let my head rest against his warm, comfortable chest. If it were possible, I would have melted into the ample flesh of his huge body and disappeared. When he tapped my shoulder, it was almost like waking from a dream.

'I'm so tired, Robert,' I said.

'There, there, love,' he replied.

I let him get away with that and he followed up with the perfect line.

'Come along now. Drink your tea.'

We sat down together at the dining table. He took off his jacket while I shivered. I had the heating on but I felt cold. I wrapped my fingers around the mug to warm them, but my body felt like a ship that had sailed into a floating plain of ice.

'I know I should care,' I said, 'but I don't. It's like he died in someone else's house. I don't even feel I'm here myself. Not now. Even though I feel that I have become this place. I am this place. You look around and you see the contents of my head.'

I glanced at the new floor and the old wallpaper, the unpacked boxes and empty cupboards, the dog without a proper name. Robert fiddled with my pack of cigarettes.

'You're not eating, are you?' he said.

'Sure I am. At Richard's.'

'You're getting thin.'

'I'm always thin.'

'And pale. Your eyes have dark rings under them.'

'I didn't have much sleep last night.'

'What about the other nights?'

'I don't sleep well, no.'

'How many times have you been out of the house since the accident?'

'Plenty.'

'Upstairs doesn't count.'

Tears welled in my eyes and I looked away from him.

'You should see a counsellor, Georgina.'

I stared out of the French windows and struggled to control myself.

'They do home visits, yeah?'

'When's your follow-up appointment at the hospital?'

An image of Dr John Walker slid into my mind, arming me for a moment, until it segued with a shade of the faceless man who had first called me up. Another followed, but this one was looking at me through a car windscreen. I could see them both but not their faces. My heart began to race.

'How can I go to my appointments when I can't bring myself to go out?'

Robert flicked open the top of a pack and offered me a cigarette. I took one and he lit it for me.

'I've heard about something called EMDR. Eye Movement Desensitisation and Reprocessing,' he said. 'It's a new kind of treatment for post-traumatic stress disorder.'

'You looked it up? For me? How sweet.'

He ignored me. 'It's a technique that helps the mind to process bad memories.'

I started paying attention. Processing bad memories was what I had been trying to do all by myself in my dreams, rewriting them to help me remember. My way didn't seem to do anything but keep me awake, but maybe the principle was right. Maybe what I was doing was the right thing.

'This clinical psychologist noticed that when she got a disturbing thought her eyes shifted to the side. The movement seemed to shift the thought from the consciousness, because when it came back again, it wasn't as troublesome.'

'How does it work?' I said.

He shrugged.

'No one seems to know. What happens is the therapist asks the patient to think of an image of the traumatic memory and experience the emotions that go with it. The patient then moves their eyes back and forth following the therapist's hand. Then they repeat the exercise with positive thoughts.'

'Don't the positive thoughts get dissociated as well?'

Robert stared blankly at me.

'It's got something to do with the way the brain processes traumatic events, and how it differs from the way the brain processes normal events. The eye movement helps desensitise the painful memory. It helps the brain digest the event.'

'It says here,' I said.

'It was just a thought.'

'What're the alternatives?'

'Benzodiazepene.'

'Now you're talking.'

Robert pulled out a crumpled sheet of paper on which he had scribbled some notes.

'Benzodiazepene is good but you build up a tolerance.' He glanced up. 'Interacts with alcohol.'

I shook my head.

'Antidepressants – numerous side effects.'

'Any good ones?'

'No.'

'Selective Serotonin Reuptake Inhibitors—'

'Prozac?'

'Could make anxiety worse to begin with.'

'No.'

'Buspirone – OK, but takes a while to kick in. Beta blockers – block the symptoms, slow the heartbeat. That's the one the snooker players were using back in the eighties to calm their nerves.'

'What else?'

He crushed the paper into a ball.

'Cognitive behavioural therapy. You know, eliminates negative thinking through counselling and desensitisation.'

'And eye wobbling.'

'Eye wobbling.'

'Where'd you get all this stuff?'

'The Internet.'

I pushed my chair back from the table and got up. I went to the long windows and looked up at the tower block, trying to find the window where the light had been and where the man had stood. The daylight revealed nothing.

'I appreciate this, Robert. I really do. The thing is, I might feel a bit better, but none of it's going to find the person who ran Richard over and tried to kill one or other or both of us. He's not an image. He's real. Right now, I don't want to forget about it and move on. I want to remember. Most of all, I want that DC to do his job.'

I sucked on the cigarette.

'Did you give him the postcard?'

'It's dealt with.'

'Where's Kuthy right now?' I said.

'He's in Zurich.'

'How sure are you?'

He pushed at his steel glasses, which had slid down his flat nose.

'Ninety-nine per cent.'

'One per cent. That's the zone I'm in, and right now, I need information, not therapy.'

He blew out his cheeks and gave a great sigh.

'He's got a job, as far as we know. One of those corporate detective agencies. He's got the skills they want.'

'Which agency?'

'Kendall Associates.'

'Oh brother.'

Kendall was the biggest and baddest corporate detective agency in the business, and one of the top three such agencies widely used in the computer industry. Kendall investigated individuals, corporations and countries. It did everything from surveillance, protection and political risk analysis to industrial espionage. These were the guys who would find out what colour underwear you wore to your tenth birthday party and who you played doctors and nurses with if they needed to know. You really want them to be on *your* side. A man with Pal's background was perfect for them.

'I had a strange phone call the other day,' I said.

'Who from?'

'A fake doctor. He got my name and number from the hospital.'

'What did he want?'

'To take me out for a drink.'

Robert's mobile phone played the William Tell Overture. He held it to his ear in a hand so large that it looked as if he had nothing in it and had simply cupped his fingers to hear a whisper. His eyes focused on the message he was getting and his plump lips formed a straight line.

'Right,' was all he said.

He got up quickly and picked up his jacket.

'What's going on?' I said.

'There's been another bomb,' he said.

CHAPTER EIGHT

# BLUE SHIFT

I was online when I heard the helicopter pass overhead forty minutes later. I was tempted to run outside to look up at it, but I waited by the windows at the back of the house instead, straining my neck to catch a glimpse of it. I couldn't see it. All I could see was a dull sun behind a bullet-grey sky, but I could hear the sound of pulsing blades all around me. The man in the tower block came to his window. He was wearing a red sweatshirt and he was drinking from a cup. As I stared up at the building, seven more people showed themselves. A woman held up her child. I watched them all face west, gazing at the invisible air ambulance skimming the rooftops below them. As I looked up, the man raised a pair of binoculars to his eyes and I watched him track from where the helicopter was to where I was. My eyes locked on the distant lenses and I had the feeling that I was being sucked into the sky.

The bad news came up on the radio. The song that was playing faded out and the announcer's voice cut in to say that there had been a second explosion in London's East End and that there would be more details on the half-hour. I phoned Richard.

'There was a newsflash on Richard and Judy,' he said.

'What did they say?'

'That there had been an explosion. You know as much as I do and as much as they do.'

'This changes everything.'

'Let's wait and see. Are you OK?'

'I'm OK. Why?'

'You seem a little on edge.'

I thought about the man at the window. I'd been scared by him, and that worried me. Was it getting so that I didn't even want to *look* outside?

'More than usual?' I said.

There was a pause.

'Do you want something to eat?'

'No.'

'You should eat. Come up.'

I put the receiver down and closed my eyes. I was exhausted. There was some pain far bigger than mine prowling the streets, but I couldn't help myself. I couldn't think about anyone else's pain. I could only think of my own. The helicopter became a faint pitter-patter in the distance. Dr John Walker would be preparing to do his stuff now. I could picture him, leaning over the bloody bodies to check their wounds, and I wondered if he had worked on Jo Casey and what it took out of a person to see what he had to see: the torn lips, the blasted skulls and the shredded torsos of the unborn.

I wanted to remember the sound of his voice, but in the replay in my mind, I couldn't. It disturbed me that I couldn't remember whether it was the phoney Dr Lane or the real Dr Walker who had an accent, but I knew he was going to call again. I wanted him to. He knew that.

Three online news sites said that there had been at least one casualty, a woman. Not one could confirm a link with the Gecko Samuels bombing, but all said that the police were considering the possibility. If there was, then Gecko was the stone's throw from which the ripples spread. My body shivered as I recalled the time when we had been together – one hurried fumble in a hotel room after a foreign press trip. It was forgettable, but he hadn't forgotten, because Cherry knew and who could have told her but him? He must have had a hundred encounters since and not lied about a single one in the name of his kind of love. One certainty fuelled my unease. One bomb was an incident; two was a campaign.

Richard cut the ciabatta and stuffed it with salad and mozzarella. He managed pretty well in the kitchen, hobbling between the chopping and cooking zones, resting his elbows on crutches and counters to support himself on his vast, plaster-encased leg. I'd stopped jumping up and offering to help. Watching me prepare food got on his nerves. He said the food just passed through my hands. I countered that I was better able to eat food that I hadn't formed a relationship with. We left it at that.

'Danny had a problem with the drink,' he said.

I held my head in my hands.

'One fuck of a problem, Richard.'

'You know what I mean. He drank. It wasn't your fault.'

'I never thought it *was* my fault.'

'That's right. It wasn't your fault. That's what I mean.'

'Just cut it, Richard.'

He lurched across the kitchen and as he slid on to his seat, I got up and fetched the plates of food.

'The guy could have frozen to death outside my door,

but I let him in,' I said, placing the large, unstable sandwiches on the table and sliding his towards him as I sat down. 'I left him lying in the hall. That was the full extent of my hospitality.'

'You did the best you could.'

'No I didn't. And now he's dead.'

Richard was at a loss. He would have liked to look away but his neck brace had fixed his position.

'It's not your fault.'

'For fuck's sake, Richard. I know,' I said. 'He was nothing to me and it wasn't my fault. He would have died outside but I let him in and he died inside. Either way, he was a dead man and I was part of his fucking fate. I know I didn't, but it still feels like I killed him.'

I took quick and greedy bites of my sandwich, tearing at it like a starving animal. The tenderly prepared filling and soft Italian bread scarcely registered. I gnawed and chewed and fragments of food fell from my lips. I looked across at Richard. He was staring at me, an appalled look on his pasty face. I swallowed a little and spoke, my mouth still loaded with food.

'I didn't, if that's what you're thinking,' I said.

I took another bite and stopped mid-chew. He was still looking at me. I realised then that my half of the ciabatta had almost gone and Richard had yet to start his. I placed the small remaining piece on my plate and wiped my mouth.

'When did you last eat?' he said.

'I'm sorry.'

'No, eat. Go on.'

Richard waited, but I wouldn't touch the plate. I felt embarrassed.

'Go on,' I said. 'I've finished.'

He bit into his own half of the giant sandwich.

'I gave the postcard to Robert Falk,' I said.

A muscle in Richard's jaw twitched and he stopped chewing.

'I reckon if it's anybody it'll be Kuthy. You remember him?'

How could he forget? I had first moved in to Richard's place to get away from Pal Kuthy.

'Robert says he's in Zurich. Ninety-nine per cent sure. He's got a job with Kendall Associates. Can you believe it?'

Richard put down his sandwich and carefully wiped his mouth with a piece of kitchen roll. 'Shall I tell Max you can't do this story? That you're working on something else?'

I pressed my lips together. If Richard said that, I was finished.

'Thing is, he wanted to know what you were doing, what you'd picked up. You could have gone with Bob Falk, followed the ambulance, you know what I mean? I didn't expect you to, but Max did.'

I looked away. I couldn't face him. His voice mellowed with pity.

'I'll tell him you were really upset over the Danny business. He'll understand. I'll make him.'

I didn't say that I wouldn't count on it. I didn't trust myself to speak. I chewed at my thumbnail instead, and the silence grew inside the warm kitchen like a puffball on a balmy autumnal night. The tick of a clock and the barely perceptible flow of passing traffic underscored the sudden quiet. The road that skirted the park at the front of the house was a regular but lightly used route east and west that avoided the congestion of the Mile End Road. At the end of the road was a small roundabout, and we listened in silence as a motorbike changed down to negotiate it and pulled up outside.

The heavy footsteps strode to the steps and the dog began to bark and growl downstairs. There was a pause, and though I was expecting it, the sound of the doorbell cut through me. Richard didn't move, but my hand trembled against my lips.

The doorbell sounded again.

'Are you going to get it?' Richard said.

I sat there without speaking and without looking at him while the bike's engine marked time and the dog got into her rhythm. Finally Richard leaned on the table and levered himself upright. He grasped the grey metal crutches to steady himself and swung one stiff leg and then the other to move steadily towards the kitchen door that led to the hall. He had just reached it when the courier lost patience and ran back down the steps. He stopped as the engine revved and the motorbike accelerated away.

I got up and squeezed past Richard as he leaned against the door jamb, into the hallway that was coloured red and blue by the daylight that shone through the stained-glass panels of the door. There was no card on the mat.

'No card,' I said.

'OK.'

'Isn't that strange?'

'No.'

'Do you want me to clear up?'

'No.'

'Thanks for lunch.'

I gripped my fingers around the door handle.

'I'll try and keep Max happy,' Richard said.

'Whatever,' I replied, and opened the door. The cold

air blew against my cheeks and my hands grew slimy with sweat. I glanced around. Nothing had been left on the step either. I had clear passage. I focused on my gate and jumped the steps down.

The *Six o'Clock News* confirmed that there had been an explosion in Camber Street and that a woman was dead. Her name was Dinika Patel. She had been a machinist outworker for a clothing factory, twenty-six years old, the eldest girl of a large family, unmarried. She'd been working at home alone when the nail bomb was delivered to the house. Neighbours had heard a motorbike arrive fifteen minutes before the explosion.

Detective Superintendent Daniel Spencer was on the scene. Smoke hung in the air, and he looked less composed than he had done before, standing alone as a silent crowd of brown faces pressed around without touching him. A voice wailed in the background, but apart from that solitary keening there was nothing else. The explosion had sucked the life out of the street.

Spencer was not to know then that the victim was dead. He said that she was seriously injured and had been taken to hospital by air ambulance. He did not know who was responsible for the attack, and no one had claimed responsibility. If it was a single individual, he said, that person was clearly disturbed, but it was too early to say what the actual motive was.

'Was it a racist attack, Detective Superintendent?' the reporter demanded, her microphone seeming to sprout from the heads of the people for whom she spoke. Spencer repeated what he had said already, that he had no evidence that it was, adding that the police were keeping an open mind and asking the public to remain vigilant.

An Asian youth in a baseball cap was more forthright.

'Cherry Shankar. Asian. Dinika Patel. Asian. What's wrong with this picture, man? Believe. That first bomb was for Cherry Shankar. We know. We live with this kind of shit every day on the street. What's bin done about it?'

His eyes filled with righteous tears. The reporter turned to another Asian, a more restrained young man whom she described as a community leader. She asked whether he suspected that the first bomb had indeed been for Cherry Shankar, and whether this was the work of a Far Right group. His answer was almost as restrained and cautious as the detective superintendent's.

'Whenever there is an attack of this sort, we receive calls from any number of Far Right groups either congratulating the perpetrator of the atrocity or claiming responsibility. Remember, there are at least two ongoing high-profile investigations into alleged racially motivated attacks in this neighbourhood. It remains to be seen whether this latest outrage falls into the same category.'

The newsreader recapped the details of the previous nail bomb attack that had killed Gecko Samuels, Jo Casey and her unborn child. The studio provided a clip of Cherry Shankar leaving the Gecko Games press conference with a heavy escort. The newsreader highlighted the race motive and said there was increasing speculation as to whether these two bombings represented a turn to overt terrorism by various far-right Neo-Nazi groups such as Combat 18 and White Wolves, although none had yet claimed responsibility.

The newsreader cut to a telephone interview with the

Assistant Commissioner for the Metropolitan Police, a stiff-backed man with ruddy cheeks, who emphasised that there was no evidence at this stage that the attacks were linked in any way to the extreme right-wing groups, although the possibility had been factored into the investigation. A professor from a northern university was brought online to give a thumbnail sketch of the kind of 'disturbed' individual that Detective Superintendent Spencer had in mind. The bitter well of acts of terror, the little man said, was resentment, towards someone or something, and it had its source in childhood. Extremism and intolerance were found in marginalised groups and/or individuals who defined their own hate targets. Whether or not he, and it was likely to be a he, was a member of a neo-fascist group or not, the professor said, he was likely to be a social malcontent. A diagram of a small box filled with nails and wires then came up on the screen.

The newsreader explained that what both bombings had in common was this type of crude nail bomb and the fact that both packages had been delivered by motorbike courier. No city courier firms had been able to show details of any deliveries scheduled for either address, so it was increasingly possible that the bomber was posing as a courier. The police were advising the public to be diligent.

I looked at my watch; it had been six hours since the air ambulance had passed overhead, and it was dark outside. The second bomb had gone off at midday and a courier had rung Richard's doorbell twenty minutes later. It was possible.

I felt a tremor of fear, like something I couldn't see was coming towards me at speed and I had to think which way to jump. The car that had hit us clicked into my mind like an image caught by the flash of a camera. I called Richard.

'The other day, when that courier came and I didn't open the door, did he leave a card?'

'What?'

'You said you were expecting something.'

'Yes.'

'Did he leave a card?'

'Yes.'

I was strangely disappointed.

'The courier today didn't,' I said.

'So? They don't always.'

'Those two bombs came by courier.'

Richard sighed.

'What have you got in common with Gecko Samuels and a twenty-six-year old Asian outworker, Georgina?'

'What had Gecko?'

'Cherry. An Asian woman.'

'You think it's a race attack?'

'Yes, I think it's a race attack.'

'And Jo got caught in the crossfire.'

'Yes.'

'And Danny sold his story for nothing.'

'Not exactly for nothing, but yes, pretty damn close. But you know what? Life's like that.'

'The courier today didn't leave a card.'

'George, please.'

'The invitation to the press conference.'

'What about it?'

'The postcard.'

'Yes.'

'They came to your house.'

'Yes.'

'They were for me. They went to the wrong address. The postcard went to the wrong address.'

'What about the bills and other junk? I'll say it again. What have you got in common with Gecko and Cherry Shankar, and a twenty-six-year-old Asian outworker?'

'Abdul Malik?'

'Another weird boyfriend.'

'An *Asian* boyfriend, Richard.'

'A dead Asian boyfriend. Get real. Who'd have known you went out with him?'

'Anyone who read the story. Anyone obsessed enough to keep a database of these stories.'

Richard paused. I thought he was beginning to think it made sense. He took his time, and when he replied he spoke slowly and clearly.

'I think you are suffering from post-traumatic stress disorder. It can manifest itself as agoraphobia and in feelings of paranoia. There's this treatment called EMDR – Eye Movement Desensitisation and Reprocessing.'

'Which you found on the Net.'

'Right.'

'The technique itself involves an individual holding in mind a representative image – pictures, sounds, feelings – of the problem, while watching a clinician's left–right hand or finger movements in short sets.'

'I have two fingers raised, Richard.'

'Just trying to help.'

I was sitting on the floor by the splinters of table on which the telephone had rested when I caught sight of the spiral notebook that had belonged to Danny and which I had swept in among my own. I picked it up and flicked it open. Inside were pages and pages of neat

Pitman's shorthand. It was a rare sight. I was surprised to see the reporter's universal code in his book. It wasn't a skill that most technology journalists had. I didn't have it.

Most techno journalists carry a tape recorder for long interviews and rely on a lightning scribble for everything else. The shorthand in the notebook meant that Danny had either taught himself or had been trained on a local paper. The only thing I could read in the notes was the date at the top of certain pages, which indicated a new story or interview. I flicked to the back of the book. The notes continued on the flip side. Technology journalists never used both sides of the paper, but journalists trained on a local paper made sure nothing was wasted by turning the book over once it was full and using the unused reverse side of the pages.

The final date caught my attention. The last notes Danny had taken down were on 30 November. I knew he had gone to the police press conference on 2 December, the day after Gecko and Jo were killed, but this notebook had no record of it. He could have used another book, but if so, why had he had this one on him if he'd finished with it?

I called Richard.

'Did Danny know shorthand?'

'I don't think so.'

'Where'd you get him from?'

'Nowhere. He came straight to us from university. Did the three-month trial. Got him on the standard news- and feature-writing training schemes.'

'Who else do you know that knows it?'

'Mary,' he said.

I paused.

'Who else?

'Jo Casey knew it. She came from a local paper. Why?'

I was about to tell a lie, but I heard another motorbike in the road. The sound of its engine slowing and the final pull on a brake tied an invisible garrotte around my throat. Girl tore down the hall and began to bark.

'Are you by a window?' I said.

'No.'

I dropped the phone and slunk around the walls in the dark until I reached the front room. The motorcyclist was standing by my gate, empty-handed. He still had his helmet on, a black full-face version with yellow flashes. His head was turned towards Richard's house. I waited and watched through the curtain as he ran up the stairs and rang Richard's doorbell. He rang it again a minute later and waited. The bells battered my heart.

I saw him come down the steps and wait by the gate. His helmet was unclipped. Richard must have got to the door and called after him, because he turned and raised a hand. When he took his helmet off to speak, I saw his matted blond hair with the black roots.

CHAPTER NINE

# PUSHERMAN

I had forgotten how beautiful he was. It was another hole in my memory, like the face of the driver in the black car. The sepia images that remained of that night were of a passing car, Richard's contorted body, and a young doctor with blond hair and dark roots who was shining a light in my eyes.

This man was almost six foot, with a clear forehead and a straight nose. He was dragging his hand through his hair and turning his head towards me, but it was dark in the room and he didn't see me looking at him from behind the curtain. He waved his thanks to Richard and put his hand on my gate and pushed it open.

He looked so young and fresh for someone who worked all hours in one of the toughest A&Es in London. He should have looked like death, but instead he looked as if he had just stepped off a surfboard. I looked like death. Richard told me daily, but he didn't have to, because I could see it for myself in the mirror. How could I open the door to this man when I looked like death?

The doorbell rang and the dog lunged forward and began to slaver. I gripped her collar as I counted thirty seconds and the doorbell rang once more, loud and penetrating. I was almost bent double trying to control her as I snapped open the door to make the ringing and the barking stop.

'Hi,' he said.

I threw the dog backwards and made her sit. When I straightened up, I thought I saw a flicker of disappointment in his face as his smile faded.

'Georgina?

'John.'

'Is this a bad time?'

'On a micro and a macro level, yes, it is,' I said.

This time the disappointment was more evident and I felt a little better.

'I see. Another time then?'

'No,' I said, and I opened the door wide.

It was the usual stuff.

He complimented me on the flat and asked if I had just moved in, and I told him it had been more than a year and he said these things took time.

'Take your jacket off,' I said.

He shrugged it off and I took a good look at his body. He was wearing a thin fleece top tucked into his leather trousers. He started to put his hand inside the top to pull it out so that it hung loose around his hips. I saw his navel and I think I was meant to.

'What can I get you?' I said, and he asked for a beer.

'Is that the Grand Union?' he said, pointing out of the kitchen window at the canal.

'Yes.'

'Have you got a boat?'

'No.'

'Wouldn't that be great? Just leave by the back door

and paddle off somewhere? It must be wonderful in the summer.'

I glanced out of the window and walked out of the room. He followed me into the lounge. I had found my cigarettes and was lighting up. I offered but he refused.

'Tough day?' he said.

'I'd say, but you have a tough day every day, don't you?'

He shrugged.

'A bad day is a good day, if you know what I mean.'

'What about the woman, the bomb victim?'

He looked away then, and said, 'Yeah.'

I thought about the psychological theory on bad thoughts and shifting eyes that Robert and Richard had told me about. People did do that. He'd just done it, and I did it. I wasn't sure about the theory that it helped the brain absorb what was hateful to it. It seemed to me to be more to do with the mind not wanting anyone to see its pain.

His hands rested on his hips as he hung his head for a minute or so before putting the bottle down and straightening up. He walked to where I was. He didn't say anything. He just looked at me.

'I look like shit, don't I?' I said.

'You look as if you haven't slept. I know what that feels like.'

I tucked a strand of hair behind my ear in a pathetic attempt to make it more presentable. It wasn't what I'd wanted to say. It wasn't going to set the mood, I knew that, but I went ahead and told him.

'Someone died here today.'

His eyes met mine. This time I looked away, pointing at the scene of Danny's demise.

'He fell into the hall. He was drunk and I thought

he'd passed out. I was awake half the night and I didn't know he had died.'

'Who was he?'

I looked back at him.

'Gecko Samuels' ex-boyfriend.'

'*The* Gecko Samuels?'

'You know another?'

He took a deep breath. He didn't say it wasn't my fault, he didn't ask me how I felt. He just left it. I liked that. I mean, what else was there to say? Shit happens.

'Are you hungry?' he said.

'Yes.'

'Let's go out.'

I thought about it and almost convinced myself that I could make it out the door on his arm.

'I'd rather stay here,' I said, and he smiled as if he knew what I really meant. I felt like a phoney.

He ordered an Indian. It would be forty minutes, so I asked if he minded if I had a quick bath. Late as it was, I wanted a fresh start to the day. He gave another one of those smiles and said that I should go ahead. I'd only just sunk into the deep, hot water when there was a gentle knock on the door and he asked if I wanted a glass of wine in there with me. I said no, thank you, but I laughed to myself all right. He picked out Curtis Mayfield, and as sweet, grooving music filled the house, I swept the clouds of candyfloss bubbles over my body and lay back in the warm water with my eyes closed.

The drill of the doorbell cut through the mellow sax and speedy tom-toms and shattered my nerves. It didn't take much nowadays. The sound of a motorbike or my own front doorbell could do it. The thought of going outside could. I pushed my hands against the sides of the bath as I listened to John's heavy boots in the hall. I heard him speak to the delivery man and shut the door. I followed the sound of his boots into the kitchen and listened as he searched through the cutlery. He was singing along with Curtis but I was still shaking, telling myself to get a grip.

I leaned back in the bath, but the moment of peace that I had needed was gone. I got out, wrapped a towel around myself and wiped the steam from the mirror. The blue eyes that looked back were set in dark hollows, and the face was white. Whatever was happening to me was showing on my face, and what was happening was that the outside world was killing me slowly while I buried myself alive. I licked my lips and drew a finger across my eyebrow. I wanted to look better. I wanted to look beautiful, but the mirror couldn't lie. I combed my hair back, the black sweep from my forehead ending in red tendrils around my throat.

I could hear him singing along. '*I'm your mother, I'm your daddy, I'm that nigger in the alley, I'm your doctor when in need—*'

His voice was at the door.

'You OK? It's ready.'

'I'm OK,' I said, but I didn't open the door.

I waited until I heard his boots walk away before I opened it. He was standing by the dining table making sure all the foil dishes were arranged and straightening out the crockery and cutlery. He picked what looked like a cigarette out of an ashtray and took a long toke. I could tell from the deep inhalation, the colour of the smoke and the rich aroma drifting towards me that it was weed. When he saw me, he put the joint down and smiled.

'I'm going to get dressed. I won't be a minute,' I said.

'No, wait,' he said, walking towards me.

I waited until he was standing in front of me, and as much as I wanted to look away, I kept my eyes on him.

'Is this OK?' he said.

'What do you mean?'

'This. Me being here.'

'Why?'

'After all that's happened.'

'I need the company.'

'I need *your* company,' he said. 'I couldn't believe it when you phoned.'

I wondered if I had made a mistake, but he bent his head and kissed my shoulder. I drew my hand through his hair. He looked up and smiled, his face closer now. I could see the faded marks of adolescent spottiness on his chin, and a small scar on his forehead. He smelled of beer and weed and leather and Calvin Klein.

'I wanted to come last night but I thought it would be too late,' he said, starting on me quickly.

He pressed his mouth over mine, snaking a hand inside the towel. His fingers stroked my waist and his thumb rubbed the curve of my breast. I was leaning against the wall and he was leaning against me. I could hardly breathe in all his excitement. His hand pushed between my legs and I caught hold of it.

'I don't think so, boy.'

'Come on. Come on.'

'No.'

He seemed not to hear. He tried to kiss me again but I held him off until he stopped and stepped back. There was a dazed look in his eyes.

'What's the hurry?' I said.

'There's no hurry.'

'So what are you doing? Squeezing me in between shifts?'

I could see from the look on his face that I had hit the spot.

'What?' he said.

'Do you do this all the time?'

I pulled the towel back across my body to cover myself.

'You've got the wrong idea about me,' he said.

'I don't think so. You see what you want. You get what you can. Busy doctor, aren't you? No time for niceties.'

'That's shit.'

'You phoned me, didn't you? It was you. You were chancing it.'

He shook his head and went to look for his jacket. I looked at the dog, who had double-guessed us and was sitting by the bedroom door. I pointed at the front door and said the word, 'Guard,' at which she padded softly further up the hall and took up her position.

I was in the bedroom, pulling on my trousers and a top, when I heard John's walk up the hall towards the front door. He stopped when she growled.

'Good dog,' he said.

'Good girl,' I whispered behind the bedroom door.

He spoke as evenly as he could, but even I could hear the doubt in his voice. It seemed to enrage her. He called out to me above the snarls in a lonely, anxious tone that was pitched a little higher than when he had asked me to 'Come on.'

'Georgina?'

I didn't answer, and he knocked lightly at the door. That was a big mistake. I heard her body collide with his and the explosion of breath from his chest. She was a big girl and he would have his work cut out. I allowed the commotion to continue for a while before I opened the door and called time out.

He was flattened against the wall some distance from the door in a futile attempt to stretch himself up and away from the dog's tireless, snapping jaws. She hadn't bitten him, but she was working around his body to within one thousandth of an inch.

'Down!'

She dropped back smartly like a well-trained soldier and sat directly in front of him, her muscular chest tense, her ears pricked, her obsidian eyes keen and sharp. It had been pot luck finding out what she could do. Tony had trained her and I reckoned I had only scratched the surface when it came to discovering what she understood by battle conditions. I sometimes wondered if she had ever practised attaching electrodes to testicles.

'Good girl,' I said, before turning to him. 'The thing is, John, I don't get out much either. You are a complete bastard, but for this evening you are *my* complete bastard. I wasn't expecting company, but now that I have it, I'm going to keep it. Take off your jacket, take off your boots and let's eat.'

He did as he was told, but he didn't really relax. I ate like a pig while the dog sat a small distance from the table playing a canine Oddjob to my Auric Goldfinger.

'Can I go now?' he said, when I had tossed the last chicken bone in the pile.

'No. Get me a beer. Have one yourself,' I said, lighting a cigarette. 'Smoke?'

He shook his head but he got me the beer. Girl followed him there and back, naturally.

'Am I being held prisoner?' he said, sitting down again.

'You thought I'd be yours tonight? Wrong, you're mine.'

'Am I allowed one phone call?'

I shook my head.

'I need to change my shift.'

'That's a lie.'

He leaned back in the chair and held out his hands. He had a very appealing, handsome face, the sort that won people over.

'OK. I'm sorry. What can I say?' he said.

'Tell me about it. Tell me how it works.'

'I didn't make that call. I promise you. You called me.'

'You go out with your patients. You hit on them.'

'You called me.'

'I knew it was you. Your accent veered across ten counties. Anyone but me take you up on your offer of a hot date?'

He didn't answer. A red stain of embarrassment inched up from his neck and across his face.

'I didn't call you.'

He was believable all of a sudden, but it didn't help.

'But you *are* an opportunist.'

'I'm a bloke, for fuck's sake.'

'You're a phoney. I could have been anyone.'

'That's not true.'

'You have done this before though, haven't you? What's to stop me ringing the hospital now? I'm a journalist. What's to stop me doing a story on you, Dr Sex?'

He looked tired all of a sudden, more tired than me.

'Please don't do that. I haven't hurt anyone.'

'You've hurt me.'

'I'm sorry.'

'How do you think I feel? There's a road accident. My friend is badly hurt. I'm shocked to the core. I'm vulnerable. *I'm* hurt. You check me out not for my injuries but to see if I'm a good lay? In casualty, for Christ's sake?'

'It's not like that.'

'The way I'm going to write it, it's going to be exactly like that. And when I do write it, the walking wounded, they're all going to remember you and they'll form a nice disorderly queue to put in a bad word for you.'

He put his head in his hands.

'Georgina, I've done it once before. Just once.'

'Don't lie.'

'Once and then you.'

'You got away with it once and you thought, this is like taking, no, *giving* candy to a baby. I thought you had to be smart to be a doctor.'

He lifted his head but he didn't look at me.

'I work in A and E. You don't have to be smart, you have to be insane,' he said. 'I'm on call every other night. I work ludicrous hours for fuck all.'

'It's a job.'

'Two hours ago I was trying to get a urologist, any available fucking urologist, to do an emergency op on a baby who'd had half his penis sawn off in a home circumcision. No, it's not just a job.'

'My mistake. I thought you were a horny little devil, but you're a fucking saint, aren't you?'

He pushed his chair back and stood up.

'You've made your point. Write what you want.'

I ground my cigarette out in a foil tray.

'Apologise.'

He stared at me.

'I have done.'

'Apologise.'

'What for?'

'For making me feel like a service station.'

He hesitated and then he said, 'Georgina, I'm sorry. It was unforgivable.'

Damn it, if he didn't nearly make me cry it sounded so real. I held out, though, kept the tears backed up.

'That's all right, John. You can go now.'

I clicked my fingers at the dog and she came and sat by me. I nodded and he moved. I watched him put on his boots, tuck his top in, pull on his chunky jacket, pick up his helmet and leave.

The door opened and shut. Curtis Mayfield had signed off and it was very quiet in the house. I took the joint from the ashtray and lit it. It was a nice buzz. The motorbike engine started at the third time of asking and I listened to it go until the sound had completely faded away.

'I really do pick them, don't I, girl?' I said, and she licked my hand.

CHAPTER TEN

# I'LL BE YOUR DOG

Another night of broken sleep. It wasn't just him. It was everything. The hit-and-run. The postcard. Gecko. Jo. Danny Morgan. And Dinika Patel, the home machinist who'd been blown to pieces. She bothered me, because to my mind, her death had taken Jo out of the frame and brought me into it. It was possible that the connection was race and that we were all connected somehow.

I had everything going for me on this one. I knew Cherry Shankar. I knew Gecko Samuels. I worked for the same news organisation as Jo Casey. One of the senior policemen on the case was my best friend and Gecko Samuels' boyfriend had died in my home.

I was thinking of the story I would have to tell the newspapers. In the short time that I had known him, Danny Morgan had cost me. This time, it wasn't money at stake but privacy. At the very minimum, there would be a photo of the house from the outside and a caption stating that I lived in the basement flat. They might even catch me going up to Richard's. Whoever had sent the postcard to the wrong house would then have the right one.

I logged on. I checked the news site, and sure enough there was a photo of the house underneath the headline

'Gecko's boyfriend found dead'. The picture was in colour and showed the Victorian terrace, two storeys above ground and one below, with the railings in front and a glimpse of my front-room curtains and Richard's Roman blinds. Behind the row of houses was the block of flats, like some sort of watchtower. Someone knew exactly where I lived now.

I had a half-developed picture in my mind of someone in a car, a person who was trying to kill me, a person who was just one of any number of killers out there looking for people to snuff out. Killers who thought that *their victims were to blame*, who thought their victims were their enemies and that their crimes of murder were simply acts of self-defence.

I might have done something to them for all I knew. I wish I knew. All I knew was that there was at least one person out there who was taking it very personally. I didn't know what I had done to the driver of the car to make him, her, whoever it was, want to kill me. It could be Pal Kuthy but it could just as easily be someone that I just didn't know. I was right not to go out.

I was in bed when I got a call from Dr John Walker. It was two a.m. but he didn't wake me. I wasn't sleeping. I was drifting in that tricky no-man's-land between dreams and reality. He sounded tired and stressed.

'You didn't have to set the heat on me,' he said.

'I don't understand.'

'I had a visit from the police.'

'When?'

'An hour ago.'

'What about?'

'About you.'

The heavy fog of fatigue evaporated and my weary

mind sharpened up. I tried to remember but nothing came to me.

'Was it to do with Danny Morgan?'

'Who?'

'Danny. The guy who died here yesterday.'

'No. It was about you and me. I assumed you'd told him I called you. I didn't call you. You called me.'

'No one knows about it.'

'A big fat copper does.'

I only knew one big fat copper.

'Robert Falk?' I said.

John almost lost his voice.

'I knew it.'

I remembered then. I'd told Robert Falk that a doctor had called and asked me out for a drink, but I hadn't given a name. I was sure I hadn't.

'Was it just him?'

'No. He had a plain-clothes detective with him.'

'Name?'

'DC Jane Flowers.'

'I don't know her,' I said, more to myself than to him. I wondered why it wasn't the hypo-active DC who was plodding along with the hit-and-run and why Robert had taken time out from a hugely important case to check on an off-the-cuff remark I'd made about a fake doctor. I knew he was protective of me, but he was a hands-off sort of guy. He rarely did anything unless I asked him to, maybe because he knew I wouldn't thank him.

'Did he know who you were, your name, your department?'

'He came and asked if I had treated you in A and E.'

'And?'

'I said yes.'

'And?'

'What is it you don't understand?'

'Where's the leap between the doctor who treated me and a doctor who gave me a call?'

John was silent.

'I didn't tell him who you were or what you did or that we had met. I said I'd had a call,' I said.

'I assumed it was about that.'

'You 'fessed up. This is your problem.'

He was silent again.

'I thought you'd told him,' he said, eventually. A great weariness seemed to yawn down the line. 'Why else would he have come?'

Why else indeed? And why couldn't it wait until morning?

'What next?' I said.

'I don't know,' he said, and then, 'But you know this guy, right?'

There was hope in his tired voice.

'I know him.'

There was silence between us. Either he was going to ask or I was going to offer.

'You want me to put in a good word?' I said.

'I don't deserve it,' he said.

'You're right, you don't, but I have a forgiving nature,' I said, though anyone who knew me would have told him that was a total lie.

'How forgiving?'

The guy was a chancer all right.

'Don't push it,' I said, and he gave a sad laugh.

'I won't,' he said. 'Push it.'

There was no way I was going to get to sleep after that. I got up and made myself a hot drink. The dog opened one eye and sighed as I walked past her. Outside, a deep frost had frozen the grass into splinters and the trees into fists of ice. The houses across the canal were in darkness, but, up in the tower block, the red eye glowed and a random pattern of lighted rectangles shone out of the night sky. Five awake tonight, but no man at the window. I wondered where he was, if he was asleep in his own bed or in someone else's.

The notebook was on the side. It had coffee stains on the cover and some of the pages were curling up. I reckoned it had to be Jo's. Danny didn't know shorthand. There were two people on the staff who did, Mary Stow and Jo Casey, and he had better access to Jo. The last notes in the book were dated 30 November, and she'd died the next day.

He'd kept the notebook in his pocket, but now I couldn't ask him why. If he knew something then he must have got wise to it by subterfuge, unless Jo trusted him and had talked to him about what she was working on. I doubted it. I would never have done that. I'd talk about a hot story only to someone I was *selling* it to, and then they'd only get the pitch.

I reckoned Danny had known all along that Jo wasn't in the picture with Gecko the way that he had been. He'd gone along with the story that everyone was putting together for the money.

Nothing wrong with that. Money's a legitimate motivation, but it shouldn't come too soon, before everything else, before fame and righteousness. You have to want to do the right thing at the beginning because it's hard to do and that's what makes you good. When you start out, you have ideals. Sometimes you get to keep them. If you sell out when you're old, it's hard but not so bad. No one knows the trouble you've seen, right? If you sell out when you're young, then you're finished, because you'll die inside, like Danny. He never had a chance because he thought he was hip to how it was. The wave of disappointment must have hit him like a tsunami.

Danny couldn't read Jo's notes any more than I could, but he knew that they were important, or he was taking a guess that they were. I reckoned he thought that she had been killed because of something she was working on. I wish that he had told me. I wish that I had made him trust me, but he was as paranoid as I was. He thought that if he got blind drunk, people couldn't see him. It was the ostrich principle of self-preservation that I was very familiar with.

I had access to the Technology Online database and I could easily check all the stories that Jo had filed. It would give me a pattern of her interests. She'd have been given a speciality to follow – a part of the industry, a large player, or a market. I could also ask Richard or Max. I decided I'd do both: the first for myself, and the second to reassure the two of them that I *was* actually doing something.

I held the hot cup against my cold cheek. My bare feet were ice. The notebook lay before me as inscrutable as the Rosetta Stone. Who used shorthand? Journalists. Court reporters. Secretaries. Richard had suggested Mary Stow, but I wouldn't trust her with a used lipstick. She'd had me over once before and stolen my story. She'd lied to Richard about her baby and he'd thrown me out so that they could make room for a nursery. He was lucky I even talked to him. Oh yes, you had to watch Mary. She might look like an overweight Julie Andrews, but she had Bette Davis eyes.

Mary Stow was out of the question, and so was any

other journalist. It would have to be a secretary. Hiring a temp was expensive but easy enough. I could get them to come to the house and transcribe the notes. And what would they understand about a bunch of technology-related news stories?

I touched the book like it was made of glass. Who was I kidding? Secretaries were smart. They knew about everything. I couldn't risk it. Shivering, I picked up the notebook and made my way back to bed. I wasn't happy with any of the solutions that I'd come up with, but as I passed the door to my office, I glimpsed the geometric pattern of the screensaver twisting and turning in the dark. Could I trust someone far, far away?

I stood by the door and stared at the computer. I could go out there and look for someone. I cleared a space on the desk, set my cup down and clicked on. It took less than a minute for the search engine to come up with every Pitman-related web site in the world. I finally settled on a pick-and-mix genius site where you could find an expert on anything. I got several quick replies but I settled for someone called Maddy Baer because she said she lived in Virginia. She was also sixty-five years old and a retired teacher of secretarial studies. I'd forgotten about teachers. If I could scan the pages in, she said she'd work for me for twenty dollars an hour, but that I was not to worry because she could do quite a bit in one hour. Maddy, I said, with a smiley attached, it's a done deal.

I turned to the last page of Jo's spiral notebook and tore out the sections by date, working backwards. It took twenty minutes from the time I scanned the pages to Maddy's email confirming receipt of them. When she came back to me I felt a pang of doubt. There was never any guarantee of credentials anywhere, but nowhere was the risk greater than on the World Wide Web. It was a risk because you never knew who *anyone* really was. As the saying goes, on the Internet, no one knows you're a dog.

I slept for too long. When I awoke it was the afternoon. Girl came in and pushed her hairy face under the duvet to get me to come to. The first thing I did was let her out. The second thing I did was log on.

Maddy had come good. I had pages and pages of Jo's notes, typed up in Word. There were a couple of long interviews with games-company executives, nothing too exciting, some foreshadowing of future products and strategies, which she would have written up. Further on there were some short Q&As that related to a couple of multi-media product announcements. There was one page that was different. I reckoned it was about three-quarters of the way through the notebook. It was a list with a title, or at least I assumed it was the title, because the rest of the list was names of people.

The title was *The Double Devils*. The list consisted of thirteen names, all women's names, three of which I recognised: Cherry Shankar, Dinika Patel and Georgina Powers.

CHAPTER ELEVEN

# MORE DEVILS THAN VAST HELL CAN HOLD

The room was cold but I had begun to sweat. I'm not superstitious as a rule, but the fact that there were thirteen names on the list told me that there was a dark and poisonous motive in the making of it. The words *The Double Devils* struck a deep chord, but I couldn't remember where I had heard the phrase before. Anxiety began to flick its worrisome tongue inside me and my mouth was as dry as dust.

It was the order of the names that jangled my nerves. My name was before Cherry Shankar's, and Dinika Patel's was after both of us. As a list of names, it made only one sort of sense. The ones before Dinika Patel could be dead, like her, or lucky, like me, and the ones after could soon be one or the other.

My hit-and-run accident was no accident. It couldn't be, which meant it mattered now. Jo Casey must have known something when she caught my eye that night in the Crown. She'd wanted to ask me something, or tell me something. She might not have known exactly what, but she was on the case. She'd have heard about me. Maybe, after that night, she still thought the hit-and-run was an accident, a coincidence, until she found out something else that convinced her otherwise. Why didn't she call or mail me? Cherry was the next on the list, and that meant she might have gone to Cherry's house to warn her. The names again:

Catriona Ross
Joan Shepherd
Jenni Quek
Georgina Powers
Cherry Shankar
Dinika Patel
Althea Winston
Theresa Gleeson
Sinead O'Neill
Niamh Connor
Fatima Khan
Susan Draper
Claudia Bonetti

The only person I knew was Cherry. Cherry knew me but did she know the others? Did she know us all? If not, then what had we in common? My mind began grubbing for clues. We were all women. We were racially different, the names confirmed that, but the race motive was still a possibility because of who we were or who we might have slept with. I had had a black boyfriend and an Asian one. Cherry was Asian and Gecko was white. I didn't know anything about Dinika Patel. Who knew her secrets?

We could all have been Gecko's women at one time, and that might mean we could all be some sick creature's rivals in love. My hands began to shake. What love? To call what Gecko and I had experienced love was to take lead for gold. And who but Cherry could have known about it? It had been so trivial that I hadn't bothered telling anyone. Who would care? Except Cherry. Only Cherry cared, and she had known because Gecko had blabbed to her in one of his moments of 'openness'. She cared, that was why she told me that she knew, but I couldn't believe Cherry could have done this, even if she did fake all that stuff about pure love.

Love. If it was about love, then where was Danny? Why would women be the only targets if the connection was the notches on Gecko Samuels' belt? Danny had been the last of Gecko's lovers but his name wasn't there. Knowing Gecko's taste for variety, I doubted if he had been his only male lover either. Where were the men in Gecko's life? Something cold began to creep through my veins. Danny was dead and I'd presumed that he had been drunk. The post-mortem might turn up something else. I lit a cigarette. I didn't need that extra worry.

My brain began to tick through what I knew about Gecko and boys. I knew nothing. Gecko hadn't come out. That was one answer. The killer who had made this list could have been as ignorant as the rest of us. My finger circled the words *The Double Devils*. Women. It wasn't about men. It was all about women, and how many women on this list were already dead? How many injured? Where the hell had she got this list? My eyes scrolled down and fixed on the name that came after Dinika Patel. Althea Winston. Althea Winston was in trouble.

I called Robert Falk but only got his 'leave a message', so I did the next best thing and called Detective Superintendent Daniel Spencer. I had his full attention.

'Danny Morgan had this notebook?' he said.

'Yes, but like I said, I think it was Jo Casey's.'

'Why didn't you hand it to us straight away?'

'I've only just found it. It was in among the stuff that

came off the table when Danny fell. By the way, what did the post-mortem show? How did he die?'

He paused, and I could hear the caution in his voice when he spoke again.

'You've got nothing to worry about.'

'I wasn't worried.'

'Are you trying to tell me something?'

'No. I'm trying to find a common link here.'

'And you came up with what, exactly?'

'Women.'

'I'll have to see the notebook,' he said, and I looked at the single printed page in my hand with dismay. The notebook was in pieces.

He arrived an hour and a half later, and I made him wait in the sleety rain while I did my usual routine of edging along walls and around corners and peeking through curtains before opening the door to him.

'I'm sorry to have kept you,' I said.

He nodded and stooped to come in. The doorway was large enough but it must have been force of habit. He was a tall man, leaner and older than he appeared on the television, but better-looking. Rain dripped off his cropped hair and splashed on the bare floorboards. I took his coat and directed him into the lounge.

He stood by the bay window while the dog kept a respectful distance. I noticed the quick glances he shot around the flat. He was making judgements about me from the disarray that he saw. I followed his eyes to the ashtray full of cigarette ends and the unwashed coffee cups spread around my untidy, half-decorated lounge.

I offered him coffee, which he refused, and tea, which he also declined. I suspected it had something to do with the standard of hygiene he'd assessed in the few moments he'd been in the place. For a moment, I saw my subterranean flop with different eyes, and I wondered if it had always been this bad.

'Let's sit down over there,' I said.

He walked over to the dining table and put the light briefcase he was carrying on it, wiping the rain from the black leather with a paper handkerchief that he pulled from a pocket pack. Then he did what everyone did. He stood by the French windows that overlooked the garden and the canal and looked out. Christmas lights were winking in the houses opposite and throwing colours on the water like paint.

'How long have you been here?' he said.

'A year or so.'

'And before?'

'Upstairs. Richard Munroe, the news editor of Technology Online, lives there. We work together,' I said.

'And you lived together.'

'Until his girlfriend moved in.'

'She still there?'

'No.'

'What happened?'

'They split up, but she can't stay away.'

He made no comment, not about me, about them or about the dismal downpour outside the window. If he was waiting for more details, he wasn't getting them. After a few moments, he turned his back on the weather and pulled out a chair to sit down. He indicated that I should do the same.

'The night you got run over,' he said. 'Tell me exactly what happened.'

I lit a cigarette and told him how the car had come out of the night and Richard had pushed me out of the way and saved my life. I came up with more details. It was like painting by numbers. Every time you came back to it, you found a thin, unfilled sliver of space between the colours that you hadn't seen before and you filled it in. I was getting there, but the face of the driver remained a white space in my memory.

'And this was?'

'A month or so ago.'

'When did you get the postcard?'

His face betrayed nothing, but my face betrayed my surprise and he repeated the question. I knew then that he knew everything about me but he just wanted me to tell him so that he could compare my version with the one he already knew.

'I don't exactly know when it arrived. It went to Richard's place. He still gets a lot of my mail.'

'Show me the notebook, Georgina.'

I fetched it but I was embarrassed to show it to him the way it was. I'd ripped out the pages to scan them, and although I'd replaced them in the right order, it looked almost desecrated. Spencer held it in his hands, his face a blank.

'Is this how it was?'

'No.'

He had a look in his eye like a raised stick.

'It's in shorthand. I don't read shorthand. I had to give it to someone,' I said.

'You gave it to someone and they did this?'

'No. I did it. I scanned it to send it to someone to translate for me. That's why it's in pieces.'

I noticed that the first knuckle of the middle finger of his right hand was permanently bent, as if had been broken once. He wore a wedding band on his left hand, which caught the light as he flicked through the pages.

'You should have given it to us immediately.'

I said nothing.

'Why didn't you just send this person the book complete?' he said.

'The person lives in Virginia.'

He looked up.

'Why Virginia?'

'Paranoia.'

His eyes picked over the expression on my face until he said, 'Show me the transcript.'

I fetched everything that Maddy had delivered. He went through it and then separated the list of names and the page of shorthand that corresponded to it.

'Is it usual for journalists to write names out in shorthand?'

'Depends how much time you have. It makes it difficult for anyone else to read if you do, that's for sure.'

I looked at his face as he scanned the two pieces of paper that were lying before him. His eyes flicked from one page to the other and he tapped his broken finger on the tabletop. Spencer didn't look as relaxed as he had been. He was chewing and sucking at his lips and tap, tapping his finger.

'Althea Winston,' was what he said.

I could see his problem. No address, no town, city or country, no telephone number, but he had to find her. Better still, he had to make a connection between her and me and everyone else on the list.

'Do you know any of these women?'

'Just Cherry.'

'Did you know Dinika Patel?'

'No, but we all live here in the East End. Maybe Althea Winston does. Maybe all thirteen of us do.'

He looked out of the window but he didn't really see

anything, not the sticky drizzle of wet snow in my garden nor the premature lights that had come on in the block of flats and the houses that lined the canal. He was focusing on the information and how it all fitted in.

I turned the list so that I could read it, and placed my fingertip on the names of Catriona Ross, Joan Shepherd and Jenni Quek.

He looked away from the window and rubbed his broken finger across his lips. He took the list from me, turning it back around and lining up the two pages, the shorthand and the transcription.

'I have to interview your friend Richard. Then I want you to both come to the Yard and look at some photographs,' he said.

'Again?'

'Again.'

I sucked on my cigarette and looked at him long and hard.

'No.'

His face was impassive.

'Why not?'

I felt my throat thicken up as if it were trying to block the truth slipping out, but the words squeezed out like prisoners under a wire.

'I haven't been able to leave the house since the hit-and-run,' I said.

'Not at all?' he said.

'Just upstairs. I've worked out how to do that. I plan it.'

'If you can overcome your fear to help him, you can do it for these women.'

I laughed. It was almost a pleasure to wrong-foot him, worthy as he was.

'I don't go to help Richard, Detective Superintendent.

I'm no help to him at all. I'm more of a hindrance. I go there to eat.'

I noticed a small, deep scar on his brow. He said nothing, but it was as if he'd given me permission to go on and redeem myself.

'He can do without me. He blames me. I know that,' I said.

'Why does he blame you?'

'He thinks we were run over by one of my weird boyfriends.'

He gave a slight nod of acknowledgement.

'Do I have to tell you about them, or do you know all about them?' I said.

'Tell me about them.'

'How long have you got?' I said, trying to grin.

He didn't smile. I looked at him through the light cloud of smoke. Cherry was going to have to do the same. She was going to have to confess her past to this man. And Dinika Patel's family were going to have to see if what they knew about their lost daughter matched up to what he knew. Every woman on that list was going to have to give herself up to him.

As he gathered up the pieces of the notebook, I wondered what his wife was like and how she had found the key to him. Perhaps he revealed his feelings to her, but somehow I couldn't imagine Spencer relying on anyone that much.

'Whoever made that list thinks I'm dead, don't they?' I said.

I had hoped he would confirm it. I wanted him to say that I had nothing more to worry about, but his blank face told me that I had everything to worry about. He thought every woman on that list had something to worry about. 'I'll send someone,' he said.

'Did Dinika Patel know Gecko Samuels?' I said.

'We don't know yet.'

He took a deep breath.

'It doesn't seem likely, but . . .'

'So it's not about Gecko?'

'. . . but we're keeping an open mind. We don't know.'

'Race,' I said, grabbing his arm. 'What about race? Is this a race thing?'

He folded his fingers over my hand and dragged them gently from his sleeve. This time I thought I saw pity in his eyes.

'It's a possibility.'

I slumped back in the chair.

'I have to know everything about you, Georgina. Everything about Cherry Shankar. Everything about Dinika Patel. I don't know what the connection is, but that's how we're going to find out who tried to kill you.'

It was almost a relief to hear him say the phrase that paid. He held the pages up to me.

'How did she get the list?'

I'd thought about that already. Nothing got into a reporter's notebook that wasn't going to be useful. There were three explanations. She had either heard something or had been told it and wrote it down, or she had copied it from somewhere. I wasn't going to tell Spencer that. He could work *that* out. The more difficult question was the one he'd asked. How? How she had got it, who could have told her or where had she copied it from?

'She specialised in multimedia stories, you know, the games business, video-on-demand, graphics chips, sound processors,' I said. 'Richard could tell you. Or Max Winters.'

'The Double Devils? Could that be the name of a game?'

I shrugged and pulled on the cigarette.

'Might as well ask me if there's a song by that name. There probably is, somewhere. Try Cliff Richard.'

He slid the pages into his briefcase and stood up. His shirt and suit smoothed easily back into place over his well-balanced body. The only person I knew who looked as well turned out was Tony Levi, and he was a villain and as fit as a fly.

'I slept with Gecko Samuels a whole lifetime ago. I suppose you'll have to know that,' I said.

He nodded but he wasn't shocked. I wasn't ever going to shock him and he knew I didn't care what he thought.

'It was nothing,' I said. 'To me.'

'A one-night stand?'

'To call it a night is stretching it. It was more of a nightcap and about as stimulating.'

A smile crept to the edges of his mouth.

'Go on.'

'Like I said, it was nothing to me. It was nothing to him either, but he liked to blab, did Gecko. He and Cherry had this open arrangement, which only he seemed to take full advantage of. It was a drunken fumble that happened well before her time, but she knew about it. She cared enough to mention it once and I asked her if he kept a list of us all. Ironic, isn't it? Someone else makes a list of women, and Gecko, with the biggest black book in town, gets killed by the by.'

He stood with his hands on his hips for a moment or two, thinking, and then he said, 'Have you got a fax?'

I showed him my office. He said he had to make a phone call too, so I took the hint and left the room. I tried to listen to what was being said. It seemed that he wanted a check on the names preceding mine and wanted it to start locally. He wanted a search of missing persons, hospital admissions, reported accidents, assaults and deaths. He wanted it done fast.

When he came out of the office, he collected his briefcase and his coat.

'I'll arrange for you to look at the mugshots here,' he said. 'You need to be vigilant.'

'I'm not going anywhere, Detective Superintendent. I can barely open the door to people I know, let alone a stranger. Don't worry. I have a big dog and I can dial 999. It will have to do.'

'We'll make some arrangements, but . . .'

'You have a budget.'

He opened the door and the cold air blew in with the rain. I broke the end of my cigarette off and crushed it underfoot.

'Devils aren't as black as they are painted, you know,' I said.

He turned around.

'I don't believe in devils, Georgina,' he said. 'I believe in the evil that men do.'

When he'd gone, I stood there for a while listening to the rain and the dog's breathing.

'What about you? Do you believe in devils, girl?'

She loped off towards the front room.

'No. Why would you?' I said. 'It's a human thing.'

CHAPTER TWELVE

# DEAD MAN WALKING

It took me two minutes with an Internet People Searcher to find four Althea Winstons. It took much longer to contact all four. The first one lived in Birmingham and had a mobile telephone.

'Althea Winston?'

'Yes?'

The Birmingham accent had a West Indian lilt.

'My name is Georgina Powers. After we've finished talking, I want you to call this number and ask for Detective Superintendent Daniel Spencer.'

'What's this about?'

She sounded very cautious.

'Please take this number.'

I gave her the AMIP number.

'I'm a journalist.'

'I'm calling the police right now.'

'Please. A minute. It's very important.'

I counted slowly and silently to five to let her think about it.

'OK, but I'm at work, you know?' she said.

'Althea, I have a list of names of people who have been involved in hit-and-run accidents in recent months.'

'Uh-huh.'

'My name is on it, and so is yours.'

There was dead silence.

'It might not be anything to do with you, you understand? It's only your name. Have you had any accidents at all recently, Althea?'

'Oh my God.'

'Have you?'

'No.'

'Nothing's happened? No near misses? Nothing that's worried you?'

'No. Nothing. Oh my word.'

'Nothing unusual's happened?'

'My husband got a job. I'd say that was pretty unusual.'

'I'm sorry, but is your husband black?'

'What?'

'Please don't be offended. My name is on this list, and I'm white and I have a black boyfriend. You see what I'm getting at, Althea?' I lied.

'All right then.'

'Is your husband black?'

'He's as black as I am,' she said.

'And what do you do, Althea?'

'I'm an office cleaner.'

'You've not suffered any racial harassment or anything like that?'

'This week? Listen, you're scaring me here. Are you sure this is me? Althea Winston? Do you have an address? Why haven't *you* called the police?'

'I've found three other Althea Winstons and I'm calling them all.'

'Really? Where?'

'One in Bristol and two in London. Does the name Gecko Samuels mean anything to you, Althea?'

'No. No, wait a minute. Gecko. That funny name I know. My boy plays those games. Gecko's the computer man who died in the bomb, yes? Oh my God, was his name on the list? Am I in that sort of danger?'

'No, his name wasn't on the list, but he might connect the names that are. It might be that another Althea Winston knows him, but the police will want to speak to you sooner rather than later, OK? Give them a call.'

'They have this list?'

'Yes.'

'How come you do?'

'I'm a journalist, Althea.'

'You shouldn't go around scaring people.'

'Call the police, Althea.'

The second Althea came from west London and said she wasn't going to speak to any journalist, not now, not ever, but she would call the police right away, I could be sure of that.

The third Althea, from Bristol, wasn't at home but her machine asked me to leave a message.

The fourth Althea was at home sick.

I told her what I'd told her namesake in Birmingham, and she had no idea what I was talking about but she didn't like the sound of it. I did my routine and she confirmed that she was black and that she didn't have a boyfriend because she was a lesbian. She said her partner was white.

I made her promise to call the police, and I was just about to put the phone down when she said, 'You know, something odd did happen the other day. It's probably nothing.'

'Tell me anyway.'

'I got this postcard. I have no idea who from.'

My heart smacked against my chest.

'It was one of those stupid By Night ones, you know? London By Night? I didn't know if it was junk mail or what. It was addressed to me and it said 'Be seeing you' in black writing, that's all. I thought it might be one of those marketing things you get, you know?'

'Do you still live in Homerton, Althea?'

'They say it's the new Hoxton.'

I could barely speak, because up and coming or not, Hoxton was barely a mile from where I lived.

'Cherry?' I said.

'Is that you, George?'

'Where are you?'

'I can't tell you. I can't tell anyone.'

'I'm going to ask you one question.'

'OK.'

'The thing you weren't supposed to tell.'

'Oh.'

'Was it a postcard?'

She didn't confirm or deny it.

'There were just three words on it, right?'

She said nothing.

'Talk to me, Cherry.'

'How did you find out?' she said.

'I got one too. It went to my old address.'

'You had that car accident.'

'Yours was addressed to you and not Gecko, right?'

'It was addressed to me. West End postmark.'

'We're not the only ones, Cherry. There's a list.'

She didn't seem to be listening.

'It was me they wanted then. Not Gecko,' she said. Her voice sounded empty and crushed.

'Cherry, did you hear me? We're not alone. There's a list of thirteen names. It's called The Double Devils.'

I read them out.

'Do you know any of them?' I said.

'Only you. The Patel girl in the second bomb. That's it.'

'Did Gecko know them?'

'How do I know?'

'You knew about me, you see what I'm getting at?'

'Do you really think he told me everything?'

'You said he did.'

'Fuck you.'

'What do we have in common, Cherry?'

'We drink. We smoke. We take recreational drugs. We're single females. We have no kids. We work in the computer business. We live in the East End. We screwed Gecko. We went to see Pulp at the Brixton Academy in ninety-five. What in hell do we have in common with Dinika Patel? That's what I'd like to know.'

'You heard of Althea Winston?'

'No.'

'Gecko ever "share" that name with you?'

'No.'

'The name on the list after Dinika Patel is Althea Winston. I called four Althea Winstons. One is a black woman who has a white girlfriend. She got a card.'

Cherry didn't speak for so long that I thought we had been cut off.

'Cherry?'

'How'd you find out about the list?'

'Jo Casey had it.'

She said nothing, and then she said, 'I can't stop thinking about her and the baby.'

Jo and her baby and Gecko, three people who weren't on the list but they died anyway.

'What's this Double Devil thing?' Cherry said after a little while.

'I don't know, but thirteen women, Cherry, you know what I mean?'

'Lucky for some,' she said.

'Did Dinika Patel get a postcard?' I asked Spencer.

He said two Althea Winstons had phoned and that he wished I hadn't interfered.

'You knew all along. Robert took the card from me because he knew about it. Why didn't you put the word out, Detective Superintendent? You could have saved her.'

'You need to leave this to us.'

'You should have warned us.'

'We didn't know about the list.'

'You should have put it on the news.'

'Calm down.'

'What?'

'I said calm down. Talk to no one.'

'I'm a journalist, Detective Superintendent. I talk to everyone, anyone who pays.'

Spencer took a breath.

'I don't think you should be thinking of raising your profile at this time. I'm going to send someone round,' he said. 'I want you to look at those mug shots. I also want you to look at some frames from a security video.'

'Where's the security video from?'

'Don't open the door to anyone you don't know. Lock up. You've got the dog, that's good.'

'You're very reassuring,' I said.

'If he's working through this list, he won't come back for you unless you give him reason to.'

'He? You keep saying he.'

He told me once more to be vigilant and put the phone down.

I agreed with him. My gut feeling was that it was a man who had made the list. His victims were his enemies. Men, sick in heart and mind, who hate women, hunt and kill them because women are their torment and their salvation. The tarts, the whores, the bitches; the wives, the sisters, the mothers. I wasn't a wife, a sister or a mother but in some man's mind I was one of three things: a tart, a whore or a bitch. Well, I thought, a journalist is all three, my friend.

Diane Shine was unusually cautious.

'We don't want to give out information that's going to help this bastard.'

'Diane. It's going to help these women. I wish I had known before he ran me over. How are the police going to find every woman on the list and warn them in time? Althea Winston got one of these postcards. I did, and so did Cherry Shankar. It's not just a story. It's a fucking public service.'

'I agree, but if we show the card, anyone could start sending them. There're a million sickos out there.'

She lowered her voice.

'I mean, God, some of them work here.'

'I haven't told you the message,' I said.

'And you're not going to?'

'No.'

'Good.'

'No names from the list. Not even mine. Just Cherry's and Dinika Patel's.'

'Why not yours?'

'You're going to by-line me. Whoever is sending these cards out knows *our* names. The point of this is to warn people. Anyone who got a card is going to check in. What's this worth?'

'A lot.'

She paused.

'Have you any idea why you're on this list?'

'I thought at first that it might be something to do with Gecko Samuels, but now I think it might be a race thing.'

'Remind me. Are you as black as I am, girl?'

'Does Abdul Malik ring a bell?'

'No.'

'How about Warren?'

She didn't say a thing, but I knew she remembered Warren, and more of him than I would have wished. I heard her suck at her teeth and sigh.

'You know? All this? Man, if it doesn't make me anything but tired. Sick and tired. Is this a complete list as far as you know? I mean, how do I know *I'm* not on this damned list?' she said.

She had a point. I had assumed the list was complete. Why would Jo Casey write down part of a list? But if she did, how many were on the original? Twenty, thirty, a thousand? More?

'George?'

Her voice brought me back to business.

'I don't know if this is a complete list, Diane.'

We were both silent, and then she said, 'OK, I'll see what I can do. Take care.'

It was five in the afternoon, and dark as well water, when I heard someone move the Salvation Army on from outside the house. They had pumped twice on a French horn and begun a discordant attempt at 'God Rest Ye Merry Gentlemen' when the party was deemed to be over. I looked out and saw their black-ribboned hats bobbing as they ambled away through the pools of yellow light in the pale street. A minute later my doorbell rang, the dog growled and I tweaked the curtains. A squat man with dark curly hair and a portly woman with a blonde bob stood outside wearing overlarge navy anoraks. Their breath filled the small yard like steam from the flanks of a couple of hard-working drays. When the man caught sight of me, he held up his warrant card. He was the police with the mug shots, and she was a lay observer making sure there would be no funny business.

I took them upstairs to Richard's and we flicked through them without speaking.

'No,' Richard said.

I took longer. I kept the white sliver of unfilled space at the front of my mind as I ransacked the sullen images presented to me as candidates for my dreams. It was no use.

'No,' I said, and Richard took my hand and squeezed it.

'Why don't you stay here?' he said when they had gone.

'Don't you think you should come downstairs with me?'

'Why?'

'The postcard came here, remember?'

Richard's face was sickly in the half-light of the lounge. The evening news flickered on the television.

'I've got a book called *The Hidden Language of Your Handwriting* by James Green and David Lewis. "Health, Job Prospects, Sexual Attraction, Personality and Emotions . . . Revealed at the Stroke of a Pen!" It's based on the Funnel Method of Analysis.'

'Who's Funnel?' Richard asked.

'It's not a who, it's a what. Funnel analysis means you flow from the general to the particular.'

'You checked out the writing?'

'A sociable psychopath.'

'Great, so he could be a mate,' Richard said, and asked me to pass him a knitting needle Mary had bought so he could scratch his leg.

When a black card with white lettering came up on the screen a minute later, I hit volume control. They showed the picture but they didn't show the message. The next shot was of Spencer in a one-to-one with the reporter. He was saying he felt the release of the information was appropriate at this time. The card had a West End postmark, he said. It was probably purchased in London and there was a message written on the card, which they would not reveal at this stage. The writing itself was unique and had been analysed. There was one thing they were certain of. The writing was not authentic. It was copied.

'How can you be so sure?' the reporter asked.

'Because it's the writing of a dead man,' Spencer said.

CHAPTER THIRTEEN

# THESE ARE BLOODTHIRSTY TIMES

There was music playing upstairs. I'd heard a taxi arrive and seen Mary run up the steps trailing tinsel from a bag decorated with Christmas trees. She didn't ring the doorbell because Richard had given her a key. I sat downstairs logged on in the gloom and listened to them: her footsteps on the wooden floors, the murmur of their voices, his laughter and the symphonic melodies swimming and sweeping above my head like shoals of glistening fish.

Christmas was creeping towards me. There were twenty shopping days left and the cards had started to arrive by post. The split was probably about fifty-fifty between people I didn't know, like the entire staff of public relations firms, and people I did know but that I hadn't seen for years, like my mother and father. My mother had sent me an advent calendar. I opened its little stained-glass windows and ate five holly-shaped chocolates to get me up to date while I read and discarded the corporate party invitations.

It would be my second Christmas at this address. Last year, I hadn't bothered with a tree and the trimmings. I had lain instead by a shell-shaped swimming pool belonging to some foreign hotel and eaten my dinner with strangers. I met a twenty-five-year-old German footballer, who crept up to my room on Boxing Day and begged me to sleep with him. His legs were covered in scars and I liked him because he was polite and could take his drink. He swam in the sea every day and sunbathed by the pool where people stared at him because he was famous. He told me he was lonely and I said I had heard that before. I think he really was, though. I saw him on the television once afterwards taking a penalty. As he buried the ball in the back of the net, they said that Spurs wanted to buy him for fifteen million. I had his address and he had mine but we hadn't bothered, not even a postcard.

For want of anything better to do, I entered *handwriting+postcard* into the search engine and got two numbered episodes from the seventh season of *Hawaii Five-O* (1974–1975). This was what the Internet was about, the fact that someone was prepared to summarise every episode of a seventies television series, lest they forget.

Finding them was like discovering coins on a beach you'd never been to, and when the sand was scraped away, seeing your own face on the pieces of silver.

Episode 147 was entitled 'I'll kill 'em again'.

The summary read: ***Postcards** from a psychopath taunting McGarrett to remember crime victims of the past precede a series of re-enacted murders.*

Episode 149 was called 'Bomb, bomb, who's got the bomb?'

Its summary read: ***Handwriting** analysis and a psychiatric diagnosis are used to track down who is threatening the life of a state Senate crime committee chairman.*

I couldn't have done better if I had asked someone to read the Tarot. There in *Hawaii Five-O* were *postcards* and *handwriting* and the unlooked-for, but relevant, *psychopath* and *bomb*.

The phrase 'Bomb, bomb, who's got the bomb?' stuck in my mind like a tune as I followed the *handwriting* trail to *Killer Fonts*, a web site whose e-commerce pitch was flawless and by definition completely lacking in good taste.

*Everyone has those days where words won't begin to describe how you feel. Why not help your words do exactly what they want?*

*What better way to let your boss know your true feelings than by resigning with the help of* ***Lizzie Borden****?*

*How else would you confess ardent feelings of corporate takeover than through the script of* ***Genghis Khan****?*

*And everyone will know you mean business when* ***Jack the Ripper*** *writes your cover letters.*

*Killer Fonts offers you all that and more. Not only can you enlist the most notorious psychopaths to your aid, but also the weighty words of Important People.*

*Who could ignore a speech written by* ***Abraham Lincoln*** *or a poem by* ***Edgar Allan Poe****?*

I was sold, and since Jack the Ripper was available, I clicked to see. The sample read:

"Perhaps tonight
you will die" – Jack The Ripper

It wasn't a fluent script. Jack had had difficulty keeping his letters going in one direction. He crossed his 't's with sharp, confident strokes but couldn't cope with a capital 'R' in joined-up handwriting. Here was a Victorian underachiever who had wanted to be someone, anyone. A noted butcher of women would do.

A Ripper link sent me to a transcript of an original letter that had been received by a London news agency on 25 September 1888, a few days before the grisly murders of the prostitutes Elizabeth Stride and Catherine Eddowes.

It was a lurid, incompetently written taunt, its mocking tone reminiscent of the infamous 'I'm Jack' tape received by the police during Peter Sutcliffe's terrifying reign as the second Ripper more than eighty years later. The tape had been found to be phoney, but not before it was played to silent football crowds in the terraces of the North of England in the hope that someone might recognise the accent and help the police catch the man who had already slipped through their hands. People asked themselves who was worse, the man who sent those tapes or the psychopath who took a hammer to women walking alone.

Two clicks on, *handwriting* brought John Wayne Gacy to my attention. A sample of his handwriting had been posted following its analysis at the Handwriting of the Month meeting of the Graphological Society of San Francisco in July 1997. Needless to say, the graphologists concluded that Gacy was seriously disturbed, as anyone who was convicted of the rape and murder of thirty-three men might well be. But it wasn't the *disagreeable pastosity* and *the abundant signs of confusion* indicating *a strong need to satisfy urges* that the graphologists had detected that interested me so much as the funny little tail Gacy put on his letter 'b'.

It was there again when I clicked on a sample of the handwriting of Theodore Robert Bundy, who had raped and murdered twenty-eight women, the youngest being a girl of twelve. Bundy also placed an extraneous descender on his 'b' so that it hung there, like the tail of a lower primate, a lingering signal to a primitive past that had not been quite buried. It was there in Bundy's script, in Gacy's, and it was there on the postcard.

When I clicked back to *Killer Fonts*, neither Ted Bundy nor John Wayne Gacy was available for those who wanted their complaints and orders taken seriously. If my postcard writer had copied their atavistic style, he hadn't found it there. There were other places, though. Bundy and Gacy had more sites devoted to them than Tom Cruise, and samples of their writing were posted on most of them, inevitably accompanied by a graphologist's analysis in the interests of science.

Bundy had an unusual little break in his 'd' too, a trait he shared with the handsome Milwaukee cannibal Jeffrey Dahmer. But the 'd's of these diseased minds didn't interest me. It was the 'b' in 'be seeing you' that did.

And Bundy was dead, executed on 24 January 1989, his death, like his life, available online, for the record, but I didn't have the inclination to download the file and watch his head catch fire. I logged off and lit a cigarette instead.

I asked myself three questions. Was the person who had sent postcards to thirteen women that he had attacked, or planned to, a man like Ted Bundy? Or was he simply the kind of man who would copy Ted Bundy's writing to disguise his own? The third question was just as hard to answer. It was the question people had asked themselves when they had heard 'I'm Jack'.

What kind of man was worse?

*

DI Robert Falk was unavailable once again, but I got Spencer.

'It's Bundy, isn't it?' I said.

He sighed.

'I don't want to keep releasing stories earlier than I might want to, and I don't want to release any information that will encourage time-wasters.'

'I'm trying to save a few lives; maybe even protect my own.'

'I understand that you are a victim. I understand that you're a reporter too.'

'Did you find the other women?'

'We have traced all the women.'

'All of them?'

'Yes.'

'Alive?'

'Yes.'

'Did they all get postcards?'

'Yes.'

I sat back as if the breath had been thumped out of me.

'When?'

'This week.'

'Before the first bomb?'

'Yes.'

'How does my hit-and-run fit in, or am I waiting for something new and unexpected? Should we all expect to be blown to pieces?'

'I don't know.'

I tried to steady my breathing.

'Do they live around here?'

'I can't reveal that just yet.'

'What's his game, Detective Superintendent?'

'Off the record?'

'There's no such thing, but you know that, don't you?'

Neither of us spoke for a long minute. I thought I heard a lighter catch fire.

'I was hoping you'd tell me,' he said.

That's how we left it, and I didn't speak to another soul until Cherry called, much, much later.

The music upstairs had stopped, but I hadn't heard Mary leave. I tried to purge from my imagination the romantic scenes that might have resulted from a blissful evening of light opera and festive home decoration. Mary playing Doris Day to Richard's Rock Hudson with split-screen bedroom yearnings. As long as she didn't cook, she'd be on song.

Mary was a vegetarian. Nothing wrong with that, but her approach to meatless cuisine was insidious and totalitarian. She had disastrously attempted to change Richard's culinary ways, but her ruse to storm his heart via his pampered stomach had been a failure, like her wholly organic wholemeal pastry. She had been so desperate to get her hands on him that she had then worked on his masculine pride and fooled him into thinking that she was pregnant. To be kind, I think she fooled herself, and when it turned out not to be true, she couldn't bear to tell him. The lie grew, but her stomach didn't. No amount of three-bean casserole could help her then. They'd split a year ago, but it had been off and on since then, and it looked like Richard needed her kind of motherly love right now.

'Are you drinking?' Cherry said.

'I'm smoking.'

'Me too.'

'You OK?'

'He's a game player.'

She'd been working at it, just like I had.

'I think so,' I said.

'Why?'

'You first.'

'No. You.'

'Ever heard of Ted Bundy?'

'No.'

'You've *never* heard of Ted Bundy?'

'Who is he?'

'How about John Wayne Gacy?'

'Everyone's heard of John Wayne.'

'John Wayne *Gacy*.'

'Gacy? No. Who is he?'

'He was a serial killer. They were both serial killers. Bundy killed women. Gacy killed men.'

She said nothing but she hadn't drifted away. I knew she'd be working it out. I waited for her to get it.

'And they're both dead, right?'

'Describe to me the handwriting on the card you got. Think of the letter "b".'

She did.

'Gacy and Bundy wrote like that. Long left to right upward strokes before initial letters. Bundy more so. It's Bundy's writing, I think. Or rather, a copy of Bundy's writing.'

I gave her the web site address and told her to check it out. I listened in silence to her clicks and keystrokes.

'What does Spencer say?' she said.

'He wouldn't confirm or deny. He knows it's the writing of a dead man. He said so on TV. I'm willing to bet on this being what he meant.'

'How do they know it's not another shit just like Bundy?'

'Why say the writer was dead? They know that it's a copy and it's Bundy's writing. Forensics must have broken it down. They've got more than one card. Maybe the sicko made up a stamp of his friendly greeting so he could mass-produce it.'

'Did you search Double Devils?'

'No. The serial killers were kind of diverting.'

'Yeah, and American. Shall I tell you what I've got?'

'Go ahead.'

She paused.

'Myra Hindley.'

It was a name that would brook no indifference. A name that stirred more emotion in England than the freak-show horror of Bundy and Gacy. Myra Hindley was the most infamous paedophile in British criminal history. She had helped her psychopathic lover, Ian Brady, to abduct and then murder five children. If she hadn't conned the kids, they would never have gone with him. They got into his black car because of her, because she was a woman, just like she knew they would.

'Don't tell me, whoever he is, he's a fan,' I said.

'Let me read you what I got,' she said. '"It's because I am a woman and it makes me the double devil".'

'She said that?'

'Yes.'

'"It's because I am a woman and it makes me the double devil",' I repeated. 'It's because we're women? Is that it?'

'No. She said more than that.'

'Go on.'

'She said: "A woman is supposed to be the protector of children, and when she does something to harm them it is perceived as far worse than a man's crime against them." '

I'd clicked on the site, and the sullen peroxide blonde with the sixties make-up and the soulless eyes looked out at me. She was the Marilyn Monroe of the Dark Side. How was I like her?

'I'm not a Hindley. I've never harmed a child,' I said. 'I'm not anything like her.'

'No?'

'No.'

I could hear her breathing, hear her sucking on the joint and getting high.

'Could you kill someone?' she said.

I thought about it. That was an entirely different question. Could I kill someone? Well, that would depend.

'A kid? No.'

'No?'

'She helped him.'

'She said Brady made her. He abused her, threatened her family. That's why she did it.'

'Made her? Come on. It took a quarter of a century to make her tell about the graves. Who could *make* her do anything that she really didn't want to do? She did it because she was a callous human being.'

'She loved him, didn't she?'

A minute went by. I felt tense. I was about to say something about the putrid kind of love they had when she said, 'Gecko made me have an abortion. I didn't protect my *own* child. That makes me even worse than her, doesn't it?'

Her words took mine away. I didn't know what to say because what I could say was not going to help her.

She had found a logic bomb and let it explode in her face because deep down she felt she deserved it.

'Cherry, women have abortions for all sorts of reasons.'

'How many good reasons?'

'Just not wanting is good enough for me.'

'We've been found out, Georgina, and whoever has found out has made a list of us, to punish us.'

'We?'

'You and me.'

'I haven't had an abortion, Cherry.'

She paused. Her voice when she spoke was quiet and uncertain.

'You told me you'd lost a baby.'

'Not one, two. I've lost two. They weren't abortions, they were miscarriages.'

She fell silent. The camaraderie of shared pain that she'd tried to form between us had gone, and so had her solution.

'Why didn't you ever say?'

I said nothing.

'Would you have had them, if you could have?'

I didn't want to answer her. It wasn't a fair question. I had always thought I'd had a lucky break, but the older, and the lonelier, I got, the more my dreams hunted me down.

'I only really wanted one, but I'd have done what I wanted to, what I needed to, either way.'

'Not what someone else wanted, yeah?' she said.

I heard something fall upstairs and roll along the floor. There were footsteps, and then nothing.

'Spencer's traced every woman on that list, Cherry. I bet there are some mothers and virgins among them,' I said.

'It just seems to fit together.'

'What?'

'That and the Christian Love site.'

'I don't know it.'

'It's a so-called pro-life site, and the Gecko Games campaign for safe sex is its public enemy number one. Check it out. I'll hang on.'

I went looking for it and it fired up to the first couple of beats of Iggy Pop's 'Lust for Life'. It always cracked me up how the righteous stole the devil's tunes when it suited them. This site not only had Iggy, it had gifs and games. It had cheerful chatrooms, a virtual agony aunt and a disingenuous photo casebook based on the porn industry's homebrew standard, 'Reader's Lives'. There were cute animations of the rhythm method and, on a seasonal note, an Advent countdown calendar with little windows that opened up. In short, it had hip content, 'clickability' and no sense of irony.

Its theme was that it was 'OK to say no' to just about everything God-given but not to God, and it had it in for Gecko Games as a corrupter of youth. Its reviews of Gecko's 'violent' games and comments on the company announcements and press releases read like a stream of convictions.

On Christian Love's home page, you could click on a toilet icon and reveal a picture of Gecko Samuels flanked by two heavies arriving at an awards ceremony. Flashbulbs exploded around him and bounced off his shaven head. He wore a neat Vandyke beard, a Paul Smith suit with an open-necked shirt, and he looked like the devil come to town.

Click on the word *scandal* and you got a soft-focus headshot of Danny Morgan and a college graduation portrait of Jo Casey. Both the photos had been scanned from the online tabloids. Danny looked like a greased-up Bambi and Jo Casey looked about thirteen. The cut-and-paste job of a story ensured that the words *gay* and *sex* and *baby* featured in each paragraph. Christian Love had a two-line opinion that went with it: *And this is the man who wanted to give free condoms to kids! WONDER WHY?*

It stopped a thought process short of calling poor old Gecko a child molester.

Another story reported Gecko Games' £2 million donation towards the campaign by the National Family Advice Bureau – NFAB – to reduce the rate of teenage pregnancies in the United Kingdom.

Christian Love had a big problem with family planning. It wasn't natural, and your plan for a family wasn't necessarily God's plan. Everyone knew the secret agenda of family planning, Christian Love said. It was licentiousness and murder. Contraception for teenagers handed out to kids like sweets encouraged under-age sex, debauchery and disease. It was one step away from the deadly 'morning-after' pill. NFAB, Christian Love concluded, were abortionists sponsored by Mammon in the guise of Gecko Games. The site included a list of NFAB's UK clinics and Gecko's headquarters and business partners. The message it delivered was to take direct action against these organisations because they were getting away with murder. I could see why Cherry had made the connection, but I couldn't make it fit. This site related to her, to her company, to Gecko, to Gecko Games' sponsorship of the NFAB campaign. Gecko Games was seen as anti-morals, anti-children, anti-baby, but the *Double Devils* list Jo Casey had found was *anti-woman*. On this site, women were the victims.

'What do you think?' Cherry said.

'How long has this site been at you?' I said.

'Since we marketed the games with condoms. About a year.'

'Your lawyers checked them out?'

'Yes.'

'And?'

'At one time they listed the home addresses of Gecko employees on the site. It was clear intimidation. We forced them to take them down.'

'How come I missed that?'

She laughed.

'They run rape and pregnancy counselling centres up and down the country, did you know that? They've had them longer than the web site. Community Family Counselling Clinics, they call them,' she said.

'Nothing wrong with that, is there?'

'You've never been to one.'

'Have you?'

'I was five weeks pregnant. I thought they were private clinics, you know? But they have no intention of letting you have an abortion. They're not actually licensed to perform them, but they masquerade as family planning clinics to get you in there, to persuade you to keep the baby no matter what. They showed me a video of a late-term foetus being ripped to shreds. They told me that I could lose my fertility or have a nervous breakdown if I had an abortion. They told me it was murder.'

She paused and then said, 'I went National Health.'

'Is that why Gecko got into the safe sex thing and the NFAB sponsorship?'

'It was a business decision.'

I heard her suck on the joint and she felt close to me. It was as if I could have stretched out my arm to share the smoke. I had nothing to hand but a fresh pack of Silk Cut.

'What does the Bundy and the Hindley thing prove, George?'

'It proves that our man spends as much time online as we do,' I said.

CHAPTER FOURTEEN

# AN UNHEALTHY INTEREST

When she'd gone, I went looking for devils and I found them. The world was held in two hands, and on their coarse knuckles were tattooed the words 'love' and 'hate'. I learned there was a New Holocaust with twenty-seven million dead babies. I learned of the people of the world who had been removed from the benefit and blessings of God. I learned the history of Mystery Babylon and the New World Order. I discovered ninety-nine covert ways to stop abortion. I read that dead children that never were planted vengeance in the minds of others. I learned that the Rescuers had seen them with their own eyes, smiling infant smiles as they floated like cherubs above them. I learned that I could be a Remnant for God, selected out of grace and truth, in a world of gross immorality and decadence. I learned I should not trust my Church for I would find no help there to save the unborn. I should not make friends, for that could blow my cover. I was told that if I had three months to live, I could torch two baby-killing chambers a day on my path to sainthood. I learned how to make butyric acid that would turn stomachs and burn eyes. I learned how to make five types of bomb. I could buy weapons and covert materials. I could offer shelter in my home and maternity assistance to those in need. I could compile lists of those who worked in abortion clinics, find their phone numbers, their email addresses and where they lived. I could find out where their children went to school. I learned I must jubilate in the knowledge that doctors had been shot and clinic workers maimed in the name of the Family. In Amerika.

The hours hurried by as I scrolled through pitiless texts of terror, each seditious page born of sacrosanct beliefs in original sin, hell, damnation, retribution and salvation. There is only one righteous way and it is theirs. The sacred cross of our ancestors is a double-edged axe. There is no evolution. There is no history. The future is apocalyptic and woman must sacrifice herself in the war against the Beast. Woman must breed for the purity of the race and the survival of God's Remnant. She is the vessel. Life must come at any cost, and the price of extinguishing it is Death.

I logged off believing that there were people in the world who would gladly kill me for carrying a condom. It was as depressing as it was banal. Didn't these people watch daytime television? Didn't they know how complicated life was? But Cherry's words haunted me.

*Gecko made me have an abortion.*

I wanted to call her back and tell her that she was fooling herself. She had been panicked into making Gecko the Devil and herself his Double, when the truth was that she wanted Gecko more than anything. I had no doubt that if Cherry had really wanted his child then she would have had it, in spite of him. Had Gecko held a gun to her head? Blaming him was avoiding responsibility, but blaming herself for failing to protect an unborn child was turning the argument on its head. Like the saying goes: many are called, but few are chosen.

Gecko was gone for ever and the possibility of bearing his child had gone with him. I could sympathise. My lost babies came to me in my dreams. I had regrets, but in my heart I counted myself lucky. The truth was, they were safer where they were.

She'd spooked me with the thought of it, though, and the things I had seen online made anything seem possible. As Richard slumbered upstairs in the arms of Mary, I sat, wrapped in a blanket, in the dark by the French windows, thinking about the bomber and the connections Cherry had made. There were no lights tonight. Only the red lamp in the tower block shone dimly across the sky like a malevolent, unblinking eye. In the distance, a motorbike whined, its labouring engine moving closer and louder until it stopped outside. I didn't move, and I wasn't afraid.

John Walker called to me through the letterbox, his face guarded from the savagery of Girl's welcome by a small metal cage that I'd rigged up to protect the postie's fingers.

The phone rang. It was Richard. His voice was thick with sleep.

'What's all the commotion?' he said. 'Are you OK?'

'It's that doctor,' I said.

'Are you ill?'

'*That* doctor.'

'Oh, for fuck's sake, Georgina.'

The line went dead. I heard male voices, and the doorbell rang again. A stranger's mouth appeared through the letter cage and Girl's insistent barking became frenzied. Her face and body were flecked with spit, and so swollen with adrenalin that I thought she might have a stroke.

The mouth identified itself as belonging to a police officer. I got the dog to sit, and when I opened the door, John was there in his leathers, standing next to two uniformed constables. The temperature had dropped like a stone as the winter night bit, and the standing water had turned to ice. They had warrant cards in their hands and their breath filled the doorway like smoke. John's face told me he didn't know which way I was going to play it.

'It's OK. I know him,' I said, and the police melted back into the sodium-orange night.

He followed me into the front room and watched me click on the gas fire.

'Why didn't you phone?' I said.

'I tried.'

'What do you want?'

'They pulled me in today.'

'Who did?' I said, straightening up.

'Your friend. The big man.'

'What did he want this time?'

'He pulled the files on some women I treated.'

He sat down and took a soft plastic wallet filled with tobacco from inside his jacket. He rolled and lit a small cigarette with a surgeon's efficiency, and the air smelled suddenly as sweet and fresh as ripe blackberries.

'I thought we had an understanding,' he said, picking stray tobacco from his lips. 'I apologised to you. I didn't think you'd be bitter.'

'I understood you all right. Why'd he pull the files? What did he want?'

'He gave me some names, asked if I knew them. I told him I knew you and one other. He told me I'd treated three others and he wanted to know if I had had any contact with them before or after they were admitted.'

His good looks seemed worn down.

'I could lose my job, my whole career,' he said.

It took some thinking about. Spencer had given Robert Falk a list of thirteen names, and within a couple of hours he had singled out three other women and linked them with Dr John Walker. He was looking for connections and he had found them.

'Did you have any contact with them?'

'Oh, for fuck's sake.'

'What happened to them?'

'Well, I'm not really at liberty to say, am I?'

'What were they? Hit-and-runs?'

He said nothing.

'Tell me their names, John.'

'Catriona Ross, Joan Shepherd, Jenni Quek.'

'DI Falk looked at patient records?'

'Yes.'

'What did he come up with? A date of death?'

'Why do you say that?' he said.

I made two cups of coffee and poured Scotch in both.

'You'd make someone a wonderful wife,' he said.

'I did already.'

'But you're divorced, right?'

'Happily. How about you?'

His eyes told me nothing.

'The police were sitting outside,' he said. 'What's going on? Is this something to do with me or something to do with you?'

I didn't know whether to tell him about the whole list.

'Say he came up with more than one record attached to each name.'

'Which is more than likely.'

'Why these women in particular, and why you?'

'I don't know.'

'Did you hit on them like you hit on me? Tell me.'

'No.'

'But that's what he wanted to know.'

'Yes.'

I didn't move.

'And did you? Hit on them?'

'I said no.'

'What did you treat them for?'

John paused.

'A date rape.'

'And?'

'A knife attack, another hit-and-run.'

'Did you remember her? Did you remember any of those women?'

He stalled then, took a minute.

'How could I forget?' he said.

'It was before Christmas, about a year ago. December the first, an ambulance brought in the police officer.'

'The knife attack?'

'The date rape. She was half dead.'

It shocked me, but not as much as he said it had shocked him at the time. I believed him. He had written up the report. On her night off, PC Catriona Ross had had her drink spiked with GHB, a bodybuilders' drug that has made its way into the club scene from clandestine labs. GHB (gamma-hydroxybutyrate) was once sold in health-food stores as a performance-enhancing additive to body-builder formulas, but clubbers used it as an Ecstasy substitute, or a come-down off it, and coke and ephedrine and speed.

They call it Grievous Bodily Harm, or GBH, because

of its knockout punch, and Easy Lay because it will sedate someone in fifteen minutes and keep them out for up to three hours. The victim is a live sex doll. It's like necrophilia only your date stays warm. John told me he was fresh out of medical school and there were five others like him handling the evening rush. He told the story in a dull and matter-of-fact way, but I didn't buy his indifference. Listening to him was like watching a failed suicide with his sleeves rolled down.

'I couldn't do a fucking thing about it. A and E is full of people who'd be safer in the hands of their GP, you know? It's a fact,' he said. 'I knew fuck all then and I don't know that much now, but I do know how to keep everything moving. That's the main thing.'

'And very reassuring too.'

He glanced at me. I'd sat by the fire and pulled the blanket over my toes.

'The thing was, I had *wanted* something to happen. It's so fucking mundane most of the time, and in the winter, it's just crazy fucking mundane. More drunks, more junkies, more care in the communities, more abdominals. It's so trivial you're screaming for a trauma. Just something serious for a change. A real emergency. You're not even asking for a major resus, just a mildly interesting bloody emergency.'

'Like a knife attack and a date rape.'

His roll-up had gone out and he struck another match.

'Joan Shepherd was a prostitute. She had been stabbed by her front door. It wasn't far from here.'

'Where?'

'Just off the Roman Road.'

'Where had she been stabbed?'

'In the right buttock. Her skin was split like a cooked

sausage. She was lucky he didn't hit the thigh and sever an artery.'

'The hit-and-run?'

'Jenni Quek. I don't remember much about her except that she was a law student. She had a broken leg.'

'And the policewoman?'

He looked away from me for a moment and then back. This was the one. This was the one that mattered.

'She worked in Brick Lane nick. We worked the same shift sometimes. Scots lass. She left the force.'

'You knew her.'

'Like we know all the local coppers. She had delusions, amnesia, visual disturbance and acute respiratory distress when she came in. She spent a lot of time in gyne after that, but none of us ever saw her again.'

'You ever try to trace her?'

He pressed the tip of his cigarette into an ashtray that was by his foot.

'No, I never tried. Look, I don't want to talk about that any more.'

'Why'd you come here? Tonight.'

'I don't know.'

'You think I can get you off the hook?'

'No.'

'What then?'

He stared into the ashtray, his face jaundiced by the dim light of the room.

'I can't stop thinking about you.'

'I'll say I called you. I'll tell them it was me who asked you.'

'No.'

'Then what?'

'I don't know.'

He got up.

'I'm sorry I came. It seemed like the obvious thing to do. I'll go now,' he said, looking around. 'If the damned dog'll let me.'

'It's late,' I said. 'Are you sleepy?'

'Tired. It's not the same.'

'Do you believe in love at first sight?'

He looked across at me, and the smoke from his cigarette drifted towards the window.

'No,' he said. 'Just an unhealthy interest.'

I awoke first the next morning and left him naked in my bed. He was asleep, his bleached hair flattened by the pillow, and his arms above his head. I noticed the marks on his wrists then, not white scars from self-mutilation but brown stains, like little rope burns. His feet were sticking out from the covers and I quietly moved around the edge of the bed to look at his ankles. There were marks there too. It was when he turned slightly and pushed the covers down that I saw the small gold cross hung around his neck and the mottled skin around his nipples.

My doctor liked a little guilt and a little pain.

I left him sleeping and shut the door to the bedroom. The dog was sprawled on her blankets in the office, and as I passed, she lifted her head and her eyebrows.

'Nothing happened, all right?' I lied.

I went into the bathroom and washed before going into the kitchen to make some tea. The earth outside the door was frozen white and the frosted trees were sealed in ice. Too cold to go out, I told myself, and while the kettle boiled I went to pick up the morning papers in the hall. The front-page headline said three words.

THE ADVENT KILLER.

The story was by-lined *Mary Stow*. Not for the first time, by fair means or foul, Mary had got to the big story before me. The paper had hooked on to the date of the first bombing and given the killer a handle. Mary had somehow got hold of the list of women. I threw the paper down and walked back into the kitchen, opened a cupboard, took out a cup and smashed it against the wall. I took out another and another and another and smashed them all until the place looked like a Greek restaurant after a busy night. The room filled with steam from the boiling kettle. It was condensing on the windows. I looked up the hall and saw the dog first, and then the man.

'Sleep well?' he said.

I said I had, but if he had expected anything more he was disappointed.

'Is there a problem?'

I switched the kettle off as he stepped carefully over the broken crockery and into the kitchen. He saw the newspaper, and brushing the shards of china from the front page, he read the story.

'This is why Robert Falk came to see me, is it?'

I left him with it and called Richard.

'Have you seen the papers?'

He said he had.

'Did you help her on this?'

'She was on the case, George.'

'How come?'

'She doesn't work for us any more. Calm down.'

'Who told her about the women? Who told her about the Double Devils list?'

Richard remained silent.

'Who told her the dates?'

'She might be a lousy cook but she's a good

journalist. You had all the advantages, George, but she got there first. It's as simple as that.'

'You gave her my fucking story. Is that what you were celebrating? What did she promise you this time, a family of four?'

I wanted to kill him.

'You're just jealous.'

'She named me along with Cherry Shankar and Dinika Patel as victims. There's a picture of my flat. It says the *basement.* You know what that means? He knows *exactly* where I live now.'

'You mean, instead of where *I* live, George?'

I slammed the phone down. Rage was roaring like a furnace in my chest but somewhere at the back of my mind my instincts were starting to salvage the situation. We had to have something in common, the paper said. The civil liberties groups were keeping an open mind on race hate, gay hate and every other hate because all the usual suspects had phoned in.

I pressed my hands on my chest and breathed slowly. I wondered what Spencer was thinking. Robert Falk had thought it might be Dr John Walker, but I didn't believe that and the paper didn't say it. Cherry Shankar had thought it was because we were the double devils who had killed our babies, but it didn't say that either. Mary hadn't got it. She hadn't got the story. I still had a chance.

I called Robert Falk and left a message, and then I called Spencer. He said he had been meaning to call but he had been rather busy.

'How's the doctor?' he said.

A feeling came over me like a shower you think might run hot but runs cold.

'He's worried about his job.'

'I bet he is.'

His tone surprised me.

'Don't tell me. He's your prime suspect.'

He said nothing.

'It's not him.'

'Whoever it is knows more than we would like him to right now. You appreciate that.'

'I hope you don't think it was me.'

He said nothing.

'I don't give stories like that away,' I said. 'What about the postcards. Who got them and when?'

'All the women named on the list received postcards just before the first bomb.'

I caught my breath.

'At the same time?'

'Yes.'

'What makes me the same as them, Detective Superintendent?'

'I don't know. Would you consider doing an interview?'

'What?'

'We need to get control of this story. If you could say what happened to you, how it affected you – someone who knows him, someone involved, maybe even he might have some second thoughts, some remorse.'

'What about the others?'

'Cherry Shankar is the only person already in the public domain, apart from Dinika Patel.'

'And she's dead.'

'Yes.'

'And I'm an experienced journalist, so I know the score.'

'Yes.'

I said I'd think about it and left it at that. The house was as quiet as snowfall.

'Fancy a walk?' John said.

He was standing behind me, leaning on the door frame.

His presence surprised me. I'd almost forgotten about him.

'What?'

'Let's go for a walk, get some fresh air.'

The dog muscled her way into the room. She'd heard the magic word.

'I can't,' I said.

She whined.

'Work?'

'Yes. Look. You go. Take the dog.'

'Ten minutes. I want company. I want to walk with you.'

'I can't.'

He stared at me for a moment and said, 'OK.'

I heard him in the bedroom getting dressed.

'I'll shower when I come back,' he said as I walked in. I wanted to say that I would go with him. I wanted to leave this place behind and shut the door on it. I wanted to walk by his side with my arm threaded through his and breathe in some fresh air.

'I just can't, John,' I said, and he held up his hands.

The bloody dog didn't give me a backward glance as John shut the door behind them as quietly as if he were leaving a sick room. It was true. I hadn't lied. I did have to work.

I put the answer phone on and a minute later the phone rang. I was expecting it. Sure enough, it was

Diane offering me money for my story. Danny Morgan's way. 'My Brush with Death' by The Victim. If I did it, I wouldn't be a journalist any more. I'd be a mark. I'd be a victim, an interviewee. I'd have crossed over and I might as well be dead.

When her message ended, the phone rang again. It was another voice that I recognised, a low voice with an East End accent.

'George.'

It was Tony Levi. My ex. The dog's ex. I picked up.

'How are you, girl?'

'I'm all right.'

'You been messing with people?'

'I suppose I have, Tony.'

'What do you need?'

'Nothing. Not a thing.'

There was a pause.

'The big man's been round,' he said.

'Falk?'

'Yeah. And a cool sort. Black geezer. Name of Spencer.'

'What did they want?'

'They wanted to know about me and you, babe. They wanted to know if we were still friends.'

'They give you a list of women's names?'

'Yeah.'

'You know them?'

'No.'

'They believe you?'

He gave an ironic laugh and then said, 'They asked me if I knew Gecko Samuels.'

'Did you?'

He didn't answer.

'They want a connection, Tony.'

'I know. They asked me what the word was.'

I paused.

'Have I been bad?' I said.

'Let me count the ways. You've been with me. That makes you bad in someone's eyes. You and him, remember. That makes you bad.'

It was always Warren Graham with him.

'Warren wasn't the only black guy.'

'Some people don't like that. Black guys, white girls.'

'People like you?'

He sucked his teeth and then said, 'No. It was anyone with you. That's how it is with me.'

I noted the present tense but didn't want to think about it or talk about it.

'You think that's what this is about? Black and white?'

'Who knows what's going on with these sick fucks? They just need an excuse to hate women. They start off saying they're going for toms because they deserve it, and then kill a supermarket checkout girl. Maybe it's the same with this geezer. He hates black men with white women, but at the end of the day he just hates women.'

'Tony, you've been a great help.'

I was about to go and then he said, 'I heard something about that list. Do you want to hear it?'

'Tell me.'

'It's been around a while.'

'How long?'

'Word is the Old Bill's had it for a year at least. The girl Jo got a tip-off from a copper – she used to knock about with him when she was up at court, as you do.'

'You know who?'

'No.'

'And they did nothing?'

'It was just a piece of paper with names on it. No dates, no threats, nothing. They ignored it. The copper told this Jo about it in passing, because it had bugged him. Something to do with the title this scum had given it.'

'And she recognised two names on it.'

'Must have.'

'She tell them?'

'That I don't know.'

'Thanks, Tony.'

He said nothing, and then, 'They giving you a minder?'

'No.'

'You want one?'

'No.'

'I'll get you a gun.'

Twenty minutes later, John came back without the dog. His cheeks were red from cold and exertion. He stamped his feet in the hall as he tried to explain.

'I didn't know her name,' he said.

'She didn't have one,' I said.

'We got to the park, I slipped the chain and she just took off.'

'No one took her?'

'No.'

'You didn't see anyone?'

'No.'

'In what direction?'

He hesitated.

'South?'

'She's gone home then,' I said. I told him about my

ex. Tony Levi, who lived in Bethnal Green, but I didn't say what he did or that he had just called.

'He didn't give her a name?'

'Girl.'

'She didn't answer to it.'

'Tony has an accent.'

He grinned, and I offered him a cigarette.

'Will he bring her back?'

'He'll probably shoot her,' I said.

He was shocked. He was probably thinking what kind of guy would shoot a dog for nothing, and whether it was really all over between Tony and me. I understood. It would worry most guys.

'Why?'

'He likes women to do what he says.'

His eyes searched mine for clues that I might be joking, but I gave him none.

'I'm sorry,' he said.

'It's not your fault. She was overexcited. Hadn't been out in a month.'

'How about you?' he said.

I lit my cigarette.

'Me neither.'

My hands gave it away. I tried to relax, but they wouldn't stop. I felt embarrassed when he took hold of them.

'I can get you some help,' he said.

'Drugs?'

'If you want, yes.'

'Nice.'

We hung around the place not speaking for a while until he said he had to go to work and I asked him to do me a favour. The colour went from his face.

'Can you do it?' I said.

'I don't want to.'

I stepped closer to him.

'Can you do it?'

'Yes, but the question is, should I?'

'You'll come back, won't you, anyway?'

It was one of those moments when you give in and win. His lips touched mine, and thirty seconds into our second kiss, my hand slipped inside his jacket and twisted his flesh between my nails.

'I don't want to force you,' I whispered.

'Please do,' he replied.

CHAPTER FIFTEEN

# YOU GET WHAT YOU NEED

It was strange being absolutely alone. When the last faint buzzing of the motorbike faded away into the city, I lay on my bed and wondered where the dog had gone; if she had gone to Tony or just left me for freedom, any kind of freedom. I'd thought of her as an inconvenience, but now I missed her. I talked to her more than I had realised and I'd got used to her motherly concern. She would have come in and checked me out for signs of life after all the moans of love that sounded like death. She wasn't there, though, and I had no one to tell that the Stones were right about not always getting what you want but just, sometimes, getting what you need.

I felt a pang of guilt. I had been very cruel to him, but I felt better for it. He'd asked for it, really asked for it, and for a moment I wondered how a man like him could be made that way, inside his head. You'd have thought that someone who looked like he did would never have had to look to smoke and mirrors to turn him on. He said it was hard finding someone he could be honest with and he was tired of always doing the opposite of what he really wanted in the hope that that might become what he really wanted. It never did.

'Take me over,' he said. 'Just take me over.'

I asked him when he'd got the rope burns and he said

they were a month old. He couldn't really afford it, but he'd got so desperate he'd paid for them. The marks around the nipples were burns too, he said, from hot wax, which he knew was a cliché but I had to understand that with what he paid, he was at the duff end of the market. He made me laugh.

'You could have anyone you wanted,' I said.

'But not anything.'

'Why me?'

'You had looks to kill,' he said, and I whispered into his hair.

'Aren't you afraid?'

He said that he was, maybe, but that was what made it so good. I was afraid for him then, because he was saying he wanted to die, and even if it was just a game, I *was* that victim who thought that everyone was trying to kill her. I wasn't sure any more how far I would go.

Truth was, I didn't know what to do at first, and he said I could just tie him up to start with. I didn't know what to do after that either, so I just walked out, left him there naked, like a crucifixion, while I struck matches for cigarettes. When I came back, I was naked and he was trembling, and I remembered something someone had done to me once, so when I climbed on to him I put my hands around his neck and squeezed. It was me who cried when we came.

His hands came free pretty easily and held me close, which made me wonder how much power I'd actually had. We lay there for a long while, my palms flat on his warm chest and his arms about me. He told me he could love me, really love me, and I said I didn't know. We made love again, and this time it was all about tenderness and touch. He seemed to fill me up with it.

And I had no one to tell. I showered, dressed and

looked out at the garden that was still deep-frozen despite the sun, which was as pink as a Florida grapefruit. Maybe I could get a little boat, I thought, and float away when I felt like it, to the north and the west. I put my foot outside the door and placed it on the cold step. It wasn't so bad. I pushed the door open and walked out into crisp air that smelled of sulphur. I stood right in the middle of the lawn, swaying like a building in high wind, making slight adjustments with my feet to keep from falling outside my centre of gravity. The world began to spin, and when I turned back towards the house, it seemed to be swinging in the air a mile away. The water was closer but the expanse of the canal took the far shore to a distant horizon. The black shadow of a bird flew over me and struck my face like an axe. I winced, throwing my arms up to protect myself, and lost my balance. My body felt as if it was being shaken to pieces and I realised that I had made a mistake. What had I been thinking of? I saw a small black crack in the bricks of the house and found the strength to run for it. It had looked so narrow from where I had stood that I was surprised that I didn't have to squeeze in through the doorway. The door had been wide open. I leaned over the sink, nauseated, telling myself that if Dr John was my medicine, I would need a hell of a lot more of it to cure this.

I called Tony back and he said the dog had turned up. She must have run all the way.

'Just don't shoot her,' I said, and he said it wasn't on his mind.

'What happened?' he said.

'She got lost in the park.'

'Lost? I don't think so.'

'Well, she did, all right?'

There was silence.

'A friend of mine was walking her. She did a runner,' I said.

'She doesn't run for nothing.'

'So what are you saying?'

'I'm saying she doesn't run for nothing. Not that dog. Who is this guy?'

I told him not to worry about it and he said to expect her back in a couple of hours. He'd send his man and the dog would be wearing a muzzle and a coat, on account of the cold weather.

'You get me?' he said.

I said I thought I did, but at the back of my mind he'd sown a little seed of doubt that I crushed because I didn't want to blame John, for anything.

I had two stories churning in my head. One, the police had had the *Double Devils* list for a year. Two, the women. I needed to talk to the women on the list if I was going to make the story fly. They had been victims just like me and I needed to know what they could remember. I wondered if they were thinking about me, what I was like and what I had done. They'd speak to me. I knew that. They'd speak to me and maybe to no one else. I suddenly felt happy and I knew why. The thrill hadn't gone. It shot through me like a rush of coke. Me *and* them. An exclusive. How good was that?

I had tried to find them myself. They were common names, but Catriona Ross and Joan Shepherd just didn't come up on my search in London, though at least thirty came up elsewhere. John could get me those addresses. I'd asked him to do it for me, and although he didn't like it, he had said he'd see what he could do. I paged him and waited. He came back to me in about ten minutes. The sound of his voice made me hold the phone close as if somehow we could slip down the wires and meet halfway.

'Can you get me their addresses?' I said.

'I don't know.'

'You said you'd see what you could do. They won't know.'

'They have a right to privacy. You have a right to privacy.'

'That's rich.'

'How would you like me to go through your notes?'

'You already have, haven't you?'

'If you want me to help you, I have to.'

'Come on, John.'

'It's difficult. Since the police came down here and looked through the system, everyone's been on their toes and people are looking at me like I have fungus on my face. Today's story in the papers hasn't helped. It said four women on the list had been treated here.'

'I want to talk to them. I need to. You said you could.'

He said nothing, and then, 'One, I'll get you one.'

'Get the policewoman. She would be best,' I said, and he put the phone down without saying goodbye. One hour later I got an email containing Catriona Ross's telephone number.

I didn't usually get a prick of conscience before I phoned a punter, but this time it was different. I knew she would want to speak to me and I knew on what level, but how would I tell her that I was working? Could I tell her that? I lit a cigarette, and it occurred to me that this was how I'd started my big love affair with Nicotine, the God of Restless Hands.

I'd lit a cigarette for the first time in a newspaper office to steady my nerves. I'd seen the sales boys do it before they cold-called. No one smoked like they did, I'd seen them forget they had one burning in the tray and light up a fresh one, they'd been so racked.

'Catriona?'

'Yes.'

'It's Georgina Powers.'

She didn't say anything at first, and I was about to repeat her name when she said, 'How did you find me?'

'I'm a journalist.'

'I know,' she said.

'And you're a policewoman.'

'We have ways and means, do we not?'

'That's right. You have contacts. I have contacts. Have you checked out the others?'

'Yes.'

'Are we all different?'

'Yes.'

'Different ages?'

'Yes.'

'Different backgrounds?'

'Yes.'

'Married, single, divorced, what?'

'Mixed. Claudia Bonetti is fourteen years old.'

The last piece of information jolted me.

'*She* got a postcard?'

'Yes. I know yours was a hit-and-run.'

'I know yours was a date rape.'

She breathed out.

'You've been busy.'

I took a tug on the cigarette.

'You used to work at Brick Lane nick.'

'Loved it, but I couldn't do it any more.'

'Why?'

'I lost confidence, d'you get me?'

I got her all right. She didn't wait for my reply. She wanted to talk.

'I used to be sharp, used to have it, but after what happened, it all went. I just couldn't get it together. I felt such a fucking fool. Date rape. It just doesn't cover it, you know? It makes it sound like I was a fucking fool. Like I couldn't keep my legs together after a couple of drinks.'

She paused.

'He used things on me. I can't have children now. I'm lucky to be walking.'

'What do you remember?'

'I remember being in the pub and I remember a blond man at the bar. Not natural blond, that bleached look with dark roots. Big fella. I remember him. It was embarrassing, because when I got to A and E, my boyfriend was helping look after me and . . .'

'John Walker?'

'You know him?'

'He looked after me too.'

'Poor old Johnnie. I screamed so much when I saw him that they took him away. I don't know why, I think it was his hair, and I was so out of it I didn't know who was who or what was what. I was so sick and I had bad chest pains with it. It was GBH. Have you heard of it? It's a club drug.'

'Yes,' I said. My mind was looping the loop, and inside I had started to ache. He hadn't been straight with me. Not at the start and not now. He didn't tell me the policewoman he'd treated was his girlfriend. He could have told me.

'Hello?' she said.

I said I was sorry, and then I told her about me.
'Are you getting help?' she said.
'Of a sort,' I replied, and then I said, 'What do you think of Spencer?'
'Bit of a ladies' man, I heard.'
The sly dog.
'Is he a good copper?'
'Top man.'
I asked if he'd spoken to her about raising her profile.
'He spoke to me today.'
'What did you say?'
'I said no.'
'He asked me too.'
'Are you going to?'
I sucked on the cigarette and my heart started to beat really fast, because I had to say this just right.
'I thought we could do this together, you know?'
She didn't answer, and then she said, 'They've seen what a bomb can do, what more do they want?'
'Yeah, but what more do *we* want, Catriona?'
I waited, and then she said, 'Where do you live?' and I told her, and straight after I called Diane Shine to do a deal.
'They'll want photos,' she said.

I didn't have a dog to bark and let me know that someone was about, and even though I knew that she was coming, I still jumped when the doorbell rang. I had gone through a packet of cigarettes and walked back and forward to the telephone, which just kept ringing every time I wanted to pick it up and call John and ask him why he hadn't told me about her. Meanwhile, my answerphone was filling up with offers to tell my story.

She was about five six, a little shorter than me and a little wider, but a real redhead, a true Highland copper, not like the expensive designer red of Cherry Shankar or the cheap gothic bleed that I was growing out. She wore a big, shapeless anorak over a sloppy sweater and thick black leggings that were tucked into short black boots. She was already smoking a cigarette when I opened the door.

She glanced around the place like a copper would, and I showed her into the front room.

'Where's your dog?' she queried.

'It's gone.'

'Only I noticed the bowl in the kitchen.'

Which means you don't miss a trick, I thought.

She had a face that could be described as sensual if it wasn't for the tough-guy outlook. Her jaw was square, her mouth wide, and her lips had a natural high colour. They were pursed most of the time. She had a fringe that kept getting in her greenish eyes and she squinted through it as if she didn't want you to see their colour, the whites, nothing.

She told me her story. She said she worked as a nursery assistant in a primary school, which was OK because she liked the kids, but she'd always wanted to be a police officer. It wasn't that anyone in the family was. Her father was a lorry driver and her mother a nurse, and they came from Aberdeen.

It wasn't her first job either. She wasn't that great at school and she'd got a job as a barmaid and then as a typist.

'I thought I could be a teacher, but I wanted some action. I came down south, waited on tables, thought of joining the army, but in the end it was the police. I joined when I was twenty-three.'

She was twenty-eight now.

'I could calm down a pub quicker than any man, I can tell you,' she said. 'Which is saying something this close to the City. The boys with the money are arrogant, and they get violent. You've got to prove yourself. Still, all over now. He might as well have torn my uniform off me.'

'He didn't kill you.'

'No. He didn't do that.'

I offered her a coffee. She drank it black with lots of sugar.

'And it's nothing personal, is it?' I said.

She looked at me for a stunned moment and then she started to laugh. She had a dirty laugh. I could imagine her out with the lads.

'No, nothing personal. He's got it in for us all, hasn't he?' The joke went sour and I said, 'And what difference does that make, right?'

She put her hand to her lips suddenly, and I saw that her nails were chewed to the quick.

'What sort of piece were you thinking of doing?' she said.

I said I wanted to show the impact he'd had on her life, and mine. I wanted something that would work for us, make someone come forward with something. I asked if what she knew now had awakened any memories of the night she was attacked, something that could explain why we had been targeted.

'We always have to give up our lives, don't we? Us victims,' she said, and I said yes.

She thought about it. She'd dreamed about it, like I had. She'd tried to paint in the white space of her nightmares, hoping she might relive the moment that would unlock it and blow all the foul air away and leave a clear sky in her mind. I watched her blinking and tapping her fingers on her knee, transmitting her anxiety to me.

'I just don't remember. Like I said, I remember the pub. I was waiting on some friends to meet me there. We were going to go on to a club up West. I remember talking to this big blond fellow. Then I remember being some place dark like a church, I just don't know where. I certainly don't know how I got there. It was like a horror movie. I woke up near the bins by a block of flats – these kids found me and then someone called an ambulance. The guy was never traced.'

'You think it was him?'

'I don't know. I don't remember enough.'

I told her I couldn't see who was driving the car that hit me either, that I kept thinking I was just about to remember but I never did. She nodded like she understood.

'I heard the police had the list for a long time,' I said.

She sat back from the edge of the seat and smoked the rest of her cigarette down to the filter before grinding it out in the ashtray.

'That's the way it goes. What can you do with a piece of paper that arrives with just a list of names on it? Could be anything. Still, it's evidence now. Forensics have got it.'

She stuck her hand in her pocket and pulled out her cigarettes. I offered one of mine but she waved me away, and took her own. She accepted a light.

I waited while she inhaled, settled, and then I said, 'What do you think we have in common, Catriona?'

She laughed again then, and I felt like a phoney because at the back of my mind I wanted to say, 'John Walker.'

'I dinna know you, do I?'

'Did you know Gecko Samuels?'

'No.'

'Ever been out with a black guy?'

'A few,' she said. 'Have you?'

I said I had.

'I got pregnant by one, a fireman,' she said. 'A one-night stand.'

She looked at me and I said nothing.

'Got rid of it, didn't I?'

She looked at me again and took a nervy pull on the cigarette.

'I was twenty-three years old, just started on the job. I didn't want a kid. And I certainly didn't want a half-caste. That was then. That's how it was then. I didn't regret it, but God, how times have changed.'

She covered her face as it crumpled, and I waited a couple of moments to give her some time, some space. When she pulled them away, her face was clear and composed.

'Four of us have been treated by Dr John Walker,' I said.

She looked steadily at me.

'Do you think that's meaningful?'

'I don't know.'

She shook her head.

'He couldn't handle what happened to me,' she said, and looked away.

John Walker, she explained, had treated her although he shouldn't have done. It couldn't be helped. It was busy, and events took over. She said he had dealt with it afterwards by remaining detached, but it had felt like indifference. She hadn't wanted that.

'I think he felt guilty,' she said.

'Why?'

She shrugged.

'He was no fucking use, was he?'

We were silent for a while, and then I said, 'Cherry Shankar had an abortion.'

Her face sharpened with interest.

'Have you?'

'No.'

'Well then,' she said, disappointed. 'Then it's something else. It has to be something else.'

'It could be random.'

She shook her head.

'This man's got religion. I know it,' she said, and she began counting off the facts on her fingers like she was telling a former colleague.

'I was assaulted on the first of December last year. Joan Shepherd was attacked on Christmas Eve last year. You were attacked when? A month ago. November. I think that reporter got it right. I think the dates have meaning for him.'

'November? He missed Hallow'en,' I said, trying to sound even-handed though I would have loved to blow Mary's story out of the water.

'November is the last month of the church year. He has a plan. He started with me in December. December is the beginning of the church year. He started with assaults and escalated to killing exactly one year later.'

'Advent is the beginning.'

'December the first is St Andrew's Day. It commemorates the first and second comings of Christ, the first coming to redeem, the second to judge.'

'You mean, last year he was only joking, this year he's serious?' I said. 'He tried to kill me.'

'Are you sure? Why use a car when you can make a bomb?'

'You think he just wanted to damage me a little?'

'Yes. Like he just wanted to damage me, a little. With a little punishment, we might be redeemed. He was being magnanimous. He was playing fucking God.'

We sat together in silence and I had no doubt we were both contemplating how successful he had been.

'Do you believe in God?' I said.

She brought the cigarette up to her lips and sucked hard. Her words came out with a cloud of smoke that drifted across the room in the weak lamplight, drawing out the motes of dust that hung in a sphere of brightness above our heads.

'Of course. What would be the point if there wasn't a God?'

'The point of what?'

'Existing.'

The sound of rush-hour traffic ate into the silence of the room. Someone said once that each age, each society, creates its own God and puts its own mask on His immutable, ever-present, ageless face. I wondered then what mask Catriona Ross had placed on her God that would make all this suffering worthwhile. I wanted to ask her if the mask of her God shone with love and forgiveness but then she'd ask me what I believed. I didn't want to tell her that I couldn't even see a mask, only the dark and terrifying void behind it.

'Would you mind having your photograph taken?' I asked.

'I will if you will,' she said, and I knew she had the measure of me, because there was no way I was having my picture taken for a newspaper. I didn't want my tormentor to see me, how I was. It'd make the bastard think he was winning.

'How about some old ones? You in uniform. The publicity shot of me for Technology Online,' I suggested, and she said that she could live with that.

CHAPTER SIXTEEN

# LOVE IS ALL AROUND

I told him not to come. I told him he had lied to me. He said he hadn't lied, but I wouldn't listen. He said I should try and understand, and I said that I did. I did understand.

It was only when I had put the telephone down that I had my doubts as to who was in the right and who was in the wrong. I reminded myself that he hadn't had a relationship with her *after* she had become his patient, but before. There was nothing wrong with that. The question I couldn't answer was why I didn't tell Catriona Ross that I was sleeping with her ex.

I felt deflated and empty even though I had written two stories and filed them. I had done something to help myself at last and I should have felt better because someone somewhere might read Catriona's story tomorrow and be moved enough to give up the Advent Bomber. We would be safe at last *and* I was going to get paid. I should have been ecstatic, or at the very minimum happier, but the truth was, I was miserable. My heart felt as if it had been cut to ribbons. It was Cherry who dragged me out of my deep pit.

'You liar,' she said.

Her voice pressed against my ear like a gun to my head. I protested, but the chamber clicked.

'You fucking liar.'

She didn't give me a chance to speak. She was not listening. She told me that she knew all about me, that she had been straight with me but that I was too much of a coward to be straight with her.

'You're no better than me, you know?'

'What's this about?'

'Five years ago you went into the London for an abortion,' she said.

I asked her where she had got her information, and she told me that if I thought she was leaving something as important as this to the police I was mistaken. She had Kendall Associates on the case.

'I know someone who works for them,' I said, thinking of Pal Kuthy for the first time in a while.

'Don't change the subject. I got them to investigate every single name on the Double Devils list. Every single one.'

'Including the fourteen-year-old?'

'Including the fourteen-year-old.'

'Dinika Patel?'

'Why not her?'

'What did they find out?'

'That you're a fucking liar. We do have something in common. You just didn't have the guts to admit it, not even to me.'

She kept on like that until she realised that I wasn't answering. I'd stopped bothering to interrupt. Her voice had become so much white noise in my head. I tried to think how Cherry and I could both be right.

'George? Are you fucking there?' she said.

I didn't answer. I put down the phone and poured myself a large Scotch.

I'd been in hospital a few times in my life.

I'd had my tonsils out.

I'd fallen out of a tree when I was a kid and broken my collarbone.

I'd been beaten up more than a few times and had my throat cut.

I'd had two miscarriages.

I'd wanted one abortion.

I couldn't argue with that. I'd made up my mind and been admitted, but I couldn't go through with it. I had wanted the baby.

I'd gone to the ward with my overnight bag but I'd carried on walking to the second set of lifts on the far side. I should have stayed. I had nothing going for me. I wasn't with the father and I was living on the fifth floor of a hard-to-let in Bow. I was just getting back to work after being a kept woman for a while. I wanted to be independent. I didn't want responsibilities. I could barely look after myself. I made up my mind that there was no place in my life for a baby. I had nothing to offer it, not even a father. Its timing was bad. I'd told myself all this and I still walked through the women's ward to the second set of lifts and pressed Down. What the hell, I thought. I'm going to grow that baby. We can make it.

Thing was, we didn't. I lost it within two days. Esther, my neighbour, helped me, like she had helped me the second time, got me through. It was OK. It wasn't as if I was devastated. I was sad, but I wasn't devastated, because I knew that that little clump of cells inside me had known all by itself that we weren't meant to be. Like I said, many are called and few are chosen, and that didn't just mean the child, it meant the mother too. As time passed, I realised I'd had a lucky break, but it didn't stop me wondering how things might have been.

Esther said that it happened all the time and that I wasn't to be downhearted, because there is hope in a tree, if it be cut down, that it will sprout again and that the tender branch thereof will not cease. Esther was a retired nurse who sang in a gospel choir and was given to quoting from the scriptures. She was the most Christian person I had ever met, but she was practical about life and left judgement to God.

Kendall had got its hands on my hospital records, that much was clear, but the records were wrong. I sipped the whisky and lit a cigarette. Thing was, if Kendall could find out, then maybe anyone could if they wanted to badly enough, and, right or wrong, we were all Double Devils in someone's book.

I was beginning to fill in the white space now. The man who had run me down believed in God, a wrathful and bloodthirsty Old Testament God. He believed in the sanctity of life before birth, and justice was his, but he had murdered a pregnant woman. I wondered how he felt about that. Probably nothing at all, because he had gone ahead and murdered again. This God's servant used a knife, and drugs, and bottles and sticks, and the brute force of automobiles to maim his enemies. He used nail bombs to murder and dismember the women who in his eyes had sinned. He showed no mercy for their fellow travellers. He had a computer and a modem or access to both. He had visited the Ted Bundy home page and copied his writing so he could send postcards to his victims and be taken very seriously. He had access to the hospital administration system and the clinical notes of thirteen women. I picked up the phone and called Cherry. This time I told her to shut up and listen.

'I didn't have the abortion. I was admitted but I changed my mind. I went to the ward and I walked out. Maybe the system didn't record that. It happens.'

There was no reply.

'Cherry?'

'You wanted to and you didn't tell me you wanted to.'

'That makes a difference?'

'Of course it does.'

I said that I was sorry if it would have made a difference, but I didn't know why she felt so guilty in the first place, and then she said that she was sorry and we both got a little emotional. Somewhere, though, at the back of my mind, I was working. Kendall's had hit on the reason why we were all on that hit list and I was going to have to get to the truth and make it a story, a story that really mattered this time.

'I'm scared, you know?' she said.

'How did they do it?' I asked.

She told me how all the hospital records were electronic now and every drug, disease and procedure had a code. Every hospital treatment booked in for and carried out was linked to a patient so that the administrators could deal with the contracts and everyone could get paid.

'It's easy. If I want to know how many abortions are carried out in a hospital and I know the code for terminations, I can go through the records and pick them all out. All those abortions are linked to a patient, so I can pick *them* out. Everyone has a number,' she said.

'They screwed up my record,' I said.

'You're the exception that proves the rule.'

'The hospital would have recorded that I had left.'

'Kendall's didn't just use the hospital system for this. It used the national system, the Strategic Number Tracing System. That's the one that matters.'

'That's the one that screwed up, Cherry.'

Just to make life a little easier, she told me to switch on the TV. I put the whisky down.

'That's an NFAB clinic on fire. It went up earlier today,' she said. 'There was a butyric acid attack on it two weeks ago. It's war. This is what we're up against.'

Smoke was pouring from the windows of a large, four-storey building in a suburb of Glasgow. A journalist in a thick coat was interviewing a harassed middle-aged woman outside. She was the clinic manager.

Cherry and I hung on the phone and together watched the firemen hose down the blaze. A man wearing round wire-rimmed spectacles and a dark Paul Smith suit stood in front of the smouldering building and denied any knowledge of the attack, but he said that if it proved one thing, it proved that the people of Scotland did not want death factories in their midst.

The journalist was on the ball. He asked Mr Christian Love if he had authorised the distribution of the names and addresses of staff appointed to the new clinics to their neighbours and their children's schools. Mr Christian Love said he was not in a position to authorise anything. The journalist asked him about the acid attack, and Mr Christian Love said that he did not believe in violence. He believed in direct action and he believed he had a Christian duty to persuade others that God accords equal status to life before and after birth.

It was all about love, he said. True love. Pure love. Christian love.

'Love gives us the courage to confront. If we cannot challenge one another's wrong-doing, then we do not love one another enough,' he said, and as the journalist tried to question him again on the matter of the fire and whether or not he encouraged this sort of action, Mr Christian Love held up a picture of a foetus and beseeched the world to feel its pain.

'That's lovable Craig Gibson, he runs the Christian Love organisation in the UK,' Cherry said.

'It's always a bloke. Have you noticed?'

'A white bloke, and for every ten of him, there's one who thinks he hasn't gone far enough when it comes to loving us all.'

I heard her pour a drink. It was like we were sitting in a virtual bar, only I imagined she was in the bit that said 'Gentlemen Should Wear Ties' and I was in the one that had a one-armed bandit and a pool table.

'Looks like the lassies are going to have to come south like they've always done,' I said. I was wondering about the fire and the butyric acid attack. GHB, gamma-hydroxybutyrate, was made from butyric acid.

'I'm going to get him, you know?' she said.

'How?'

'Do you think he's been to the Gecko site? You think he's a regular visitor?'

'For sure.'

'Think cookies,' she said.

And, of course, she didn't mean American-style biscuits. She meant programs that stored site visitors' personal details. If our man had visited Gecko's site, he'd have left a footprint; that is, unless he was particular enough about his privacy to turn the cookies off.

'When's the funeral?' I said.

'I don't know. Are you going to come?'

I said for sure I would and took a deep breath. It had to be done.

'This is news, Cherry,' I said.

'No way.'

'You and me.'

'If you and me, then the others.'

'Dinika Patel is dead. Catriona Ross would do it, I'm sure. We can go public because we already are public. We can say what connects us and that he made a mistake with me. If he doesn't feel guilty, then someone close to him, who knows, might.'

'So you look like a fucking martyr and we look like we deserved it.'

'Dinika Patel's the martyr. So's Jo Casey. So is Gecko and so is Catriona Ross, who can't have kids any more.'

'You won't get Dinika Patel's family to agree. Never. Ever.'

'Think about it,' I said, but I got no reply, just the dull drone of a line made suddenly available for another call.

I was about to pick it up and call her when the doorbell rang and my whole body jerked. Goose pimples prickled up my arms but I didn't move. The bell rang again. My heart ramped up its beats per minute and I began to sweat and shiver. I wiped the bubbles of perspiration from under my nose and took a slug of the Scotch.

Baz Williams' bulky frame filled the doorway. He wore a large anorak the cuffs of which almost covered the stubby gold-ringed fingers of each hand, a round woollen hat with a big yellow Nike tick on the front, and £100 trainers to match. He was holding the dog on a short but substantial chain. Her face was muzzled and she was wearing a designer-brand quilted coat that matched his. It fitted snugly around her back and under her belly.

'Georgina?'

'Baz.'

'All right?'

'Good, yeah. Yourself?'

'Good. Yeah. Tony sent me.'

'Yeah.'

'Here she is then.'

'Thanks.'

'Tony says she needs more exercise.'

'Yeah?'

'You should take her out more. Put a coat on her, in this weather.'

'Right.'

I took the lead and Baz pointed his chubby finger at me like a gun.

'Her coat, right. Tony wants her looked after.'

I took the dog and shut the door.

She was pleased to see me. I think she would have licked me if her mouth had not been wrapped in steel. I took off the guard and patted her head, and then gave her an awkward hug as she pushed into me affectionately, banging her tail around. My arm slipped under her, and unless I had the wrong dog, the long, hard object tucked underneath was a gun.

I'd almost finished a half-bottle of Scotch as I sat on the sofa holding the 9mm Browning semi-automatic.

I'd held a gun before, but I'd never used one. It occurred to me that the Advent Bomber hadn't either. With a gun, you point it at someone and shoot. That's it. Do it right and they're gone. Where was the fun in that? It was too quick, and too clean in comparison to an exploding parcel of nails or a broken beer bottle or a blade.

I thought about the phone call from the phoney doctor. Had to be him. The man that filled the white space in my mind was vindictive. He was arrogant and he was confident, and why wouldn't he be? He believed he had God on his side.

'You bastard. I see you, I kill you,' I said. The phone was ringing and I let it. It stopped and rang again and I got up to answer it.

'It's me.'

'Tony?'

'The brown dog's nine years old. Needs looking after. Don't be afraid to exercise it if you have to.'

'Tony,' I said.

The time had come and I knew it. It was like I was beginning to slide. I'd hit the sludge on the slippery slope and I was on my way down. I couldn't stop myself.

'Tony, I need to tell you something. You might hear something. I want you to hear it from me.'

'You've had a drink. Save it.'

'Tony, I can't.'

'You better tell me then.'

I told him how Cherry had got a private detective to find out what we all had in common, and he'd discovered that we'd all been admitted to the London for the termination of a pregnancy. Even the fourteen-year-old, I said, and the Asian girl who worked from home. I thought I heard him swallow. I lit a cigarette and he heard me flick the Zip.

'You should give up, girl,' he said. 'They're bad for your health, don't you know that?'

'You remember when we were together the first time?' I said, and in a soft, weary voice he said, 'Don't tell me, George. I don't need to know.'

'It was yours.'

He told me again that he didn't want to hear, but I said he had to because people could get the wrong idea poking around in people's private business, and some-one had got the wrong idea about me.

'Did I?' he said.

'What?'

'Did I ever have the wrong idea about you?'

I thought about Cherry and how she said that Gecko made her have an abortion. Tony would have made me keep it. But it wasn't up to Gecko and it wasn't up to Tony. It was up to Cherry and it was up to me because only we could know when the time was right to change our bodies and change our lives.

'I changed my mind. It's on record that I didn't, but I did. I walked out of the place and went home. I lost it two days later.'

'You wanted the kid?'

'I wanted it but it was my choice if I did or I didn't. I was right when I walked in and I was right when I walked out. '

'Why'd you want it?'

'I thought we could make it.'

'You and me?'

'The kid and me.'

There was a long, long silence and Tony spoke first. His voice hadn't changed. It was the low, matter-of-fact monotone that he delivered no matter what. The only time it was different was when he lost his temper, and then his delivery just seemed to lose the matter-of-fact part of it.

'I've got a kid. He's fifteen years old. I never told you. I'm sorry,' he said, and was gone.

I sat down and gazed at the screen. The gun lay on the mouse mat. My head was spinning. I glanced at my watch. It was closing time. Outside there was life. People would be wearing funny Santa hats, hailing cabs, hurrying for trains and running for buses. I missed real life. I missed real things. I hated the man who had brought me to this. I had done nothing. I hadn't broken the code he lived by, and even if I had it would have been none of his damn business. I picked up the gun and I thought of Tony. This was how he sorted things if he had to. It was his way, get someone else to do it, as a rule. My way was different.

CHAPTER SEVENTEEN

# A MILLION DEATHS IS A STATISTIC

It was late Saturday morning and the pain behind my eyes was intense as I spoke to Catriona Ross. I'd meant to ring her first thing, but the booze had revived me to a false dawn at about three a.m. and I'd drifted back into unconsciousness until late morning with the Browning tucked under my pillow like a book. I told her what Kendall Associates had done and what they had found out, and when I'd finished all she could say was, 'I see.'

I kept silent, and then she said, 'Why did you lie?'

'I didn't,' I said.

'I had Spencer on the phone first thing.'

'About the piece?'

'Yes, but he really called to tell me what you just told me. He didn't mention this Kendall bunch at all. He just told me what we all had in common.'

I sat back in my chair and stared at the wall. I hadn't told my friends or my family about what had happened to me. I hadn't even told the father. Only Esther knew, and the God she prayed to for me.

'They were checking out John Walker. They must have spotted another connection apart from him,' I said.

'It's the only connection between us.'

My heart jumped at the irony but I said nothing.

'How confident are they?' I said.

'Spencer's pretty confident.'

'I didn't go through with it. I discharged myself.'

I heard her suck on a cigarette. I wondered how she managed her habit all day at the school, or whether she saved up her craving so that she could chain-smoke later. She smoked more than I did, and I wondered if she drank more and if she ever went out to do it any more.

I told her that a computerised system could be audited and the when and where of a request for the details of thirteen women would be tracked down.

'The "who" is the big, big problem,' I said.

I asked her straight out.

'Will you go public again?'

She laughed, but not through any sense of fun.

'Good story for you?'

'Of course it is.'

She was walking about with her phone and I could hear the noise of people walking above. She lived in a flat like I did, alone.

'Spencer asked the same thing,' she said. 'You'll be getting a call no doubt. He wants all of us to do it but he wants our permission. He doesn't need it. He'll do it without if he has to.'

I began to rock in my chair. I hadn't got much time. Spencer would be going for an official announcement any time soon. He'd tell everyone what the connection between us all was. We'd be stripped naked for public consumption. He wanted to control the situation but so did I. I heard her turning pages. She must have been looking at the newspaper, at herself in her uniform and me in the publicity shot they'd got from Technology Online. She looked fresh, smart and happy under her hat, and I looked Generation Xed with my hair a peroxide crop. Those were the days.

'There's you, me, Cherry Shankar and Dinika Patel. He doesn't have to identify everyone else. We've already been identified. What's the problem?' I said.

'You didn't have an abortion.'

Here we go again, I thought.

'I was going to,' I said. 'I changed my mind.'

She said that people didn't like to talk about abortion, they didn't like to think about it. Even those who thought it was the woman's choice believed it was a necessary evil.

'I work in a nursery,' she said. 'I don't want my colleagues, the mums, the kids, most of all the kids, to know I've had an abortion. What if Dinika Patel's family didn't know?'

I hesitated.

'There you go,' she said.

Dinika Patel's parents had been on TV. Her father made his pleas for information in broken English and her mother never spoke at all. She stared around at the cameras and microphones, her eyes wide and uncomprehending. I could just see them sitting on a couch in their front room having it explained to them by Spencer, with a translator standing by and a policewoman like Catriona Ross on hand to put an arm around the mother while the father sat there, taking it in, wondering if he really knew the girl who had spent twelve hours a day in a corner of the dining room sewing clothes on piece work.

'Well?' she said.

'Dinika Patel is dead. Her parents would have wanted her alive. They wouldn't have wanted someone to kill her for having an abortion.'

'They might have done it themselves if they had found out she was pregnant.'

It was complicated but I had already made up my mind. I had the edge. I had the story and I wanted to sell it. I knew what I wanted to say, and when it came right down to it, our feelings didn't matter as much as those of the man who had done all this and those of the people who might know him. He'd made a mistake with me. He had to know that, and if he had friends, they had to know that too. Someone, if not him, would lose their nerve when they saw that they were as fallible and bloody human as the rest of us.

Spencer was thinking the same way, I was sure of it, but he was under pressure. He had to make sure all the risks he took came off. I felt excited and anxious at one and the same time. I needed to get off the phone and talk to him, make him an offer. I wanted him to deal with me and not Mary Stow.

'Think about it,' I said.

'What's stopping you? You don't need our permission. You don't need our approval. Just do it,' she replied.

I knew Diane wasn't going to be at work, but I had her home number and her mobile. I glanced at my watch. It was eleven-thirty a.m. and she would either be at the gym or at home. I phoned her home number and got the machine, so I called the mobile.

'Yes?'

She was out of breath. I heard a man swearing in the background.

'Seventy-five per cent of people will stop having sex to answer the phone,' I said.

'This better be *fucking* good, George.'

'Better than what you got now, girl.'

'Go.'

'The Advent Bomber.'

'You got me.'

'I know why he picked us,' I said, and I heard her say, 'Get off,' but not to me.

'Give.'

'We were all admitted to the London to have a termination. Every one of us. We're on his Christmas list. No, we *are* his Christmas list.'

'Jesus.'

Whoever it was who was trying to take her mind off the call was told to stop, and I heard a creak and a mutter.

'How'd you find out?' she said.

I told her how Kendall's had gone three times to the hospital and had found out that what John Walker had told me was true. Password security was relaxed. People left their machines logged on and their passwords taped to the underside of the ward PC's keyboards. The Kendall's detective was sympathetic. A&E was like a transit zone in a small war, he had reported, but medicine was a co-operative business and people just didn't have time not to trust each other.

He had wandered into the hospital and noted that every ward had a PC that acted both as a terminal to a central database and as a local machine so that nurses and doctors could create and print documents from it and email their colleagues and friends. The hospital had 2000 of these machines linked to an intranet – an internal network – that was in turn linked to thirteen other hospital sites across east London.

'That means he could have got access at any one of these terminals, at any one of those sites.'

'Wait. It gets better.'

I explained that Kendall's had discovered that the hospital also shared its internal network with its medical school, which in turn plugged into the Joint Academic Network, a creaky old network that linked every university in the land. The hospital internal network was also linked to another nationwide network, NHSnet, the National Health Service's own private internet. This, in turn, linked to yet another nationwide network, the family doctors' Healthnet network. Ultimately, NHSnet connected to the Department of Health, into whose databases it channelled all the statistics on everything that had ever happened to anyone under the entire National Health Service so that the government would know how sick we had all been.

This infrastructure was going to make the holy grail of the government's computerisation program, the Electronic Patient Record System, work. It would mean that if I had been involved in a hit-and-run anywhere in the country, the hospital doctors could have pulled up my medical notes and found out everything they needed to know from my blood type to my drug allergies, if I had any. It also meant that the Advent Bomber didn't have to access an insecure PC in the London to get to our notes. He just needed access to any insecure terminal, anywhere in the country. In theory. Kendall's man had said that, *in theory*, the London's hospital security was good. Not just anybody could walk up to a terminal and access the system. They had to have a password. GPs logging in from outside the hospital, for example, had to have a smart card, and their passwords and user names were changed every ninety days. Even when they got in, they couldn't roam around the hospital system at will. The hospital's core administrative computers were protected from outsiders by a demilitarised zone of special security hardware and software.

Unfortunately, the Kendall man said, the problem arose not from people coming in from outside the computer network, but from within. Being a hospital, security was relaxed at best because staff had more important things on their minds, like saving people's lives. Staff usually logged off the ward computers when they'd finished using them. But they were often distracted by an emergency or a colleague needing information. They tended to forget that they were logged on and would walk away from the machine. Someone else could then step up to the computer and assume their privileges. If that someone tried to access certain patients', or departments', records that the legitimate user had no permission to see, then the system would warn them. There was no ear-piercing alarm or anything like that, just a few lines of admonition onscreen. The software wouldn't even lock that person out. It simply warned that the computer would audit any changes made to the records and that the user would be identified and held accountable. As long as no changes were made, the trespasser just received a warning. He or she could browse to their heart's content. In other words, there was no harm in looking.

'So what happened?' Diane asked when I had finished.

'Kendall's guy walked up to a ward computer that had been left logged on and asked the system to download a list for him. While he waited, he slipped a disk into the "A" drive. When the list arrived, he saved it to disk and, just to prove a point, sent it as an email attachment to Cherry Shankar. It took less than ten minutes,' I said.

'You're kidding me.'

'That's just someone, anyone, walking by with the bottle to do it. It doesn't have to be a member of staff. Just someone who notices a doctor or a nurse at a terminal walk away without logging off. And the terminals are standard PCs with drives, just like I've got. Anyone familiar with a PC could cope.'

'I want that. I want that. People walking by. Who else could do it? How many? Who's got *legitimate* access?'

'The police investigating a serious offence, naturally; the people who work there, of course, the doctors, the nurses, the clerks. The rest of the time it's available for use by the extended NHS community.'

'What does that mean?'

'Your chiropodist.'

'You're exaggerating.'

'No. People get referred to them, don't they? How about pharmacists, counsellors, dentists, social workers? You never know, your aromatherapist might have an "in".'

And then I remembered Richard's letter from the National Road Traffic Accident Claims Centre, but I didn't have time to tell her. They were complete outsiders, but the hospital had thought nothing of sending the details of Richard's accident to them without even asking him.

She told me to stop and think. We had to get a grip on what we were going for. What I had described was a system that was wide open to anyone wanting personal information. Everyone knew that for a few hundred quid slapped into a willing palm you could get the details of someone's bank account or find out if a soap star had had breast surgery, if it wasn't obvious enough. She'd done it herself, she said.

'The breast surgery?'

'The bribe.'

'This is different,' I said.

'Yes, this is different. This is different. This is telling the general public that a psychopath had access to their local hospital. He knows where they live and where they used to live. He knows their secrets and their children's secrets. He knows if they are white or black, if they are immigrants, if they are drunks or junkies or blind or sterile or impotent or dying. And it's worse than that, because if he had access to the local hospital network, he could have had access to every damn network in the National Health Service. I need statistics. Horrible statistics. How many women are at risk? Is everyone at risk?'

She sounded excited rather than shocked. I wasn't about to judge her. I knew this was probably sounding as good for her as the promise of a line, and she liked that, a lot.

'I don't know. Is anyone listening to this, Diane?'

'He's in the bathroom,' she said.

'The bomber thinks I had an abortion, but I didn't.'

'How come?'

'I was admitted. I went to the ward and walked out.'

Diane stopped the quickfire interrogation and started to think. I could hear her clicking her teeth and flicking her nails. Her nails were always long and manicured. She didn't smoke and she worked out, did all that stuff with steps to keep her black body fit and her mind sharp. When we worked together on Technology Online, Mary Stow had told her that as women we had to be twice as good as men in our business, and she had told Mary that as a black woman she had to be ten times as good as *she* was, and she was. That's why she took Charlie once in a while, because if you're ten times as good, it makes you feel twenty.

'This man could have accessed the hospital database via a terminal.'

'Right.'

'Once you are admitted to a ward you are a hospital statistic. As far as the hospital is concerned, you had that abortion and you were discharged. Then where does that information go?'

'To the Department of Health. All the stats go there.'

'Anywhere else?'

'I don't know, but I presume all this data is anonymous. Statisticians work with numbers and events, they don't need to know any personal details.'

'OK, but *potentially* the Advent Bomber had access to millions of records, millions of women.'

'Yes.'

If he'd accessed the London's database, he'd have seen that you didn't have that abortion. At some point, maybe not right away, but at some point they would have recorded that you had discharged yourself and that the operation did not go ahead. It would be on your records. So he *couldn't* have got his information from the local hospital's database. He must have got it from somewhere else. Maybe, once you're actually admitted to a ward, the computer sends the information to the central networks and then the information can't be changed. You have to check that out. It doesn't make sense otherwise. You have to find out why he didn't see that you had walked out of there. There must be a point in the software beyond which you walked and became a statistic.'

I couldn't speak for the numbers that had begun to build in my mind. I should have seen it when Cherry said that Kendall's had used the Strategic Number Tracing System. They might have got in through a hospital terminal but they must have got access to a national centralised database. And why? I guessed that they had done it before. They knew it was the best 'people searcher' and privacy buster around. What Diane was saying was that the Advent Bomber had got access to it too.

'The big story is what? How many women have abortions each year, George? Eighty thousand, a million? And how long do they keep records – ten years, twenty?'

I waited while she sized it up and told me what she needed.

'No one else has got this, right? I have to check if we can reveal this personal stuff. I mean, there's a fourteen-year-old kid involved. If we can, we'll just do the four of you and the local angle first. Hospital security and all that shit. Make a point of the mistake he made in your case. You know what I want but you find out the other stuff. Let's get paid,' she said, and then she paused.

'You OK?' she said.

I said I was.

'This is bad. Just about everyone I know has had an abortion,' she said.

'How about you?'

'No, I've never been caught like that. I looked after three brothers and sisters, and who knows how many nieces, nephews and cousins. That was enough. I don't want my own kids and I don't want anyone else's.'

'You might,' I said.

'Don't bet on it.'

'You get back to what you were doing.'
'No kidding,' she said, and checked out.

It was Saturday and I had to work. The sun was shining and the dog was in the garden, sniffing around her shrunken world like an old lag in an exercise yard.

When Richard called I told him I was busy. He told me Max wanted me to stop working for newswires because all he could see was stuff I was doing going elsewhere and nothing coming in for him, and I said that was fine, but I might have something for him. Richard said he'd heard it all before. He was trying to be sympathetic but I would have none of it. I was mad with him. I asked him what Mary was up to, and he told me she was shadowing the police investigation but I knew that, didn't I? He asked me what I was up to, and I told him I'd be mowing the lawn later and was that news enough for him? He made a half-hearted offer of lunch, which I refused, and, roughly translated, he told me to suit myself.

He could go hang. Diane wanted statistics and I found them for her from the Department of Health web site.

The latest figures showed that around 180,000 terminations were performed annually in England and Wales, and 12,000 in Scotland. Ninety per cent of them were handled by just nineteen of the 105 health authorities. In other words, a lot of women were going private whether they liked it or not because their own hospitals didn't have the funding or the inclination to provide a timely service. I could forget the private sector for the time being. I had almost 200,000 women at risk on a government database for Diane Shine.

*

Those were the numbers, but did he really have access to them? I needed to know how the system worked. I was logging on again when Spencer phoned.

'Will you go public?' he said.

'On your terms or mine?' I said.

He hesitated.

'What are your terms?'

'I file first. Mary Stow files second.'

'I was thinking of a measured statement at a time of our choosing, taking the status of the victims and the feelings of the victims' families into consideration.'

'I know what to say. I'm a victim, remember?'

'Of course.'

'You think he'll bite?' I said.

'It'd give him something to think about.'

'You mean he might want to check his facts?'

'Maybe.'

'How would he do that?'

'Will you do it?'

'Sure,' I said, and he said he'd get me the statement he had prepared by tomorrow.

The receiver went down with a click. Read it and weep, Detective Superintendent. It would be in the Sunday papers.

The answers I needed about National Health databases were online, of course, on separate sites from separate departments. A piece here and a piece there and you got what the intelligence community called aggregation of data. A network of spies will collect it for you in months, maybe years. A computer network will turn local vulnerabilities into global ones because anyone, anywhere on the network can exploit them. The

Internet pulled what I wanted together in less than an hour.

I let the dog in. The sky was bright with winter light and the air was still and pungent with the smell of fried onions. I could hear laughter rising up from the park where people had taken their children to feed the ducks. There was a distant boom of traffic as the Roman sucked in cars to its street market. Up in the tower block I could see no one, but a voice inside told me that that didn't mean they couldn't see me.

But I felt good. I had a story and I had a gun.

CHAPTER EIGHTEEN

# HOW THE COOKIE CRUMBLES

Robert's round face, with its sweetheart mole high on one cheek, was tense with the after-effects of prolonged concentration, long hours and, after one week, no result. I offered him half a glass of Scotch in return for a special chow mein and some fortune cookies.

'Don't do it,' he said.

He was exhausted. He'd taken off his jacket, loosened his tie and slipped off his enormous shoes. He lay back on the sofa, the soles of his black-stockinged feet pressed together and his broad knees splayed. The golden glass of Scotch dangled in his large hands between them.

'Why not?'

'You're the goat he's tying to the tree.'

I'd thought about that. How many people were going to look at the photos of us four, see me, and think, *The good victim? She's the one that didn't even have an abortion and she got hit*. Despite the horror of pain and murder, of rape and bombs, there would be people who'd be untouched, people who would believe that I was harder done by than Dinika Patel, who was dead. I was the supermarket checkout girl in the Ripper's list of whores, the soft target to whom he owed an apology, and Spencer wanted to make him try and deliver it.

'Spencer thinks he'll try and contact me?'

'He's got that sort of profile,' Robert said. 'Likes to be right. Likes to dominate. Caught out, would want to justify his actions.'

'Who are we talking about here? Spencer?'

Robert adjusted his glasses. His gingery freckled skin was pasty and his hair shone like straw.

'Just don't do it. No story, nothing. He'll convince himself he was right somewhere along the line. It's too risky.'

'Why do you think that?'

'He knew he'd killed a pregnant woman. If he'd had some humility he'd have stopped then but he didn't. He went out and did it again.'

'You and Spencer disagree on this, don't you?'

'On the risk, yes. And it's not just him. There are others.'

He took a slug of the Scotch while I sucked the yellow noodles from my plastic fork. Ted Bundy's lower-case 't' showed he had a low opinion of himself, but the break in the bottom of the 'd' that he shared with Jeffrey Dahmer proved he could rationalise almost any action. While I thought about how the killer could square killing a pregnant woman with his holy war against all women who had had an abortion, Robert began to talk about the trails they were following in the hope that forensics would throw up a lead.

The postcards had been posted in the West End. It was possible he had bought them there. They were tourist cards so they were focusing on the central area of the city. He was confident they'd get a print from the cards or the packages. They were peeling off the stamps and testing the adhesive for DNA, but Robert didn't think our man would be fool enough to have licked them.

They were checking the scraps of paper that had wrapped the bombs for indentations – a trace of a phone number or a line of an address. The remains of the bomb mechanisms might produce more clues: the style of wiring, the method of detonation, the fuse, the explosive, or any fibres or hair that might have entwined themselves in its wires. The nails in the bomb were another clue. They were ordinary masonry nails and had been shown on TV.

They were revisiting the statements of the hit-and-runs and checking the dumps, the body shops and the second-hand dealers. They were checking car hire firms. They were searching through security videos that monitored the traffic and checking any that might have snapped a registration number. The hospital security videos were being played through. The hospital computer systems were being audited. I tried to imagine the manpower.

'You checking the list the world forgot for a year?' I said.

'We're checking the ink, the paper. We're talking to everyone the thirteen women ever knew. Ex-boyfriends. Ex-girlfriends.'

'Better leave mine until last if you're pressed for time,' I said.

Robert let my little joke pass.

'You're checking the pro-lifers, I suppose?'

'We know who they are.'

He sipped the drink and swilled it around his mouth before swallowing.

'How are you getting on with the doctor?' he said.

'You got a cam set up in here too?' I said.

'Don't be bloody stupid. I'm doing my job.'

'Is he a suspect?'

Robert said nothing.

'How about the guy that phoned me? Did you trace that call?'

He got up and walked over to where I was eating to pick at the leftovers in the tray and pour himself another Scotch. The day had faded suddenly into black and he switched on the light. Our reflections moved against the background of fairy lights that shone out from the fake snow scenes on the windows of the houses opposite.

'I hear you went to see one of my weird boyfriends,' I said.

'You're too hard on yourself. Tony Levi is Mr Normality compared to some.'

'You like him, don't you?'

'Not really. I'd nick him tomorrow if I could.'

I took one of four fortune cookies and cracked it open.

Inside, there was a message for me.

*Let every man mind his own business.*

I showed it to Robert.

'How are *your* cookies doing, DI Falk?' I said.

He had some cigarettes in his jacket and he dug them out.

'Want one?' he said.

'I know what you're doing. I just want to know how.'

'For information only?' he said.

'For information only.'

'Don't write this up.'

'Confirm it.'

It's how it goes. Robert Falk was probably one of my closest friends, but he was a policeman and I didn't trust him, and I was a journalist and he didn't trust me. Those were the parameters we worked within and within kept our friendship alive. He wasn't sure that if I told him something I wouldn't sell the information, and I wasn't sure that if he stumbled across the stash I had hidden in an empty tin of travel sweets in the kitchen he wouldn't go ahead and caution me. He threw me his cigarettes.

'I love you, Mrs Powers,' he said.

My eyes felt a little watery.

'And I love you too, DI Falk.'

I lit one. We were in no-man's-land now.

'OK. What do I do?' he said.

I told him he gathered criminal intelligence on organised crime.

'Correct. Therefore, I monitor activists. I monitor people who believe in single issues and direct action and pose a threat to democracy and the realm. I also help them communicate, and then I watch and I listen.'

'You run bulletin boards for them?'

'And counterfeit web sites and phoney anonymous remailers. We get to know our customers very well.'

'Cool.'

'We have a pro-choice and a pro-life site. Everyone who clicks on them gets a cookie, if they haven't disabled this valuable feature on their browser, and whenever they go online, the cookies report back to our server. We know where everyone who has clicked on the site is and what they are browsing, but if you write about it the game's up.'

Open up my temporary files and I was probably losing a megabyte of storage to cookies, little computer instructions used by web servers to make your life easier when you log on to a site. You visit a web site and its server makes a note of who you are, the web page you were at before, the browser you use and if you have visited its site before. It will then send you a cookie – which your browser will store on your computer to save time the next time you log on to the site.

When you visit the site again, your browser consults the cookie and grasses you up. The server can then monitor your browsing habits, just like Robert said. It will know how many times you've been to the site and what files you've looked at. If you have registered with the site, then the cookies store your user name and password. This is handy for easy navigation of sites; if you're reading *The New York Times*, say, and you don't want to keep putting in your user name and password every time you click through to another page because servers on the WWW can't remember who you are from one click to the next. By giving the browser a cookie and then asking for it back, the server can remember your virtual face.

'Our man would disable the cookies, wouldn't he? Someone like him would be hip to that.'

'Ever tried to live a full life on the web without them? It's a royal pain. But yes, it's a possibility that he'd have disabled them, though we've been tracking some interesting people nevertheless. We're gathering their email addresses, their Internet Service Providers, unique identifiers of their PCs, the software they use and, most importantly, their browsing tastes. We know who they are and what they like to do online. Gecko's doing the same with its banner ads.'

'How does that work?' I said. 'With the ads?'

'If the site has a banner ad, your browser will connect with the ad agency's server so that the ad agency can get a feel of what interests you and send you ads that you might like. Any time you fill out a form online, your email address is supplied. It's a public service, George. because people will never get to see an ad that they are unlikely to respond to. How good is that?'

'Fantastic.'

'With your email address, the ad agency can cross-reference your name and address and other personal details from other computerised databases, resell the information and/or target you with junk mail. Like I said, it's a public service.'

'So Gecko is doing what? Cross-referencing the email addresses it gets from ads with its customer database?'

'They're checking the online information they get from cookies against names of their customers.'

'And he would have bought a Gecko game?'

'That's right.'

'Is that likely?'

'I don't know about likely. He might have done. We need to address that possibility. The Mrs Whitehouse Syndrome. You know, watch all the filth in order to be appalled. He could be a true fan, though. That is very possible.' Robert smiled. 'He could be their number one fan.'

I didn't think that our man would be that dumb. I imagined that when he went online he might as well have been the white space that I couldn't fill in my head. He'd be anonymous and untraceable, or lost in a crowd. If he had an identity at all it would be someone else's, like Bundy's or Gacy's or Jack the Ripper's, or mine.

I poured myself a Scotch this time, and the dog came and sat at my feet. 'Are you allowed to do that?' I said.

Robert lit a cigarette. He'd given up for years, but every now and then he broke open a pack and smoked a lot, like a binge alcoholic saving up to go on a month-long bender.

'Tell me where I've been then,' I said.

'You got an email from Dr John Walker. I know that.'

That got me. I'd been trying not to think about him.

'He's not your man,' I said.

'Nor yours any more.'

I stared out of the windows and watched the Christmas lights winking. Red, green and gold reflections flickered on the water. I tried not to show the hatred I felt when I turned back to face him, but he wasn't a fool. He knew what he'd done. He wasn't smiling. He had to tell me about what he did and what he knew, make me understand how far he could go and where I couldn't.

'Are you and Gecko Games comparing notes?' I said.

He said nothing, but his look said it all. Of course they were. I got up and flicked on the TV. The sports reports were coming in. Robert's eye was drawn to them. He supported Third Division Leyton Orient because, he once said, he had to feed the pessimist in himself.

'What's the motto? Use for good not evil?' I said.

Smoke billowed around his bulky body as he stood holding the Scotch in one hand, cigarette in the other, waiting for the scores. He turned and drained the glass.

'How'd they do?'

'Two nil. To us,' he said, his plump ruby lips wet and shiny with whisky. 'We triangulated that phoney call to you from a mobile at the London. It was a pay-as-you-go but we're getting close. You don't need to take risks.'

He put down his empty glass and looked for his coat.

'And you can't quote me either,' he said.

'Wait a minute,' I said. 'You know Kendall's compromised the hospital system, don't you? Their man just walked in and downloaded a list of our names from a national database.'

He stopped looking for his coat and focused on me.

'We know that. We did it ourselves.'

'You pull my file again?'

His face flushed with embarrassment like I'd caught him going through my underwear drawer.

'Says I discharged myself on the hospital system, doesn't it? I was admitted but I didn't have the abortion.'

Robert sat down on the sofa. He looked tired suddenly.

'So where did he get his information about me, Robert? Where did he get the *wrong* information?'

He pushed his steel-rimmed glasses back up to the bridge of his nose.

'There isn't just one place. There are many, many medical databases that hold this sort of information. The NHS calls them registers and the NHSnet links most of them, it's about all it's really useful for. The information on these registers is used for statistical and research purposes.'

'But how did he find us? Don't they strip the identifiable data out for research and stats work?'

Robert asked me what I would consider to be identifiable information, and I told him anything that might link me to the medical details in the record. 'Name and address?' he suggested. 'How about your postcode? Gender?'

'You can't identify someone by a postcode. And I share my gender with every other female in the country,' I said.

'Georgina, the patient data that travels from the hospitals and doctors' surgeries to the Department of Health includes your name, address, postcode, date of birth, sex, HIV status, details of sexually transmissible diseases, abortions, and fertility treatment. Only the names and addresses are removed before the information is stored in any government databases. This is what the government means by "anonymising" data.'

I felt a mixture of relief and disappointment. Relief that my privacy was being protected and disappointment that one avenue I was chasing for my story had disappeared. How had the Advent Bomber got the wrong information about me and the right information about Cherry Shankar?

'So if he didn't get us from a central database and he didn't get us from the London's database, where did he get us from?'

Robert didn't want to look me in the eye.

'What are you saying, we've got a hacker or something, intercepting stuff?' I said.

'You're asking the wrong question, Georgina. Ask me what "anonymous" means.'

'What does "anonymous" mean?'

'All that's left of your identity in your centralised National Health record is a date of birth, sex and a partial postcode. That might sound anonymous to you, but you can identify ninety-eight per cent of the population with that.'

I said that I didn't believe it.

'In the last few years, everyone has been issued a new NHS number so that records can be searched for by computer. It's effectively a national ID number. With the new NHS number attached, you can identify everyone, including the remaining two per cent of the population: twins, people of the same age and gender in multiple-occupancy accommodation, students, soldiers. The National Health Service's Strategic Number Tracing Service holds the administrative details of everyone registered with the NHS in England and Wales.'

'You use it. Just like Kendall's does.'

'We get a warrant to use it, but we're certain the Advent Bomber, either through the local hospital or in some other way, has had access to a Department of Health database of some sort *and* the NHS Strategic Number Tracing Service. He knew the code for an abortion. He searched the database for files with code attached and with the new NHS number and the Strategic Number Tracing Service. He found the names and addresses of thirteen women, including you. Your information is incorrect because once you are admitted to a ward for a procedure like an abortion, it's logged. Only the local system is correct, which is why we know he had access to a national system.'

'When was this search system introduced?' I asked.

'The software for that was rolled out to ninety-eight health authorities in the summer.'

'Catriona Ross was attacked last Christmas. He must have had access before that. Where and when were the pilots?'

'Cheshire and East London and City health authorities, last year.'

'He could be working out of anywhere that has a link into those health authorities.'

'All the incidents have been in London.'

'He's local, then.'

'We think so.'

'Who ran the pilots?'

'A private consortium.'

'It was outsourced to a third party? Who? Are their staff vetted?'

'AHS Limited, British subsidiary of AHS Corp, had the contract.'

'AHS gets a lot of government work.'

'Yes, but it's had its problems.'

'Like what?'

'In the early days thousands of people were issued with duplicate numbers.'

'Duplicate numbers.'

He was like someone standing on the brink and wondering if he should jump off. He was wondering whether we had stopped playing our game in no-man's-land and whether we had both walked back to our lines.

'Which one of us, Robert?'

He really didn't want to tell me.

'Dinika Patel,' he said.

CHAPTER NINETEEN

# STRANGERS IN THE NIGHT

I had to ring Diane. She was on the late shift.

She said, 'I was right.'

'You were right, but the bomber screwed up. I checked back through the Technology Online database. The computer glitch that gave duplicate NHS numbers was corrected six months ago. It's a mess. He got the wrong Dinika Patel.'

'Bob Falk give any indication that they were homing in on this guy?'

'They've got information overload right now, but they're getting there, I think,' I said.

'Wait,' she said, and put me on hold with Sinatra singing 'Strangers in the Night'. He was just hitting the high notes when she came back to me. She was buzzing.

'Jesus, George, it's all over. I think they've got him.'

My mind jumped back to Robert standing there and telling me not to do a thing. They'd been closing in and he'd interrupted his schedule to come and give me a little friendly advice. I was relieved, really relieved. The tension began to seep out of me and I suddenly felt weak and exhausted. Soon I would see his face and fill in the last piece that was missing from my bad dreams.

'Hold on,' she said.

Ol' Blue Eyes was soaring, letting fly with the vocals above a steep bank of violins when she came back.

'A man is helping police with their inquiries. That's all. Listen, I really need the story if you can straighten it out. It's gold. I'll let you know when we know. I'm pleased for you, George.'

I asked if it would affect the deal if I sold a version of the story to Technology Online. She said it wouldn't and put down the phone. I wasn't about to double my money, but it was better than nothing, and Max would stop feeling neglected. I wondered whether I might put in the details of Robert's phoney web sites and cookie spies now that they had the man. I should check with him about that, I thought.

The dog was lying down by my feet, her black lips resting over her solid paws. It was quite possibly the end of a nightmare for her too. If they'd got him, I could go out, I said, but to myself, so that she couldn't hear. I looked around my back bedroom office and seemed to see it for the first time. The ashtrays were full and the desk was piled high with paper and unwashed coffee cups. The wooden floor was a mess of files, folders, old newspapers and magazines, and the shelves that held my reference books and boxes of software were thick with dust. Tomorrow, I told myself, you can start on it tomorrow.

I got up and made my way to the kitchen door. I looked out of the glass at the dull houses across the canal and up at the block that overshadowed us. There were no lights on any floor, not even in the flat where the red light was, where the man lived who couldn't sleep at night. I opened the door and felt the cold touch of air. The dog sat behind me and I said, 'Go on then,' but she wouldn't move.

'Go on.'

I looked out into the garden again as fear crept over my skin and lifted the hairs on the back of my neck. I shut the door and turned to her. She laid her ears back and licked my hands.

'Jesus, don't you start, girl.'

I wrote the story, but before I filed it I rang Cherry to tell her that they had made an arrest. She knew already.

'It's someone who worked at the hospital,' she said. 'A doctor. Can you believe it? A bloody doctor.'

My mouth had gone so dry that I couldn't form words. The white space in my mind filled with the face of John Walker, but it was a bad fit.

'They tell you more than that?'

'No. I'm checking with Kendall to see if they can get me a name and the guy's history,' she said.

'The police have been interviewing a doctor who treated us all in A and E.'

'You think it might be him?'

It was possible. Everything was possible. I thought about the fake phone call. He'd thought he'd straightened that out with me, but in my heart I had always thought it was him. He'd got my telephone number from my files. But I never thought that he could have done this thing to me, to Cherry, to Catriona, to Dinika Patel.

It made sense. He had access. He knew all about the new National Health numbers, hospitalisation codes and the Strategic Number Tracing Service. He had to have done. The whole system was designed to help him to help us, after all. I felt like a fool as I saw them all, all my weird boyfriends, flash before my eyes like the Ghosts of Christmas Past. Dr John Walker joined the parade, another one for that sanctimonious Richard to crow about.

'No,' I said. 'Not him.'

Cherry said nothing, then, 'I wanted to catch him, you know? I wanted to corner the rat myself.'

'And what would you have done then?'

'I don't know, get him.'

I told her I knew exactly how she felt, but I didn't tell her that I had a gun.

'Vengeance is mine, sayeth the Lord,' I said, but she said nothing.

'I suppose we should be grateful,' I said.

'Why?'

'That it's over.'

'Yes,' she said, and for a while we said nothing. We sat there together miles apart, thinking about what we would do next, now that it was over. I don't know about her, but I was thinking of the outside, the big, wide, terrifying landscape of the city outside the walls of my flat. I wanted to ask her a favour. I wanted to ask her if she could check with Kendall Associates about Pal Kuthy. I didn't feel quite safe yet, I wanted to say, but then I thought I was looking for excuses not to face the world.

'You know what I'd be doing on a Saturday night, George?' she said.

She wasn't really expecting an answer.

'I'd be waiting for Gecko to come home.'

Saturday nights, she said, meant dropping her home while he went on to a club, something like the Met or the White House, where there would be music and people and coke and E.

'I got tired of the scene, you know? I liked to be home. Gecko didn't like that. He didn't know what to do when he was home and he didn't have people around. I played around with the software and he'd watch TV. He said it was like sitting in with an old lady and her knitting. He was right. That's what I'm doing now. I'm not doing anything different. The only difference is Gecko isn't coming home. I don't even have a home.'

I hated to hear her cry. I couldn't comfort her, put my arms around her. I couldn't even look sympathetic. All I could do was say something, and nothing I could think of was going to make any difference. Tell you the truth, I felt like crying myself.

'Listen, Cherry. Did you ever regret it until now?'

'What?'

'Did you ever regret the abortion?'

'I thought about it.'

'Regret, Cherry. I'm talking about regret.'

'Before Gecko died? No. No, I didn't. Not really. But I had hope before,' she said.

Another phone started ringing somewhere where she was, and I heard someone answer it. She apologised and I said it was all right, but she had stopped listening to me and I had frankly stopped listening to her. Someone was talking to her and I was trying to make out what was being said. I couldn't stop myself doing it. I had eavesdropped on other people's conversations all my working life. It was an essential skill for a journalist, like being able to read upside-down writing.

'Can I get back to you, George?' she said, and she was gone.

Diane was pumped up. She'd sold my piece to a major Sunday tabloid for a five-figure sum, and she'd got a name on the guy. The receiver hung loosely from my fingers. Come on, hit me with it, I thought.

'It's a doctor,' she said. 'His name is John Walker.'

It was still a shock, like a punch to the stomach. I wanted to put the phone down, hold my head and cry, but I couldn't do that. No one could know how I really felt.

'I know John Walker,' I said. 'It's not him. He treated me.'

'He treated four of the victims, George.'

I couldn't speak. My throat was closing.

'George?' Diane said.

'Has he been charged?' I said.

'No.'

'Can they place him at the scene of each attack?'

'I don't know. You OK?'

'Yes.'

'Doesn't seem possible, does it?'

'No.'

'What an ordeal.'

'Yes.'

'You sure you're OK, George?'

I wasn't OK. I was hurting and I couldn't decide for myself whether it was because he had made me feel good or made me feel a fool. I couldn't decide what was worse.

I had noticed him the first time when he was moving through a silent vigil of veiled women with their sick, brown-eyed children. He had reminded me of one of those volunteers that you see beamed in to a TV screen near you from the refugee camps of the world. One of those tired but calm medics, committed and methodical in the face of the overwhelming needs of humanity placed before them by natural disasters, man-made wars, ignorance and poverty. I couldn't see him building bombs so that he could have an emergency. The way he talked, he'd felt guilty just having wished for one once because he'd got one, in the bloody, battered shape of Catriona Ross, and he'd never been able to forget it. Her brain had been addled with drugs. She remembered nothing of that night, just a blond man that she had confused with her own boyfriend when he had tried to help her. John couldn't have done it. He couldn't have been in two places at once. I told her I didn't think that he was a killer. Not John.

'It's just been a strain, you know?' I said.

'Sure.'

'I don't think it's him.'

'Whether it is him or not, Georgie girl, there's something they don't like about the guy,' she said.

I couldn't argue with that. It had to be the stupid phoney phone call. He'd lied to me. He'd got my number off my medical records and pinched his colleague's name to chat me up on a pay-as-you-go phone. He must have done it before and thought it would work. The phone call would be easy to explain away. It couldn't be the only reason. They must have found something else, something worse. I felt sick. I felt sick knowing the police thought that he was the man, sick that I had let him touch me and that I still wanted him to.

I couldn't sleep, but I wasn't the only one. Max Winters was wide awake too. He called me.

'Nice story, Georgina,' he said.

I thanked him once I'd recovered from the shock of the compliment.

'I have something for you, it might help with a follow-up,' he said.

'I thought I wasn't working for you.'

There was a sucking sound and a small wet wheeze as Max pulled on a cigarillo.

'It was also the last thing Danny Morgan pulled from the database. It might be relevant. Shall I read it or email it?'

I told him to do both.

The story Danny had been researching appeared to be a plain vanilla announcement of the final stage of a major upgrade to the National Medical Research Database, one of the largest and most important NHS databases run by the Department of Health and one of the biggest repositories of medical information in the world.

The database held hundreds of thousands of medical records and the equivalent of twenty-five million man years of information. The multimillion-pound contract to upgrade and commercialise it had gone to the British subsidiary of an American computer consultancy, AHS Corp. The original story was three years old and it was by-lined Mary Stow.

The clue that an insider had tipped Mary off that all was not as kosher as it might be came in the paragraph that told us it was an unpublicised contract award to AHS which would allow the anonymous files containing medical records, identified only by the new NHS number and postcode, to be queried not only by academics, drug control agencies and medical authorities, but by 'suitable vetted' researchers for a log-on fee. In other words, the thing was going discreetly into business and AHS was standing behind the till.

'These are Danny's notes. Professor Ronald Highfield. You know him. President, AHS. Prominent right-winger. Director-in-Chief, Christian Community. AHS telephone number in Boston as follows.'

I played catch-up, scribbling the words down at speed until Max said, 'The last words he wrote were – Christian love?'

I wrote *Christian Love* with a capital L and automatically drew three lines by the side.

'Christian Love,' I said.

'That's right.'

'Christian Love's the pro-life site that's been giving Gecko Games grief,' I said.

'Then it looks as if Danny was on to something.'

'What do you want me to do with it?'

'Usual rates, Georgina,' he said, and he was gone.

Cherry vetted my call on the machine and picked it up halfway through the recorded message that said she was unable to take calls and the press should call another number.

'Any news?' I said.

'Doctor's name is John Walker. He treated four of the victims. He treated you.'

I told her that he was Catriona Ross' ex.

'Do you know him?' I said, and she said that she didn't.

'How could he have got back to the hospital to treat you? To treat that Catriona Ross?' she said.

'He had to have a car. You can't be the hit-and-run driver without a car.'

I tried to imagine him in the car, but I could only see him on a motorbike. It didn't reassure me. The bombs had been delivered that way.

'Even so. They work long shifts. How could he come

and go without anyone noticing? He has to have an alibi. Unless.'

She paused.

'Unless what?' I said.

'Unless he wasn't working alone.'

I had thought of it but I didn't want to think about it. I had fast-forwarded to the moment when they would realise that they had made a mistake and that John would call me and explain and I would forgive him for the fool that he was. I didn't want to think about him working me over with someone else. I didn't like to think they were still out there.

'Professor Ronald Highfield. Have you got anything on him?' I said.

'President of AHS, that creepy consultancy that the government is farming out half its IT departments to? Wanted to run for President? Type of person you listen to and think makes a lot of sense until he goes on for a minute more than he has to and you realise he's one crazy fucker. Director-in-Chief of Christian Community. It backs legitimate direct action against abortion. It gathers huge crowds to pray outside the clinics in the States, makes a big song-and-dance about responsible Christianity. Works very hard to keep its good image. Means it gets taken seriously in Washington.'

'Danny Morgan had pulled an old story about AHS winning an unpublicised government contract to upgrade a database.'

'So?'

'It was the National Medical Research Database. His notes mention Ronald Highfield. Christian Community and Christian Love. Danny had held on to Jo Casey's notebook. He was on to something.'

'Wait a minute.'

She was walking across a room. I heard her sit down and then I heard the musicality of a modem dialling out, as familiar and satisfying as the sound of frying sausages.

'Christian Community sponsor ethical medical research. You can go to the Christian Love site and read about it,' she said.

I clicked on to it and on to the glowing button that said *research*. There were a few paragraphs of testimonies but the bulk of the text was a report entitled *Post-Abortion Syndrome – What is it?*

Women who have suffered an abortion, the report said, typically go into denial for five to ten years before emotional difficulties surface. They experience drug and alcohol abuse, personal relationship disorders, sexual dysfunction, recurrent nightmares, repeated abortions, communications difficulties, damaged self-esteem, and have a higher than average attempted suicide rate.

'I've got most of those and I've never had an abortion,' I said.

'I never experienced any of it until Gecko died, but put me down for drug and alcohol abuse and recurrent nightmares.'

At the bottom of the page was a blue hyperlink that read, *Christian Community for Ethical Medical Research*. I clicked on that and was shunted to the clean lines of Christian Community's American web site. It looked authoritative and responsible and it repeated the clinical research that had featured on the British Christian Love site. It didn't say how many women out of a hundred or a thousand had had those problems before, or anything that might put the story in perspective. Right down at the bottom of the page there was also a credit which read, *Source: National Medical*

*Research Database of the Government of the United Kingdom.*

I could almost see Danny's size-twelve footprints in the virtual sand.

'You reading what I'm reading?' I said.

'I see it.'

'It's a conflict of interest. Danny picked up on that. Christian Community could have got access to an AHS-run database legitimately, of course, but it's still a conflict of interest. AHS is responsible for the security of that database, for the vetting of its users. Highfield's on the board of both.'

'He wasn't a complete fool then.'

'Who?'

'Danny Morgan.'

I thought it was harsh but I said nothing.

'I don't know,' she said. 'Christian Community has worked hard to establish its reputation. It wouldn't jeopardise it by playing around with fringe extremists like Christian Love.'

'Someone saw the data that was used for this research, Cherry, and used the NHS Strategic Number Tracing Service to hunt us down,' I said. 'Someone who thought it was time to stop pussyfooting around in Washington, and Westminster.'

'This doctor and his friends?'

I didn't even want to think about it. Every time I did, I hurt inside.

'Got time to chat?' she said.

'Always.'

Some say that the real Internet is the Usenet collection of newsgroups and not the World Wide Web's linked pages and sites. The Internet, of course, is the network to which just about every computer on the planet is connected. The global network that began as a military exercise in invincibility and an academic dream of shared knowledge has instead become a parallel universe of Trivial Pursuit. There is more than one way to travel in this universe. Those who use the WWW like their information to come packaged with click-on signposts to help them find it. Those who use Usenet like to see the plain text of their own voices discussing everything from Star Wars to Stalinist utopias. For Usenet is the world of newsgroups, and for newsgroup read discussions and what used to be called SIG – special interest groups. The special interests of alternative culture were filed under *alt.* for 'alternative', which, for those who know better, stands for anarchists, lunatics and terrorists.

Cherry took me to a newsgroup called alt.christians to meet someone called john@qcms.org. I didn't want to see the name John, no way, but there it was like a slap in the face. 'We threw this guy off the Gecko Games site three years ago for abusing our chatroom system. He had a number of handles. One anonymous ID we traced back to the server and leaned on it. He never came back.'

'What was his problem?'

'He'd followed one of our customers to our site from an alt.games discussion. Kept harassing him. I'm going to email you something.'

It took ten seconds. She'd sent me a list of email names and addresses.

derve@nym.alias.net
commentator@nym.alias.net
gp@aol.com
remnant@aol.com
rool@aol.com

jayque@mardigras.com
catross@mardigras.com
shankar@hotmail.com

'They're all from about three years ago. You'll notice Shankar. Catross. Jayque. GP.'

It was hard not to, and it meant that whoever this was had had an interest in Cherry and Catriona Ross and Jenni Quek and me for a while.

'Can you believe it? We've been bugging him all this time.'

'Do you know who they really are?'

'*They're* all one person, George. They're him. John the Baptist here used all these handles as pseudonyms. It's not even that simple. They're him but he pretends that they're all *different* people. Their function is to agree with him, make him feel like an intellectual. He even humiliates some of them, the ones playing devil's advocate, makes them look small. He was always looking for cheats on Creature game levels. Some intellectual.'

'What's qcms.org?'

'Queen's College Medical School. It refused to give us a name at the time. Thought the incident was too trivial to breach its student's confidentiality. They said it was a free speech issue. That medical school account is dead now but he's back. He just can't keep away.'

'How can you be sure that it's him?'

'Same MO. He appears with his pseudonyms. AOL, Hotmail, nym are his favourite hideouts. They participate in the same discussion threads as they used to. When his alter egos are not sharing discussion threads with him, they're off discussing the same subjects somewhere else and praising him in his absence. But they're all him. It's him all the time. Check this out.'

She sent me two sample posts, one from alt.abortion and one from alt.games.creature.

'The alt.abortion is about a month old but he's calling himself Peter, not John. JD is some poor sap he's cornered. All the rest of the "participants" are him. The alt.games thread is three years old. Just compare them.'

Peter kicked off the thread for alt.abortion with: *But who is the murderer?*

*JD:* The abortionist.
*Peter:* He is merely the agent of the devil.
*Cat:* Ha. Ha. Isn't it funny how people like you, JD, accuse the choice crowd of being pro-murder and reject the idea that women should be prosecuted for it? Where do you really stand?
*JD:* The woman is his victim. He cons her.
*Peter:* Is not the principal of wrongful conduct at least as culpable as her agent? Is she not the double devil?
*Jitters:* The religious right hates to think about that one, Peter. I wonder why?
*Peter:* I wonder too. They want to punish the agent of the iniquity, the doctor, and excuse the principal. The hypocrites place the moral blame for an abortion on the doctor who performs it and ignore the evil motive of the woman who orders it. Even the most radical religious right groups wish to excuse the woman who *ordered* the abortion and punish only the doctor who is acting out her instructions. And yet they set themselves up as *defenders* of the foetus. They state that the foetus is a human being and this makes them hypocrites.

The ancient alt.games.creature thread had the Catross pseudonym handling much the same discussion.

*Catross:* The pro-lifers maintain that abortion should be prohibited by law but they refuse to treat the foetus as a person in law. If the foetus really was a person, then abortion would be murder.

*GP:* I have always wondered why the hypocrites of pro-life do not care about punishing the aborting woman. Maybe John has an opinion on this?????? It's clearly a form of hypocrisy. The pro-lifers argue that abortion is murder. They also argue that women who abort are blameless or have less blame than the abortionist. How can you take them seriously? She is a devil twice over.

*darth:* Man. How did this damn thread get into the Creature newsgroup?

*hammerskull:* Guess everyone's killing time until Creature II.

*Squint:* Someone, GP????, asked where John was? Someone else digs up his latest thread on abortion, a comparison between number of foetuses aborted and number of Jews killed in the Holocaust. We get a terminally tedious abortion thread featuring this bloke's fucking morphs. Thread turns to the topic of when a foetus becomes a person and people (who shall remain nameless) start arguing over what's the definition of a person. Someone asks how this all got started. Someone else with no life responds.

'I kind of like old Squint,' I said.

'Yeah. Top man.'

'Surely Queen's will check its old accounts now?'

'Queen's have: john@qcms.org is John Walker.'

I took a cigarette out of the pack and got a really strange feeling when I heard her strike a match.

'Is she not the double devil?' I said.

'She is a devil twice over,' Cherry replied.

I asked why she was convinced that the new Peter was the old John, and she said they had used style analyser software on all his discussions.

'He chooses a biblical name for his main character, that is, himself. He overuses the word "hypocrisy". He also forgets who he's supposed to be half the time. That's the trouble with multiple personalities. You ready? I'm going to email something else to you. It's a profile of his interests.'

I got the list as quickly as I had got the last. It read:

alt.activism.religion
alt.activism.children
alt.binaries.pictures.foetus
alt.games.gecko
alt.christnet.prayer
alt.culture.internet
alt.crime.bundy
alt.christnet.christianlife
alt.religion
alt.activism.animals
alt.bodybuilding
alt.drugs.ghb
alt binaries.pictures.foetus
alt.med.ob-gyn
alt.politics

This was the picture that felt right. I could almost see his face, but as I gazed at the list, I didn't see John Walker. He still didn't fill the white space in my head, but maybe I just didn't want him to.

'It's not John Walker,' I said.

'Come on, George.'

'Someone could have used his account. It happens all the time.'

'Yes, but what makes you so sure?'

I hesitated for a moment, and then I told her.

'Because when he chooses a fantasy world, he doesn't like to be in charge.'

CHAPTER TWENTY

# ONE DEATH IS A TRAGEDY

Just in case I missed him at the Boston office, it being a Saturday, Cherry had given me every number that I needed for Professor Ronald Highfield: his home number, his direct line, his pager, his mobile, his weekend retreat, his mother's and his mistress' numbers and the number of his hideaway in Bermuda. It was interesting how Kendall Associates were always there when I needed them, one step ahead of me.

I thanked her and sighed. It must have sounded like my soul was tired of living.

'You OK?' she said.

'Yeah.'

'You make it with this guy?'

'Yeah.'

'You miss him?'

'Yeah.'

'I miss my man too. We should sleep together tonight.'

I laughed, and then I asked her, 'Do you feel safe, Cherry?'

'Knowing that they've got the doctor?'

'Knowing that they've got the doctor.'

She inhaled. I exhaled.

'Put it this way. I haven't made Kendall Associates stand down.'

It was six p.m. on the East Coast, and I reckoned even a God-fearing man like Highfield with a deeply ingrained work ethic would not be at the office, so I called him at home. It seemed he wasn't there. He was on business. I called the office and got a selection of numerical choices, which I knew would lead me to that electronic cul-de-sac of our times: voicemail. In the end, I reached him on his mobile.

He seemed to be expecting me, or if not me, someone who would be asking questions he had to be well prepared to answer. A big Kahoonaburger like him would not have given me the time of day ordinarily. He would have had at least twenty vice-presidents he could have let pass me around. Forewarned is forearmed, and I wondered which Fortune 500 corporate investigator he was paying to keep ahead of the game.

I got to the point and told him I was interested in the arrangement that AHS had with the National Medical Research Database. He explained what I knew already and what, as he pointed out, had been press-released: that it was an outsourcing contract from the British government and that the main thrust of it was to enable properly vetted researchers to log on to it and exploit the data contained in the medical records for a fee.

'It's a wonderful resource. We have nothing like it here in the United States,' he said.

I agreed that it was a wonderful resource and asked him to explain how it worked if, say, Christian Community for Ethical Medical Research wanted to research Post-Abortion Syndrome, for example.

He didn't miss a beat. He told me that his recollection

was that Christian Community sought consent about three years ago for just such an analytical study.

'You don't think there was a conflict of interest?' I said.

He said I had to understand that Christian Community was an entirely separate entity. AHS did not own it. It was a registered charity.

'Of which you are a director.'

'That is correct.'

'Who ensures the confidentiality of the medical records, Professor?'

'We do.'

'AHS?'

'That's right.'

'Who else?'

'Researchers guarantee confidentiality, and Christian Community is no different to any other research group.'

I pointed out that Christian Community was a political and religious group, but he was on a roll.

'Christian Community has acted in accordance with the principles set out in the British Data Protection Act of 1984 and the British Medical Research Council's statement for Responsibility in the Use of Medical Information for Research. In the case of British NHS patient records, the NHS is responsible for ensuring that those whose medical data might be used in research are informed and given the opportunity to discuss this and object, subject to overriding public interest, of course.'

'I didn't give my consent.'

'Excuse me?'

'I said that I didn't give my consent for anyone to look at my records.'

Highfield remained silent. He might have been saying

a prayer for my soiled immortal soul, damning me to hell or merely counting to ten, but when he'd finished, he spoke more slowly and more carefully.

'Accredited researchers are permitted to scan the database for a sample to study without the consent of the subjects.'

'Are the records in the database identifiable in any way?'

'No, they are not.'

'Are you saying there is no identifiable data whatsoever in those records?'

'No. There is always some identifying data.'

'The records are identifiable, in that case,' I said.

'Some are, yes. De-identification often rests with the researcher.'

'De-identification?'

'The removal of identifying data.'

'Rests with the researcher. Christian Community, for example.'

He did not reply and I updated him on the local difficulties with death and destruction that we had been having in the UK, but he couldn't see how there was a connection between the Advent Bomber and perfectly legitimate research carried out by Christian Community. AHS had nothing to hide and Christian Community had nothing to hide either. I said I suspected that raw data from the database had been accessed, legitimately or illegitimately, to identify women who had had an abortion, and that an assassin had got his hands on it. I asked if Christian Community researchers were vetted, and he said they were.

'By whom?'

'By AHS.'

'Anyone else get a say?'

'The ethics committee and the Medical Research Council.'

'Do researchers share their raw data with anyone else before they've de-identified and studied it, Professor Highfield?'

'Researchers routinely share selected raw data with trusted collaborators.'

'Do you vet trusted collaborators?'

He said that they did.

'Was Christian Community the only sponsor of this research, Professor?' I said.

He said the co-sponsors included a major pharmaceutical firm, a private healthcare provider and a health insurance company.

'Why the healthcare insurance company?'

'They just wanted to be involved.'

'Did they access the data? Did any of the sponsors access the data?'

'They had access to the final *study*, not the data.'

'AHS made the database accessible online to researchers.'

'Did a medical student called John Walker work for you, Professor Highfield?'

There was silence at the end of the line.

'Professor Highfield?'

'I do not have that information to hand.'

'Can you get that information to hand?'

He said nothing.

'Do you concede there might have been a leak from this study, Professor Highfield?'

'AHS has received no complaints of a breach in confidentiality. Christian Community has received no complaints. If there has been a breach of confidentiality then we will investigate it.'

He ended it there and I settled back in my chair, stuck a cigarette in my mouth and lit it. My hands were trembling. It could have been that I was overtired. It was one o'clock in the morning, after all. It could have been the stress, but that seemed to be permanent. I went over what I knew.

Danny had pulled this story. It was definitely relevant. He'd hung on to Jo Casey's notebook. It was possible that they had discussed something.

John Walker was definitely connected. John Walker's email account had been used in newsgroups and chatrooms to express strong views on abortion. Highfield wouldn't confirm or deny it, but his reaction made me think that he knew the name. I had to face the fact that the police probably knew more about John than I did, which was why they had pulled him in. I felt sick to my stomach.

Cherry had said they'd thrown Online John off her site three years ago. It must have been John Walker's final year at medical school.

'Let's go, George,' I said, and spread my fingers over the keyboard as the modem sang like a bird.

'Search. College. Graduates. Name.'

A minute and there it was, the roll-call of students who had their final year at Queen's College three years ago. I looked for his name among the thirty. It wasn't there. I went to the year directory. I clicked on it. The page gave me a choice of postgraduates and graduates. I clicked on postgraduates, and the list that turned up was shorter, about ten names, and John Walker was one of them.

The names were highlighted in blue. I clicked on John Walker and a page gave details of his research project.

As I read it, the walls of the room seemed to crowd in on me.

I called Professor Highfield back, but he wasn't as relaxed as he might have been.

'I've already spared you as much of my time as I am going to.'

'Shall I call back, Professor Highfield?'

'Call my office on Monday. I'm entitled to my weekend. I'm entitled to a holy day.'

'How about if I call this number?'

I read out his mistress' number that Kendall's had so thoughtfully provided.

I thought I heard his teeth clamp together, but it could have been noise on the line.

'Get on with it.'

'John Walker.'

'What about him?'

'Was he the medical researcher on this project?'

He took a long, long time before he said, 'He was the medical research *assistant*.'

'Who was the principal?'

'Dr Andrew Miller, a well-respected Boston gynaecologist.'

'How about your sponsors?'

'Lander Pharmaceuticals.'

'The insurance company?'

'Standard Health Insure.'

'And the healthcare provider?'

There was another long silence.

'The healthcare provider, Professor.'

'The Community Family Counselling Clinics.'

'Is that connected in any way with the Christian Love organisation here in the UK?'

'I believe it is.'

'Does Christian Community have any sort of relationship with the Christian Love site or its clinics?'

'No, it does not.'

'Did it ever?'

'No.'

'Christian Love has a link from its site to your site.'

'Many pro-life sites have links from their sites to the Christian Community site. We provide a forum for rational discussion and the most up-to-date scientific research.'

'You have no connection with the Christian Love site?'

'No.'

'Did John Walker collaborate with anyone at Christian Love?'

'John Walker withdrew from the study after three months.'

'Why?'

'There were differences of opinion.'

'Concerning what?'

'The research methods.'

'Can you explain?'

'No.'

'What was the purpose of the study?'

'The truth about abortion and its effect on women.'

'Who replaced him?'

'I don't recall.'

'Who else worked on this project, Professor?'

He gave me two names, and the addresses were American.

I was done with him. I pushed back the chair and walked away from the phone and the screen. My flesh was crawling. John Walker had withdrawn from this project. He had seen the raw data and it was possible that he had copied and kept it. Whoever was working with him would have seen it, which meant someone working for Christian Love could have. It was possible that they had copied it and kept it, which meant that any number of anti-abortionists had a definitive identifiable list of all the women in the UK who had had a termination. Just like John had.

I stood by the kitchen door and stared out at the night. The permanent glow of the city had blanked out the sky and the stars. Three flats in the tower were lit, and the red light tempered the darkness in another. I had one question turning in my mind. I had to ask myself on which side of Christian Love did John Walker fall, on the extreme side or the other? Did he think Christian Love was hypocritical? Did he think that burning a clinic did not go far enough? Catriona Ross had said that John had been indifferent to her pain. I'd taken it to mean that he couldn't face what had happened to her, that he had felt inadequate. It seemed that way to me, to hear her talk about it and him talk about it. The John I knew wanted to be punished for failing. I think he wanted to die a little every day because he thought he had failed her. It was hard to think of John as a man who might think that she deserved that pain. It was even harder to think of him as the man who had delivered it to her. My breath fogged up the glass in the door and I looked at my watch. It was two a.m. and my body and brain were aching. I needed to sleep but I kept thinking of the little gold cross on a chain that John wore around his neck. It didn't help.

It was the incessant ringing of the telephone and the sound of my own voice taking messages that woke me. I was lying on my bed and my whole body was stiff with cold. It must have been late, because the sun had reached high enough into the winter sky to penetrate a gap in the curtains and illuminate the subterranean gloom of my bedroom. I didn't feel that I had been to sleep, but here I was waking up. A glance at my clock radio told me it was twelve-thirty p.m. and the afternoon already. I hadn't wanted to sleep this long. There was work to do.

The day was one of those cold, still, apricot-coloured days of winter which make the birds look as black as charred paper against the sky. I flicked on the central heating and pushed my face close to the glass in the kitchen door. The man was at the window of his flat high up in the tower block. He was talking on the telephone. I wondered if I could just step out into the garden and stand there. It might be a way forward, to go out there and stand there for a minute, and the next day, stand there for two, and the next, three. I made a bargain with myself. If you think it was John who drove the car at you, do it. If you don't, then don't do it.

I didn't move. I was momentarily excited until I told myself that it didn't prove anything and went to pick the Sunday papers up from the hall to have a look at my story. The dog came running from the garden then. She stood by me, her skin twitching. It wasn't that she thought I was leaving. She'd heard someone arrive. I held the papers to my chest and looked through the lens of the front door. Robert Falk was standing in a piebald slice of shade and faded light. He was just looking at the door, his big shapeless arms hanging by his sides. He looked sunken and defeated, like a punctured football, and he was making no attempt to ring the bell.

I waited, looked again, waited and finally I opened

the door. He blinked at me behind the cold lenses of his glasses.

'Were you ringing before?' I said. 'I'm sorry.'

He said he hadn't, and stepped inside. There was something wrong. I offered him the usual, tea, coffee, beer, something harder. He shook his head and went into the lounge. The atmosphere was a bit formal and I wondered if he and Spencer had had words about me going public in my own time.

'If you're going to tell me off about the story, I'm sorry. If I'd cleared it with Spencer he'd have given it to Mary Stow. I don't trust him. I had a right to this story. It was my story. You think you've got him in the cells. I don't know. Wherever he is, whoever he is, let him read it and see how badly he screwed up.'

'It's not about the story, Georgina,' he said.

He asked me to sit down. It was bad news.

To his credit, he got straight to it. He said he was sorry, very sorry. I said how, and he said that it was hard to keep a man alive who wanted to die, especially a doctor. I didn't say anything, so Robert kept on talking, explaining why things had happened as they did. He said they had searched John's place and found his address book. It had Craig Gibson's name in it, Mr Christian Love, along with other contacts in right-wing Christian movements. John had insisted that he had worked with these organisations on a research project that they had sponsored, but when he saw how they wanted to twist the facts, he had walked away from it, and them. He had said that he barely believed in God any more, but the police couldn't ignore the connection, not with the access he had had to hospital files and the fact that he had treated women on the list. He admitted he'd made that call to me and impersonated Dr Lane. I told Robert that I had always thought that that was John, but that the man that I was afraid of had got the wrong address and the wrong information. John Walker had always been in the position to get the right information. I asked him if, for all that, he thought that John Walker was the man they had wanted, and he said that he didn't know.

I hit him as soon as he had said that, that he didn't know and that John was dead. He let me, didn't even lift his arm. He could have done me for it I suppose, but like I said before, we were friends, though I told him then not to come around for a while, a good long while. When he had gone I tore at my clothes. I remember that. I tore at them hoping I could pull my heart out of my chest and get rid of the pain.

I watched Spencer face the cameras on TV. He should have looked like he had swallowed a snake, but his manner was brisk and confident. John Walker's death had been a regrettable incident, he said. The circumstances of how he could have been able to take his own life would be fully investigated, but he said he felt sure they were close to making a breakthrough. He said that inquiries were in progress relating to breaches of the Data Protection Act and computer misuse.

Catriona Ross called me an hour later.

'You've heard?' she said.

I said that I had. I had a little trouble speaking normally and I said I was a little tired when she asked me if I was OK. She said she was bearing up when I asked her.

'He was a Catholic, you know? Lapsed. Said he had to be, the hours he did, couldn't ever get to Mass. It was just a joke. He didn't believe. Not as much as I did.'

'Was it him? Did he maim you and run me down?' I said.

'Hard to imagine, isn't it?'

'Try.'

She was quiet for so long I had to ask her if she was there, and she said she didn't think he'd attacked her, and if he hadn't attacked her, then in her mind he couldn't be the bomber.

'He didn't agree with abortion, I know that,' she said.

'Did you talk about it?'

'It came up. He said women had free choice but so had he. He wasn't a fanatic.'

'Did he know about you?'

'I didn't tell him.'

'Didn't mean he didn't know,' I said.

I told her what I had found out from Ronald Highfield.

'Did he ever tell you about that project?' I said.

She said no, and then she asked me if he had ever mentioned it to me. I asked why would he and she said that she knew that he had been seeing me.

'I wanted John to be happy,' she said, and I felt like there was no hole deep enough for me to fall into.

When Cherry called to ask how I was, I choked up more than when I had spoken to Catriona Ross. We really had something in common now but we left that fact unspoken. She waited while I wiped my nose and stuff.

'You think it was him?' she said.

I told her that he'd done some stupid things but he'd done them to get to me. I told her what had happened between him and Catriona Ross.

'He couldn't have faked how he felt about that. It was eating him alive,' I said.

'Until he found you.'

'I don't know. We had something, but it was only just beginning.'

I had started to cry again.

'You had something. I hear you, but do you think it was him? Do you think he was our man?'

I said no, definitely no, and she said that was OK because she didn't either, and when I asked why, she said, 'Because our man was having a little chat with himself this morning.'

I logged on to alt.abortion like she told me to.

There he was. This time his name was not John nor Peter but Rem. He was under pressure from a number of people who had read the day's papers and he was using all his pseudonyms to form a protective shield around himself while he defended the indefensible. Women who aided the murder of their children were not victims, he said.

'Can you trace him?'

'It's going to take time to dig him out from there and my bet is the trace will go back to a proxy server. We've got something, though. He still likes to play Creature.'

'How does he square playing Creature with trying to kill you, Cherry?' I said.

'Kendall's profilers tell me he can't. He loves Creature. I made Creature. He hates me. He can't square the circle. They call it cognitive dissonance. It creates a kind of unpleasant tension.'

I felt a little rush. It made me ashamed that after all that had happened I was still chasing the story down. John was dead and I still couldn't stop. Cherry's laughter was a little thin, because she knew what I was thinking.

'Got your paper and pencil, George?'

'Sure.'

'Call him Peter, Catross, GP, John Walker, Rem. Whoever. He downloaded three pieces of software from the Gecko site this year. We've pattern-matched aliases, read the cookies, checked the client database, and we found three attached to one address.'

It was in Whitechapel, Jack the Ripper country, not far from the hospital, not far from the two bomb blasts and not far from where I lived. She said they had a credit card reference too and they thought it was real. The guy had good credit. It was almost funny. The only time he was straight with himself and everyone else was when he was playing games. Players took their games seriously. Like they say about football, it's not a matter of life or death, it's more important than that.

'Man by the name of Sulliman lives at that address now, but he still gets mail addressed to one Declan Campbell.'

Declan Campbell. The white space in my head had a name but still no face.

'You think it's him?'

'I don't know yet, but we can find his new address. We can check him out. I'm waiting on Kendall. It's too easy, isn't it, George? We know that.'

I told her everything, what Highfield had said and the fact that the police had found John's address book with Craig Gibson's name in it.

'He was a researcher for them for a while. He walked away.'

'Why?'

'I think he had a problem with their research ethics.'

Cherry said nothing, and inside myself I thanked her for not saying it, for not telling me what I already knew. That because I wanted to believe it didn't make it true.

'Declan Campbell and John might not have known each other even if Campbell was using John's medical school account. All we know for sure is that he had access to Queen's College's computer system.'

I gave her the university site and directed her to the year list. Campbell wasn't there.

'He wasn't a medical student,' I said.

'Academic. Employee. Easy enough to check.'

'Friend. Dealer,' I said. 'Christian Society?'

'What we need is John's address book. If Declan Campbell's in it then he is our man.'

'A little black book,' I said.

'So *retro*, you know?' she said.

'The police have it.'

She was silent.

'Let me give Ronald Highfield a call. I want to know who replaced John Walker on the team. It might have been Campbell,' I said.

Highfield told me he didn't know any Declan Campbell, but he was weary enough of my attention to tell me that I had to understand that not everyone who believed in the sanctity of a baby's life was as temperate as his organisation was.

'There are a lot of angry people out there,' he said.

'And they don't work for you?'

'No, ma'am, they do not.'

The line went dead.

I searched the Christian Love web site for a contact number and put in a call for Craig Gibson. I was given the impression that hell might freeze over before he called me back, but I mentioned Professor Highfield's name and got a call in less than half an hour.

Craig Gibson was a softly spoken man with a sincere manner. He was sympathetic to my situation but told me I had to understand that he couldn't remember everyone he had ever met in his ten years of campaigning. If I hadn't seen him on the TV, I might have been convinced of the purity of his motives.

'Did you know John Walker?' I said.

He said the name didn't mean that much to him until I told him that he had been arrested in connection with the two London bombings.

'There was a joint research project that you sponsored three years ago. I spoke to Professor Highfield about it and he confirmed that Dr John Walker had been a research assistant. Maybe that's why your name was in his book.'

He grabbed at the safety line that I had offered him.

'I believe he left early on and was replaced. That's why I didn't remember him. I'm sorry about the woman. The young journalist. Her baby. That was terrible.'

'Why did John Walker leave the project?'

'He wasn't sympathetic to our views. He was ambivalent, let's say. We needed someone who felt more comfortable with the sponsors of the project than he did.'

'Who replaced him?'

'I don't recall.'

'Was it Declan Campbell?'

He hesitated for a second, and when he spoke again, he spoke more cautiously.

'No.'

'Who was it?'

'It was a woman. I just don't remember her name.'

I felt the dry taste of disappointment in my mouth. There went the straw I had been grasping at.

'Do you know anyone by the name of Declan Campbell?'

Gibson blew out a sigh.

'We are a very moderate organisation. Some who join us are not satisfied with our approach.'

'You do know Declan Campbell, don't you?'

It was getting complicated. He could see that. There was a pause as he considered how best to keep his nose clean.

'Declan Campbell was one of our supporters. There was some conflict. He wanted us to take a stronger line.'

'What did he do? Was he a doctor? A medical student?'

'He was a Queen's University computer studies student.'

I took a flier.

'And he worked on your web site.'

He said nothing.

'Until when?' I said.

'Until about a year ago. We had to let him go.'

'And that was it?'

'There were some hostilities. We reported it to the police.'

'Any idea where he lives?'

'The last I heard it was Whitechapel.'

I sat alone with the posts on alt.abortion staring at myself, as Declan Campbell wanted me to be, spouting his beliefs, playing the camp follower to his Christian soldier. Here was a man who thought Christian Love was too moderate, that setting fire to a clinic and terrorising its employees was too tame. He'd gone further. He had used his victims' names and cloaked himself in them. He'd stolen John's name and John's life. He probably knew how to make a date-rape drug like GHB from butyric acid and a bomb out of nails.

'Show yourself, you bastard. Show yourself,' I said, and my eyes came to rest on one email address in a post in alt.games.creature that read *peter@caffnet.co.uk*. It had been posted on the morning of the day that Richard and I had been run down in the street.

I logged on and searched for caffnet.co.uk. It turned out to be an Internet café on the Whitechapel Road. The site had gone for a bright sixties pop design with hip and breezy-looking graphics. I searched for an address, a real, offline address, and a number that I could call to check out if they had a security video. One with a tape in it would be nice. But Caffnet did better than that. It had a real address and number and one nice extra touch. It had a webcam.

I picked up the phone.

'Hey Cherry,' I said. 'Get a load of this.'

CHAPTER TWENTY-ONE

# A SHOT IN THE DARK

I downloaded emails in the dark while I smoked a cigarette – I was limiting myself to ten a day and managing. If I had a drink, it went up. I couldn't resist a cigarette when I was drunk. The mails came in and I checked my watch. It was seven p.m. If it was going to happen it would be about now. He liked to post about now.

There were ten machines in the café and I got a view from the door that did a slow pan across the room. The bar was at the back and three people manned the joint: a slim brown girl with long dark hair, a short A-line skirt and a polo-neck jumper; an Asian dude with Michael Caine specs; and a geeky-looking white guy wearing baggy jeans and an oversized sweatshirt. There was a plump, veiled Moslem woman sitting at one machine and a tall white guy at another. He wore a loose tweedy-looking coat, and was losing his hair. They had their backs to me.

You looked at the scene and wondered why anyone would bother logging on to see what was happening there. It was tedium with a capital Z. There was more happening in the fonts on the home page. After about an hour, I began to notice that the geeky guy did all the work and the Asian fella with the Michael Caine specs was kind of sweet on the brown girl. He made a big effort to make her laugh and she pretended she was too serious for him. It had potential as a kind of soap, if you had the time and someone else was paying your phone bill.

I was watching it and I was waiting, but I got to thinking about John. The news that he had died in custody had been everywhere. He was gone and all that was left of him was a lingering suspicion that he had once been connected with an extremist group. It was left to his family and Catriona Ross, for whom the press had a fascination because she had been his lover and could have been his victim, to say that he was a good man and a good doctor and they would miss him. No one asked about me because no one knew about me except for Robert Falk, and I was glad, because I didn't want to talk about it.

When I'd finished with Gibson and told Cherry, I'd put on my coat and opened the back door, and as usual, the dog hustled and ran out before me. Somewhere overhead I could hear a helicopter. It was close; the sound of its spinning blades growing louder and softer by turns as it circled above. My first thought was that there had been another bomb somewhere in the city. My second thought was for Althea Winston, the next on the list. Then I thought of John, who wasn't going to be there to tend the ill and the injured. I was sick at heart for him and for myself.

The dog had stood in the middle of the muddy lawn, staring up at the grey sky, her ears pricked and her eyes alert. I went and stood by her. It wasn't so bad. It wasn't good but it wasn't so bad. I had the gun in my pocket, and that made me feel better. I felt better about whoever might be there lurking in the canal, in the submersible, ready to up periscope. I poked fun at myself. It helped.

I promised myself that I would stand out there every day at the same time. I would take my time, breathe in the heavy city air, swing my arms, get myself better. I wanted to come alive and I had to take a chance to do that. I said this out loud to myself and then I looked up at the tower block and there was the man who kept me company, staring down at me. I thought about waving at him but changed my mind. I took my time, waited for my heart rate to start to climb and turned to the house before it had reached the point of terror.

Declan Campbell, in all his guises, had a habit of talking to himself online at more or less the same time. I'd made the bold move of interrupting him. I'd posted a mail and told him that the Advent Bomber had, frankly, screwed up. He had killed only the innocent – a man who had done nothing, a woman with an unborn child, a woman who had probably never even had sex. He had hurt a woman whom he had mistakenly identified as a child killer, I said, and a friend who had tried to save her. He had ruined another woman's chances of bearing any children at all. He had ruined the lives of countless others, including two lonely men who couldn't live with themselves because they had a conscience. God would judge him, I wrote, for presuming to judge for Him. I wrote whatever I thought he wouldn't want to hear. I was betting that he was an arrogant man, too arrogant to be cautious in his opinions. He'd have to answer me, and if he chose to post at the same time then he'd use the café and I'd see him for real and fill in the white space once and for all. I sat at the screen watching the webcam feed online, and at about 7.05 p.m. the door opened and a shot of adrenalin surged through me. A bulky man in a puffa coat and a blond ponytail scraped back from dark roots came in and sat down at a free machine. He looked familiar. He wasn't like John; only a poor drugged woman with a distorted vision of her rapist would have thought he was. He was more like a caricature of him, a bad, mad copy. He nodded at the girl and she brought him a coffee. He ignored her. I saved that shot. There he was in black and white and I could see him in the car. I had seen him. I was sure of that. I had the whole picture. He logged on and I waited. I saved that shot. The window to alt.abortion was on screen next to the webcam window, so that I could read the answers to my thread. I'd had five replies since I had posted but they didn't mean anything. They were on my side. I was watching the back of this man's head and watching my screen and waiting.

Five minutes later, I saw—

peter@caffnet.co.uk wrote: *Whatever the Advent Bomber has done, his motives were pure. He was forced to act. There are casualties in every war. This is a Holy War for the Innocents.*

My hands were steady as I wrote: *Declan Campbell, no one else here agrees with you but you. Smile, you are on worldwide webcam.*

I sat back and waited. The Moslem woman next to him got up and said something to the girl behind the coffee bar. The geek and the guy in the Michael Caine glasses who were sitting behind the bar looked up suddenly. They seemed to be paying close attention to her as she walked around the bar area. They got up and the boy followed the girl through a door at the rear of the bar, and the woman followed them and shut the door behind her. I didn't know what was happening and I was worried that Declan Campbell would get spooked and leave, but he stayed, and so did the man in the tweed overcoat. Both men were staring at their screens, but only Campbell's arms were moving. He loved the sound of his own texts, the clickety-clack of his yackety-yack. I sat and watched and hated him. I hated the shape of him, the back of his head, the greasy-looking ponytail and his lumpen arms. It was going to take a few minutes for my post to register. I had to be patient.

After a minute he stopped abruptly and turned, staring up at the camera. I realised then that I knew him. I'd seen him in the dark against the light and during the day with the sun in his face. This was the man in the tower block. This was the man who had watched the air ambulance skimming over the rooftops with his victims on board. This was the man who had watched me through a pair of binoculars to make sure I ran inside. I'd seen him that very afternoon, watching me like I was a little bug he had trapped in a box, making sure that I stayed put.

He wasn't smiling like I'd asked him to, but I saved the shot all the same. If he was smart he'd get out of there, but he wasn't smart. He had to have the last say. He turned to the screen once more and his hands worked at the keyboard. From behind, it looked like he was strangling something.

As I dialled 999, I watched the man in the tweed coat get up. He seemed to shake his arm. It looked casual, but as Campbell was typing, the man's arm pointed at him and jerked twice. Campbell fell from his chair. I saw now that the man in the tweed coat had a strangely unnatural beard and that he wore dark glasses and dark gloves. He stepped across the back of Campbell's chair, and, with his back to the webcam, shot Campbell again. I had been too stunned to move the first time, but this time I saved, and as he left the café, with his head down and one hand in his pocket, I saved again.

I sat in my chair watching the webcam, watching the police arrive too late and the people who ran the joint coming in from the back. The woman in the veil was nowhere. My brain felt numb, but I had the beginnings of the intro running in my head. It was a powerful force of habit. Two minutes later I got a call.

'Did you see that?' Cherry said, and I said that I had.

'Was that him?' she said.

'Who?'

'Campbell, of course. Did you recognise him from before?'

'I think so,' I said.

'Great,' she said, and that struck me as a little odd.

'He lived in the tower block that overlooks my garden. He was a fucking neighbour.'

'Well, he's fucking dead now.'

'Did you save anything?' I said.

She fell silent.

'Cherry?'

'You didn't save the shot, did you, George?'

I thought about it for a moment and something tickled at the back of my neck, and I said that I hadn't, no, I hadn't saved it. I was wondering if she had because the police might want to know.

'Someone must have, though. Someone else might have logged on. Maybe they did,' I said.

'I doubt it,' she said.

'Think they had a security video going?' I asked.

'No,' she said. 'No, they didn't.'

Her voice sounded distant and distracted.

'You didn't save anything, did you, George?'

'I told you,' I said, but I didn't want to ask why it bothered her so much.

'That's it then,' I said.

'Yeah. That's it,' she said. 'Game over.'

When he called, Spencer was suspicious of me, but I told him the truth, most of it anyway. I said I was investigating a story and this was as far as I had got. I hadn't expected the man to get whacked before my very eyes. He said whacked is what you got in American crime movies. He said the man had been *executed*, and what I had seen was a contract killing. As if I didn't know. As if I couldn't make a fortune selling the evidence of my own eyes. I realised then that Spencer didn't have intuition, because if he had he'd have asked the relevant questions, which were: did you save the webcam pictures, and did you know the man in the tweed suit?

I did know him, but Cherry Shankar wasn't to know that I did, and Kendall Associates or whoever the hell he worked for weren't to know either. I sure as hell couldn't tell Spencer it was Pal Kuthy, as I lived and breathed, a little older and with a stupid false beard instead of the thick, glossy moustache that I remembered. I couldn't tell anyone that it was Pal doing what he did best.

I was faced with a dilemma, maybe two, maybe more. One was moral. I'd seen a murder. I knew who the victim was, who had murdered him, I had a good idea who had ordered it and paid for it. No matter what I felt, I wasn't judge and jury, any more than Declan Campbell had thought he was. I could do the right thing and report it, go with it, get my name in the papers again, get paid, put my friend in jail and bring the whole house down: Cherry Shankar, Gecko Games, Kendall Associates and all.

I didn't know if I would be better off keeping my mouth shut. She and I would have a secret but I didn't know if our friendship could survive it. I asked myself the question, how much does she trust me? But I couldn't give an answer that gave me any great deal of confidence. I needed her to trust me, but it wasn't just her. I needed Kendall Associates to trust me, and worst of all, I needed Pal Kuthy to trust me. And after what I had done to him, that wasn't ever going to happen. I didn't even want him knowing that I had been watching. They all had to trust me, because if they didn't, I could end up as dead as Declan Campbell. I asked myself the important question. Do I trust them?

I heard something like a small explosion, and the dog's ears pricked up. I hurried to the back of the house, from where I thought the noise had come. I looked out of the French windows and into the wintry sky. Flames were licking from a ragged hole that had held a window where Declan Campbell had once stood and gazed down at the suffering he had caused.

I felt a sting of fear. It had begun. His life was being erased. There was going to be nothing left of Declan Campbell to link him to anyone of any importance, not to Cherry Shankar, not even to Professor Ronald Highfield and his friends. They had had to be quick, very quick, and I was going to have to be very, very careful. I heard the sirens wail and stepped back from the window.

I lit a cigarette and went into my office to start backing up my hard drive. It was seven-thirty. I reckoned about ten minutes from the tower block to my basement, as the crow flies. *You're paranoid. It's all over*, I told myself, but a little voice inside told me to wise up and go get the gun.

I had the labelled zip drive in a Jiffy bag that I had addressed to Max Winters and covered with more stamps than was needed. I wrote *First Class* on it and hoped the Post Office would take me seriously. Inside was a note to Max telling him to put the drive in the company safe and unzip the contents when I told him to or when he felt the time was right. I had the dog on a lead, my mobile phone in one pocket and the gun in the other, and I was standing by the front door.

The perspiration trickling down my front and down my back was freezing me. My heart didn't just seem to be beating but spinning. If I didn't get a grip soon, I knew that I was going to faint. I told myself I was going upstairs to Richard's and somehow that got me to snap open the door and get moving. Instead of turning right at the top of my steps, I turned left, and the dog was pulling me into the dark street that glowed with the orange from the streetlamps all the way to the postbox that was shining dimly on the corner. It was a hundred yards that seemed like a hundred miles, but the dog was out in front and I held tight.

I got to the end of the street and posted the envelope in the gaping grin of the letterbox. I thought it had begun to rain, but it was sleet, and it fell in weak, white crystals that clung to my eyelashes. I was calmer now. The dog was sniffing the ground and I snapped the chain around her neck so that she would come to heel.

'What now, girl?' I asked. 'Do we go home?'

I didn't want to, and when I turned I could see that there might not be much point. In the distance there was smoke coming up from the basement and drifting into the lamplight.

I called Richard on the mobile and he said it was coming out the back too. It was worse out there. I told him that I was coming to get him and he said he'd already dialled 999.

'Where are you?' he said.

'I've been posting a letter.'

'Now? You crazy bitch. Did you set this fire?'

I didn't answer. I could see Pal walking up the street towards me, in a different coat and with no beard or glasses. The seventies moustache had gone. He was clean-shaven and wearing a hat, but one thing had remained the same. The closer he got, the wider was his grin. I put the phone in my pocket and closed my fingers around the Browning. He was smiling like he always did, like he'd heard a great joke that he wasn't going to share.

'Georgina.'

'Pal. How are you doing?'

'Good. I'm good. Busy, you know.'

'You finish up back there?'

'Yes.'

'I need to get my friend. He lives upstairs. Got a broken leg.'

Pal nodded.

'Who sent you?' I said.

He laughed.

'You still working on those little stories?'

The smoke was billowing out of the basement now.

'I have to go now,' I said.

The dog whimpered when she saw the gun in his hand. She'd disliked guns since her partner had been shot in an incident that Tony had taken them along to. I kept a good, tight grip on the Browning and tried to remember how to use it. Tony had shown me once, a long time ago. He had told me that the most important thing was to keep cool. I heard something like the quiet rush of an express train. The chain went taut and heavy, and I fired.

I hadn't given it a second thought. Once upon a time in a hotel room with him, I had stopped to wonder if I could do it. He had given me his own gun and told me to do it. He had called my bluff. He knew I wouldn't fire it. This time my hand was aching from the recoil, and the smell of bullets was in the air. Lying in the slush, his face was almost yellow, and I could see that his hair had greyed. He sighed, the European way, with a kind of ache in it.

'You shot my dog,' I said. 'You shot my fucking dog.'

'Your fucking dog. I had one summer suit – you remember the one? That was it. One summer suit in the whole stinking world. I go to Zurich to collect my money. Guess how much? For all that hard work, you remember?'

I said nothing. I looked at the dog. Steam was rising from her motionless body. I could see the fire engines by the tower block. They were evacuating people from the building. I could hear sirens but no one was coming to this street. I had to get to Richard, but Pal had hold of my coat. 'Three hundred and sixty-five dollars. Can you believe it? They cleaned me out. And everybody's dead, so who can I kill? I came looking for you but I found her. She was a little like you, you know? But she changed everything.'

I stretched over and pushed the gun with the silencer from his fingers. I had to be sure. The man wasn't dead yet.

'What are you talking about?' I said.

'I wanted to retire. Do something else. She had a baby inside her but the bastard killed her.'

Pal lay dying just like Danny had done, with his legs splayed and his mouth open. But it was blood, not booze, staining his shirt, and his chest bubbled like a blocked drain underneath. He still had that stupid grin on his face while my mind was exploding with the realisation that I had done it. I'd shot him.

'You've learned something since I've been gone,' he said. 'That's good.'

I leaned over Pal, but his eyes were closed and he looked old enough to be my father. Danny had said that it wasn't just him; that there had been others. I remembered Jo's look too. She wasn't looking at the great Georgina Powers. She was looking at herself.

'It was personal then,' I whispered.

'It was business,' he said, and the smile died on his face.

All Orion/Phoenix titles are available at your local bookshop or from th
following address:

Mail Order Department
Littlehampton Book Services
FREEPOST BR535
Worthing, West Sussex, BN13 3BR
*telephone* 01903 828503, *facsimile* 01903 828802
*e-mail* MailOrders@lbsltd.co.uk
(Please ensure that you include full postal address details)

Payment can be made either by credit/debit card (Visa, Mastercard, Access and Switch accepted) or by sending a £ Sterling cheque or postal order made payable to *Littlehampton Book Services.*
DO NOT SEND CASH OR CURRENCY

**Please add the following to cover postage and packing**

*UK and BFPO:*
£1.50 for the first book, and 50p for each additional book to a maximum of £3.50

*Overseas and Eire:*
£2.50 for the first book plus £1.00 for the second book and 50p for each additional book ordered

---

BLOCK CAPITALS PLEASE

*name of cardholder* ..............................
..............................
*address of cardholder* ..............................
..............................
..............................
..............................
*postcode* ..............................

*delivery address*
(*if different from cardholder*)
..............................
..............................
..............................
..............................
*postcode* ..............................

☐ I enclose my remittance for £ ..............................

☐ please debit my Mastercard/Visa/Access/Switch (delete as appropriate)

card number ☐☐☐☐☐☐☐☐☐☐☐☐☐☐☐☐

expiry date ☐☐☐☐ Switch issue no. ☐☐

signature ..............................

*prices and availability are subject to change without notice*